ABOUT THE AUTHOR

Aimee Alexander is the pen name of bestselling Irish author Denise Deegan. She lives in Dublin with her husband, two children and dog. Find out more on aimeealexanderbooks.com or tweet the author at @aimeealexbooks.

Also by Aimee Alexander

The Accidental Life of Greg Millar

pause to rewind

AIMEE ALEXANDER

ISBN-10: 1503256022
ISBN-13: 978-1503256026

Pause to Rewind

Aimee Alexander is the pen name of Denise Deegan.
This book was first published as *Time in a Bottle*.

To Alex and Homer, filies meis

one

'Come on, Mum,' Charlie shouts, racing up the path ahead of me, red lights flashing on the soles of his shoes.

He makes it to the door. Jumps to reach the bell. Misses. Tries again. And Again. I lift him up. He presses the bell. Continuously.

'Charlie, enough,' I say, pulling him back and popping him down.

Still, no one answers.

'Where is she? She's taking aaages. Ring again, Mum.' He starts to hop.

'It's OK, she knows we're coming.'

It's another minute and even *I'm* thinking of ringing again when the door finally opens.

Everything stops. Even noise. I'm not breathing. Inside, organs hammer into each other.

It's him. It's been five years. But it *is* him.

Have I the wrong house?

No, I checked the gate.

Right house. And he looks at home.
Debbie Grace. My God – his daughter!

His, 'Hello?' is a question. He has no idea who I am. Something at least.

'Hi. I'm calling for Debbie? I'm Jenny. This is Charlie.'

'Oh, hello. Yes. Yes, of course. I'm sorry.' He scratches behind his ear. 'I'd forgotten about the baby-sitting. I hope you weren't waiting long. I thought you were one of Debra's friends. The door's usually for her.' He holds out his hand.

And I have to do it – shake it, touch him. I survive and die at the same time.

'Simon Grace. Simon. Come in, come in.'

Charlie bursts past him. The smell of steak wafts through the warm September air.

'No, it's fine. Thanks. You're eating. We'll wait in the car. Come on, Charlie. Charlie!'

'I was just finishing up. Come on in. Please.'

'Honestly, we're fine. Thanks. It'd be handy to have the car turned, ready to go.'

He looks as if he's trying to work out whether I'm being polite or honest.

'Just hold on a minute, then,' he says. And he's gone, pounding up the stairs, calling, 'Debra! Jenny and Charlie are here. Come on.' He disappears.

Charlie heads for the stairs.

'Charlie, come here. You can't just go into people's houses you don't know.'

He stops, turns, still holding the bottom rung of the banisters.

'I know Debbie,' he says simply.

'Yes, but this is her father's house. And you don't know him.'

'I do. His name's Simon.'

I sigh, check that no one's coming, march over, pick him up and head back to the porch. 'We'll wait here,' I say firmly.

He knows I mean business.

We wait in silence. And I think about how little he has changed, Simon Grace. Still that same preoccupied look, as if you're disturbing him but he'd hate you to know it. He's taller, leaner than I remember. A bit neglected? Although, stubble at this time of day is probably standard for someone so dark. I remember his face with a tenderness that's alarming and tell myself to get a grip. So what if his eyes are sad? So what if he looks strong and vulnerable at the same time?

There is lighter thunder on the stairs.

'I'm so sorry, Jenny,' Debbie rushes. 'I was just drying my hair. I didn't hear the door. Hi, Charlie,' she says, smiling, her voice higher when talking to him.

'Hiya, Deb!' He wriggles out of my arms and runs to her. Just before he reaches her, he stops. 'Is it OK if I go into your house?'

She smiles. 'Sure.'

He turns to me. 'Told ya.'

I laugh as if to say, 'kids'.

Debbie scoops him up and swings him round. He squeals in delight. She laughs, her sleek black hair lifting from her shoulders and moving through the air in slow motion. She has inherited his colouring – dark hair, pale skin. Her eyes are blue, though. She's the kind of girl you'd see coming through the gates of a private school on Dublin's south-side with a group of friends and a hockey stick. Her look says confident, healthy, well adjusted - everything you'd want in a baby-sitter. She settles Charlie on her hip, kisses his cheek and heads for the door. Reaching it, she turns, for the first time, to acknowledge her father, who is hovering politely.

'Why didn't you call me?'

'I did.'

'Not loud enough, obviously.' She turns to go.

'What time will you be back?' he calls after her.

She doesn't answer, so I say, 'About eleven. If that's not too late?'

'No. That'd be fine, thanks,' he says, then adds uncertainly, 'Seeing as it's a weekend night.'

'I won't be late.'

'Good, good,' he says. 'Do you have your key?' he asks Debbie.

'Yes,' she says impatiently, leaving without looking back.

'Goodnight, then. Enjoy yourself.'

No answer.

I smile goodnight, then turn to go. If Debbie's anything like I was at her age, his life is hell. Then again, her mum probably gets most of it. Mine did. You can tell he cares, though.

The door closes gently behind us and I suspect that Dr Simon Grace, paediatric oncologist, is relieved to be left in peace. *I'm* relieved – he didn't recognise me. It makes me realise just how much I've changed in five years. Back then, I was Little Miss Newshound, wonder-journalist, on her way up. Contact lenses, cropped, highlighted hair, fitted trouser suits, and heels, always heels. Uptight. Aggressive. Soulless. And her replacement? A single mum who does a bit of freelancing to pay the bills and keep her hand in; whose neglected hair has grown to her shoulders and regained its waves and natural colour, who'd like to have time for contacts but doesn't, so it's small, rim-free rectangular lenses. Suits have been replaced by jeans and hoodies, practical wear for someone who has no longer anything to prove.

Even our names are different, I think, as I follow Debbie and Charlie up the path. He knew me as Jennifer Grey, the name I still write under. Everyone, including his daughter, knows me as Jenny Dempsey.

I smile at Debbie and Charlie as I zap open the car, a clapped-out mini that I love dearly.

'Sorry about that,' she says.

I look at her. 'About what?'

'My dad.'

'What about him?'

'He's kind of anal.'

I laugh and open the back door for Charlie. He climbs into his car seat. I strap him in.

'Sit here, Deb. Sit here,' he shouts in my ear.

'Sure, Charlie,' she calls, giving me an isn't-he-cute smile as I get out of the way. She slides in beside him. 'Who's this?' she asks him, holding up his huge, bright blue, fluffy Muppet.

'Cookie Monster,' he says.

'Oh my God. I love Cookie Monster.' She makes her voice growl when she says, 'Me love cookie.'

I smile. If her father could see her now.

I slot the key into the door of our apartment. On the other side, I hear the dog snuffling and barking, his nails tapping on the wooden floor, then door. I imagine the scratch marks he's leaving and try to hurry. He rushes out and springs up on Charlie.

'Down, Sausage, down,' Charlie says, with so much authority I have to stop myself laughing.

'Go on in, Debbie,' I say. 'The dog'll move out of the way.'

I turn off the alarm, while they go ahead.

'He's lovely,' she says, a little unsure, bending down to pat his head. You can tell she's not used to dogs.

Sausage isn't fussy. He'll take any attention he can get. He jumps to lick her face. She laughs but stands, wiping her cheek with the back of her hand.

'Wow, he's friendly. What is he – some kind of beagle?'

'Mixed-breed,' announces Charlie proudly.

Debbie throws me another isn't-he-adorable look.

'D'you want to show Debbie around, Charlie?'

'Good idea,' he says, grabbing her hand and taking off. 'Come on, Deb. We've a great telly.'

I follow them in.

Debbie turns. 'Cool apartment.'

I smile. 'My gran left it to me.' Otherwise I wouldn't be able to afford it. We're on the first floor of a three-story Georgian redbrick, on a wide, sleepy, tree-lined road. Its Glenageary location is upmarket. Or so I'm reminded, daily, by my editor, who holds it against me personally – or at least he pretends to. But whatever Jack might say, I'm not complaining. It's a great place to bring up a child. Safe, leafy and near the sea. The light is wonderful on the first floor, filtering in through ceiling-to-floor bay windows. A crystal hangs in each one, breaking the sun's rays into little rainbows here and there on the walls and furniture. The floors are wooden, hidden in places by brightly-coloured rugs. I've lived here since I became pregnant and my gran insisted I move in with her.

'You need a home, Jen, not just somewhere to stay,' she said, following it up with a sigh and a faraway look. 'Imagine, Jen – me, a great-grandmother.'

She was the first person who made me feel that my baby was welcome. I knew she'd make a great great-grandmother and started to call her, 'Great'.

She didn't object.

Objections are the specialty of my mother. When she heard I was pregnant, there was no talk of homes. There was no talk at all. Not as in conversation. Just a monologue. As if I didn't already know that a) I was single b) the 'child' was fatherless and c) my career would 'suffer'. It was her own career she was worried about, her 'profile', as an elected politician. Neither of us mentioned that.

Moving in with Great *was* great. She may have been my mother's mother but they were as far apart as A and Z. I've often (understatement) wondered how Great managed to create such a cold, power-hungry...enough of the adjectives...cow. I never asked if she regretted not being close to her daughter – as soon as I became a mum, I knew.

My mother's view of Great was one-dimensional. She was a potential source of embarrassment, a political time bomb. Great said what she wanted, when she wanted. If people didn't like it, 'then tough'. This made her very popular with me. She would die rather than ingratiate herself to strangers, trying to wangle a vote out of a Mass-goer. She was fun. And warm. Interested in and enthusiastic about everything. She was my mother's mother. In all but birth, she was mine. She should have lived forever.

When I moved in, she humoured my nesting instinct, not once objecting to having her wallpaper stripped and her walls painted white or her carpets ripped up and her floors sanded and varnished. She loved the transformation, whipped out her sewing machine and made bright covers for the sofas. Together, we went out and bought an indoor rainforest. Our new life was beginning. But all this industriousness was a ploy on my part, a distraction from the fact that I was going through pregnancy on my own. If I kept busy, I wouldn't miss having a loving hand rest on my stomach, sharing the movement. I wouldn't long for someone to say, 'That's not a man's name'. I wouldn't wish to hear, 'Yes, love. The Will is sorted, the pension's organised,' when I suddenly decided that everything needed to be safe, fastened down as though a storm was coming. I wouldn't look longingly at pregnant couples, holding hands, heads together, planning. It was hormones that had me thinking like that, I knew, but something had to be done to stop it – and that was work.

I tried resenting my son when they landed him gently on my stomach that ice-cold January day. But it was no use. I caved in almost immediately. How could I close my heart to this little man with the glassy blue eyes that bore into mine as though searching for something? This kind of love was something entirely new. It hit me with force, knocked me over and changed my life absolutely.

Maybe if he'd been difficult, I could have learnt to hate him. But crying just wasn't his thing. He smiled early. Slept through the night from eight weeks. It was as if he was trying to get me to love him. So I decided, 'That's it, I'm doing this right.' I listened to the experts. Breast-fed, cuddled, snuggled, tickled, laughed and chatted with the new man in my life. When my maternity leave was up, I couldn't go back. I met with my then editor, explained my position and waited for her to come up with a solution. Or fire me. It took her two weeks and some negotiation but her offer was like Baby Bear's porridge. Just right. Move from health correspondent to contributor, writing a weekly health page, from home. I took a salary cut which turned out not to be too extreme when reduced taxes were worked out. I was lucky. The timing was perfect. The editorial execs at the paper had been contemplating a health page – they couldn't remain the last of the nationals, albeit a tabloid, without one. Tough market. So she dived straight for their Achilles heel, then topped off their insecurities with an assurance that I'd developed a name for myself in health. It worked. I owe her.

Moving from news to features suited the new me, matching my shift in interest from breaking news to breaking wind. In-depth interviews, real people with real stories, what happened, how it affected them and how they got through it, meant more to me than brief news reports that became history, every day.

With the change from news to features came a change in editor. I wasn't too thrilled about that at first because I liked working for a woman. I knew Jack well through my ex-fiancé, Dave, who used to write for the paper, but I didn't know what he'd be like to work for. I was very polite and formal at first but, in time, we resumed our relaxed, comfortable relationship. It helped that he was easy-going and encouraging. He was even open to a little slagging, which is just as well because he gave enough.

Mostly, I worked in the evenings. It suited the people I had to interview, because I wasn't interrupting them at work. And it suited me, with Charlie in bed and Great engrossed in her crosswords, glancing up occasionally with a contented smile. Not exactly what you'd call a high-octane life but I'd had enough excitement.

Then, last year, Great died. It was hard. But it would have been harder without Charlie, who kept me looking forward, focused. I still had my boy. I had to be there for him.

'D'you want to see my room?' Charlie's voice breaks through my thoughts.

'Sure,' says Debbie.

'Come on.' He drags her off. Sausage, who doesn't want to be left out, follows, barking, jumping and wagging his tail.

I take up the rear. 'Guys, I gotta go.'

'OK, Mum. Bye.'

'No hug?'

Charlie looks at Debbie, then back at me. 'Busy, Mum.'

I smile. 'OK, well, I'll just have to give you one then, won't I?'

''K.'

'Will you show Debbie where everything is?' I say, squeezing him tightly.

'Yep.'

'Good boy. See you later.' I kiss him just above his forehead.

'Debbie, you have my number, in case you've any problems?'

She nods.

'Here's where I'll be.' I tear out a page from my jotter and hand it to her. 'Charlie can stay up for another half-hour. Then it's bedtime. OK, mister?'

'OK, Mum. You can go now.'

'See you later.' I laugh to hide my hurt.

I walk to the car, jiggling my keys nervously, thinking about how quickly he's growing up. He's just started school and already he's changing. No longer my baby. Becoming his own man. It's good for him, I know. I should stop worrying. We all have to grow, build a life for ourselves. Charlie needs friends. Independence is good for him. I'm too attached. It's good that I'm going out, even if I don't feel like it. I haven't met up with the guys from work in years. I've missed every Christmas party – I've wanted to. But I need to get on with my life now. Charlie's getting on with his.

I'm not comfortable in skirt and heels and already regret the perfume. It's conspicuous, no longer me, and, I suspect, with a sniff, that it's gone off.

two

It's a dark, authentic, traditional pub in city-centre Dublin. Themed, without effort. The almost-black mahogany countertop and stools, the mirrors stained yellow from years of smoke, and the 1950s memorabilia are all genuine. This is not the place to order a Bacardi Breezer. This is Guinness territory.

We used to spend so much time in here; it was like a second office. You'd think I'd feel at home. For the first time, I walk in and hesitate. For the first time, I wonder what I have to say to these people. For the first time, I'm aware of how I look. I could happily turn around and go home.

I spot Jack and smile. He hasn't changed much. Slightly heavier, a little less hair. Suited as ever, not sharply, relaxed now that the shift's over. His familiar uncomplicated smile reassures me. He stands and waits for me to reach the table.

'How're you doing, Jen?' He pats my upper arm. It's as close to a hug as I, or anyone, will ever get from Jack.

The others smile, nod, or greet me with a, 'Hi Jenny.' Some do all three.

What was I worried about? I know these people. Well, most of them. The new faces seem so young.

Jack grabs a stool and lands it down beside him.

'Thanks, Jack.' I take off my jacket and sit, leaning my bag against the legs of the stool.

'Good to see you out, missus,' Jack says. 'How've you been?'

'Grand. You?'

'Same as ever. Here, what're you having? The usual?'

'Nah. Driving. A Coke would be great, thanks.'

'Oh, right,' he says, a bit deflated. Then he's up and off, muscling his way through the mob.

Ted, an ex-colleague who was, in all honesty, more a competitor, is sitting opposite. We started around the same time and constantly kept an eye on each other, both with the same idea – keeping ahead. I guessed he must have been thrilled when I got out of the action. Especially as he got my position.

'Hi, Ted.'

'Jenny, how's it going?'

'Not bad. You?'

'Good. Good,' he says.

'That was a great piece you did on the tribunal yesterday.' It would have been better if his ego hadn't got in the way. It wasn't an opinion piece.

'Still reading us, then?' he asks.

'Still writing for the paper, Ted.'

'Yeah,' he says in a tone that implies freelancing isn't writing. Though it's the backbone of the paper, in recent years.

I look across at Brenda who writes movie reviews. We used to go to the cinema together. Until Great died. *I must start again, now that I've Debbie.*

But do I have Debbie? Can I risk meeting Simon Grace again?

Actually, no.

But Debbie's so sweet. And Charlie loves her.

'God, it's bedlam up there,' says Jack. 'If we weren't regulars, I'd still be there. Here you go, Jen. Slice of lemon to liven it up.'

'Cheers.'

He clinks my glass, holds his in the air for a sec, then gulps a great big mouthful of Guinness.

'Any news?' he asks, wiping foam from his upper lip.

'I don't think so. No, not really. Let's see...' And then I think of it – the one bit of exciting news I have. 'Charlie's started school.'

'Oh, good. School, yeah, great. He grew up fast, didn't he?'

You can tell this isn't his type of conversation.

I laugh. 'Jack, you're nodding off.'

'I am not.' He's indignant.

'Jack.'

'All right, you've got me. Kids aren't my specialty. Your page is great, though.'

'Thanks.' But I don't want to discuss work. I'll do it, fine, enjoy it even, but I don't want to talk about it. Boy, I've changed.

A hat zigzags above the crowds. It looks like a Phillip Treacy. And when I see who's wearing it, I know it must be. Jane Peters. Our fashion correspondent. What's she doing here? She must be 'like, so stressed out' to be away from her usual haunt, the Shelbourne bar. Her eyes zoom in on me. And suddenly it seems she has a destination, a purpose.

'Jenny,' she gushes. 'So good to see you. Excuse me, Jack. Can I just squeeze in there? Have to catch up with Jenny. You know how it is.'

Her eyelash-batting is lost on him. But he does shift his stool a bit so she can get in. I widen my eyes at him; he knows how I feel about her.

'Sorry,' he mouths and makes a what-could-I-do face.

'Jenny. How are you?'

'Fine. Jane. And you?'

'Oh, super.'

I nod. I have nothing to say to this person. Nothing. Could I even list more than five designer labels?

Jane looks at me closely. And frowns. 'You look a little pale, sweetie.' I'm about to blame the lighting when she adds, 'Up all night with...what's his name...little...?'

'Charlie. And, no. He sleeps at night like most four-year-olds.'

'Sweet.' She smiles. Then frowns again. 'You sure you're not anaemic?'

I long for my apartment, the silence of it with Charlie asleep, the peace. My coffee maker. My snuggly quilt. The novel I've just bought, still in its paper bag. Like Dorothy in *The Wizard of Oz*, I want to click my heels and be back home.

'How's Dave?' she asks, though she knows we split up almost five years ago.

'I don't know.'

'Don't you stay in touch?'

'No.'

'You really screwed up that one, didn't you?'

I laugh. Because this has been coming since the minute she showed up. She always had a thing for Dave.

'He's really making a name for himself over there, isn't he?' she continues.

'I don't keep up.' For a long time, I did. Googled him way too often. Followed his career. Lurked on twitter. I told myself he'd changed, become American, so different from the Dave I knew. And loved. Slowly, I got over him. Weird, though, how you can plan to spend the rest of your life with someone and then, just like that, they no longer figure in your future. Or present. One thing – that's all it took to blow our plans apart – plans that were so certain, solid, plans I never doubted. I hope he's happy, that he's found someone else, someone who won't go and mess things up.

I stick it out till half-ten, then give the new-babysitter excuse. Next time I go out, it will be to the cinema.

three

We're dawdling up the lane to school. Charlie's taking the puddle route, like I used to do as a kid. His navy uniform and starting-school haircut have conspired to remove the last remnants of baby. Gone are the innocent blond curls, snipped off in their prime, leaving darker, smoother hair. Grown-up hair. A mistake, I know. I don't need to be asked, 'What happened his hair?' But I am. Repeatedly.

Suddenly, Charlie breaks into a run, his bag banging up and down on his back.

'Dara, Dara, wait up!' *When did he start talking like an American?*

He turns a corner.

I quicken my step.

I catch up with him in the yard.

'Hurry up, Dara's gone in,' he says to me.

'OK, there's no rush,' I say, no idea who he's talking about but glad he has a friend already.

We go inside. I help him off with his bag and coat. The orange lining is still warm. I'm left holding the coat as he dashes over to hug his new buddy.

'Urgh. Go away,' says Dara. Big guy, *must be five*, razor-tight haircut.

I feel like telling *him* to go away.

'I just want a hug,' Charlie says to him, confused.

'No way. Hugs are for girls.'

'Oh.' The corners of Charlie's mouth turn down and I'm afraid he's going to cry. But no, he fights it off. *That's my boy.*

'Don't worry,' his teacher says, leaning towards me as though letting me in on a secret. 'He'll be fine.'

'Maybe I should have sent him to playschool first.' *Toughen him up. But I don't want him tough.*

'Not at all. He'll be fine. We'll see you later.' She says it like she wants me to leave.

Charlie looks like a little lone buoy, bobbing around in a sea of new faces. I want to take him with me.

I go over to him and whisper, 'Sweetie, if you ever feel like a hug, I'm your woman.'

'It's OK, Mum,' he says in a trying-to-be-brave voice.

'OK. Bye Charlie.'

I leave, trying to be equally brave, but failing. I walk back up the corridor in tears. I've always been able to protect him. At school, he's on his own.

'Don't worry. He'll be fine in a few weeks,' says a more seasoned mum.

'Thanks.' I force a smile and continue on. I think of Great. 'Look after him,' I whisper.

I was never religious but something happened when Great died, something that made me believe that maybe there was more, that maybe it doesn't just stop when our hearts do. When Great died, her room filled with the strongest smell of roses, though there were none. The chaplain turned to me.

'Was she a devotee of Saint Therese?'

'She loved her,' I said, surprised.

He nodded as if that explained everything.

'What?' I asked.

'This often happens when devotees of the Little Flower pass away.'

'The smell of roses?'

He nodded as if it were no big deal. To me it was. It was a sign, a message. She was telling me she'd still be around. Still looking out for us, Charlie and me.

It took months for the solicitors to sort out her affairs. They called me in, one morning, to sign some documents. I was putting the date beside my signature when I realised that it was Great's birthday. She'd left me the house – on her birthday. It wasn't the only shock. I didn't know it was her house to leave me. She used to say she rented the first floor. Turned out, she rented it to herself. Great was a landlord. Actually, given the tenants (struggling artists and musicians) and the rents she charged (tiny), you could say she was a patron of the arts.

She wouldn't be impressed with the couple in the basement now. Madeleine, Swedish, works in a call centre. Her boyfriend, Tadhg, from Ballydehob, is an accountant with the same company. They have plans. They are saving. I feel guilty having broken the unwritten rule. It was not deliberate. I'm not landlord material. I can't double as a neighbour and some kind of rent collector so I hired an agency to handle it. It was they who picked Madeline and Tadhg, deeming them low-risk tenants. Great wasn't afraid of risk.

I hear her voice in my head.

'Don't worry,' she says. 'He'll be fine. I'm keeping an eye on him.'

I take a breath and hand him over to her.

I spend the morning interviewing people about sexually transmitted diseases and reassuring them that I won't be using their real names.

I have to stop myself from running up the lane when school's over.

And what's the first thing he says?

'Can I go to Dara's house?'

'I don't know, Charlie. We'd have to talk to his mum.' Who I sincerely hope we can't find.

'Hi. You must be Charlie's mum? I'm Mary,' says a smiling brunette standing next to us, still waiting for her child to come out. 'Dara's mum.'

'Oh, hi. How are you? I'm Jenny.' *Crap.*

'Dara never stops nagging me for Charlie to come over.'

'Oh,' I say, surprised.

With that, Dara comes bolting out the door. 'Hi, Mum. Did you talk to Charlie's mum?'

'I was just going to.' She looks at me meaningfully, eyebrows raised. 'He's got three big brothers who do nothing but give him a hard time. He'd love to have a friend of his own over.'

I hesitate, thinking of bigger Daras.

'Don't worry if you've something on...'

'Please, Mum, please. I'll be your bestest friend,' whines Charlie.

'I thought you *were* my best friend.'

'Please...'

'OK.'

'Today?'

Argh. I don't know these people.

'If it doesn't suit...' Mary starts to say.

'No, no, it's fine. If you're sure it's all right with you.'

'Absolutely. We'd love to have Charlie over. Phil, my husband, is off today so he'll be around to play with them a bit.'

She tells me where she lives and gives me her mobile. I give her mine and Charlie's car seat.

'I'll pick him up in an hour,' I say.

'Sure, they'll only be getting going at that stage.'

'Right then, two hours. It's his first time. He might get tired.'

I watch them walk off, Charlie chatting animatedly. He jumps every now and again, which he does when he gets excited.

I take a deep breath. And go home alone.

I can't help it. I turn up early to collect him.

Mary asks me in.

In the sitting room, a grown man rolls around the floor with two boys, one of them mine. Yelps of laughter from all three.

'We're not ready, Mum,' shouts Charlie, jumping on Dara's father's back, roaring, 'I'm taking you down.'

I laugh.

'This is Phil,' says Mary.

Her husband waves from the floor just before a cushion hits the side of his head.

'Go, commando,' shouts, *my son?*

Dara spots me hovering. 'Have a cup of tea,' he suggests. An obvious delaying tactic.

I smile and look at Mary. 'Where did he learn that trick?'

'Where he learns everything – his brothers. Come on into the kitchen. We'll have a few minutes' peace.'

'You're sure you're not making dinner or anything?'

'I'll throw a pizza on in a minute, and that, I'm afraid, will be it. It's what they like and I'm tired of arguing.'

'You seem so calm.' The place is bedlam.

'With four boys, it's a practiced art form.'

I smile. 'It must be a doddle for you, Dara starting school.'

'It's actually a relief. He hates being the baby. Couldn't wait to get going. Charlie seems to be settling in well, too?'

'He seems to love it, all right. It's me I'm worried about,' I joke.

'It's not easy, letting go. God. With James, my eldest, I spent the first week in floods.'

'You did?' *Phew.*

'I was a complete eejit. Phil had a great laugh.'

We've reached it – that point in the conversation when I should automatically talk about Charlie's dad. So I offer that silent smile I've perfected so well. And nothing is said.

'You can't stop progress, though, can you? All you can do is make the most of your free time.' She shrugs.

I nod.

'You'll get used to it.' She smiles. 'I promise.'

Bedtime. Teeth, face and hands washed, Charlie lets me carry him to his room, though there's nothing wrong with his legs. His *Winnie the Poo* decor suddenly seems too young for a boy who solemnly transferred his lifelong companion, Buzz Lightyear, from his home on the bed to the cold, lonely, toy box, as soon as he learnt (from Dara) that 'dolls' were 'for babies.'

'Did you have a nice time at Dara's?' I ask, after our story but before our goodnight hug.

'The best.'

'What did you do?'

'Played the best games in the world.'

'Did you play with Dara's brothers?'

'No. Mostly his dad. He's mad.'

'Yeah?'

'Yeah. He played lots of crazy games.'

'It's good you had fun.'

'Mum?'

'Yes, Charlie?'

'Why don't I have a dad?'

I've had years to prepare for this and I'm still not ready. *Try honesty, Jenny.* I take a breath.

'You do have a dad, Charlie.'

'Well, where is he?'

'I'm not sure, exactly.'

'Why? Why doesn't he live here with us?'

'He's got another life, sweetheart.'

'But I want a dad.'

'I know, Charlie.'

'Can't we ring him and ask him to come for a little while?'

'It's not that easy, sweetie.'

'Why not?'

'Well, he's a very busy man.'

'Doesn't he have any time to play?'

God.

'Sweetie, he mightn't even be in Ireland. I don't know exactly where he is at the moment. I'm sorry. But you know what? Maybe we can ask Dara round next week. How does that sound?'

'OK, I suppose.' His head is down and he's picking at a scab on his knee.

'Come here.' I sit him up on my lap. 'I think I feel a hug coming on.'

'Don't like hugs.'

four

My mother is on The News. I almost switch over. But, much as I want to, something stops me. This happens all the time. What is it? Curiosity? A need to keep tabs on her? I don't know. And today's news: When she was on her way to one of her clinics – from the security-driven car to the door – a poster was blown down by strong winds and struck her on the head. It wasn't just any poster. It was of an opposition candidate in the latest by-election. On camera, she jokes of a dirty tricks campaign. She is, no doubt, thrilled with the fuss and, most importantly, media coverage. Ironic, given her disappointment when I chose journalism over, say medicine or law. Not that she was disappointed for me, but for herself. I'm her only daughter, her only child. She had me and that was enough; must have realised that children take time and she didn't have any to give. And still the expectations.

The phone rings and I'm wondering who it is at this time.

'Hey, Jenny. It's Mary. Dara's mum. I was wondering if you'd like to catch a movie, sometime?'

'Oh. Right. OK. Yeah. Sure. That'd be great.'

'You could drop Charlie over to us if you haven't got a sitter.'

I think of Debbie. And her dad. But also how much Charlie loves her. And how hard it was to find someone like her. I tell myself to stop panicking. I don't need to decide right now. 'That'd be great, thanks.'

'Cool. When suits you?'

'Well, I'll have to check my diary. Such a hectic social life, you know?'

She laughs. 'Me too.'

We decide on Friday. Giving me four days to sort out a babysitter.

Trying to find someone to mind Charlie makes me realise how much my life has shrunk. One by one, I've let my friends go. Too busy to go out. Too tired. Not interested or able to party till dawn. I could ask my parents to babysit. If I spoke to them. I have neighbours. My favourite, Louis, is the keyboard player in an aspiring band called Damage. Louis wouldn't damage a fly. Neither could he mind one; Charlie would have way too much fun. I could ask Madeleine. But I wouldn't do it to Charlie. He loves Debbie. And as time runs out, I realise that I do too. I find a solution: rather than calling to the door to collect her, I'll text her when we pull up outside.

That was easy, I think, when she jumps into the car on Friday.

'Where's your dad?' Charlie asks.

'He's inside,' she says, pressing his nose.

'Oh.'

I start the engine and pull away.

'I don't have a dad,' Charlie says.

'Poor you.' In the mirror, I see her kiss the top of his head.

'He's busy,' Charlie explains.

Debbie catches my eye in the mirror. I snap mine back to the road.

'I don't have a mum,' I hear her say.

I grip the wheel. *She died?*

'Don't you?' Charlie asks, fascinated.

'No.'

'Why not?'

'She died, Charlie.'

Oh God. I'd always hoped she'd make it. I mean, I knew the chances were tiny. But I'd hoped. I feel so guilty. I already did. But I'd got over it. I had my punishment – well, not punishment; repercussion – to deal with, to keep me busy. Her name comes to me suddenly. Alison.

'Great died,' continues Charlie.

Debbie looks baffled. 'Sorry?' She looks in the mirror.

'Great is what we called my gran,' I explain.

'She died,' Charlie repeats.

'Oh,' says Debbie. 'That's sad.'

'She's in heaven now. She minds me.'

Debbie smiles. 'Same with my mom.'

'What was she like?' Charlie asks.

'Pretty.'

'Was she great fun?'

'Yeah. She used to read me stories and plait my hair.'

'Like my mum. Only she doesn't plait my hair.'

'We'd pretend I was Rapunzel. I'd throw my plaits over the side of the bed and she'd pretend to climb up.'

'Do you really miss her?'

'All the time.'

'Why did she die?'

'She got sick.' Her voice begins to falter.

'Like Great. My dad isn't sick. He's just busy.'

'Lucky we have each other then,' Debbie says and ruffles his hair.

And I think: *she will be our babysitter forever.*

I'm ready to leave. I look over at them, sitting together on the couch. Charlie in his PJs, on Debbie's lap, points at pictures in his book of whales. The hairless skin on his arms is soft and spongy, little dimples at his elbows. His feet jut out past Debbie's knees. The soles are round and squishy, not hard and flattened like adult feet. But my son is growing up. His hair gives it away. Gelled, the way he likes it now. A few weeks at school and he is officially 'a man'. No more trooping into the Ladies with his mum, not without argument at least.

'But I'm a man,' he says.

No more holding hands. 'No way.'

No more blind-acceptance of whatever clothes I buy for him – anything featuring *Bob The Builder* is a no-no.

Rude words are suddenly cool. Bottom, butt and boobies are almost as funny as willy. And let's not forget poo, the feature attraction. They love burps in Asia. Guess where he wants to go?

In the last fortnight, he's had three proposals of marriage – all from women in their thirties who always want to know if he takes after his father.

'What an unusual mix – dark eyes and fair hair.'

They have no idea what they are asking. Or how it might make Charlie feel. I go over to him now, to say goodbye.

'Where's my hug?'

He glances at Debbie. 'Don't like hugs.'

'Oh, yeah. I'd forgotten.'

'Hugs are for wimps.'

'Right.' He's been giving me hugs all week when no one was looking.

'I'm not a wimp, Mum.'

'I know but I am. So can I have one?'

He slides a finger into his mouth as he tries to decide. 'OOOOK,' he says finally. 'But just for three seconds.'

'Great. Thanks.'

He hops down and runs lightly over to me.

'Thanks,' I say, hugging him a little closer than usual, breathing in the smell of citrus shampoo.

'Oooone, twoooo, threeee. Three, Mum. Three. Time's up.'

'Oh, right,' I say, finally letting go.

He takes a quick peep at Debbie, making sure his street cred is still intact. She is scrolling away on her iPhone.

'Hey Charlie,' she says. 'There are some cool games on this. Want to check them out?'

'Doodle Jump?'

She smiles. 'You're way ahead of me.'

'What's your highest score?' he asks, climbing back up onto her lap.

'64,000.'

'You are going down.'

She laughs.

'Bye Charlie,' I say.

He doesn't hear.

Debbie looks up from the phone and smiles.

I smile back. 'Thanks Debbie.'

The movie's six out of ten. The night only really gets going when we go for a 'quick' drink afterwards. There's nothing quick about it. We chat about nothing in particular. Actually, that's how it feels, but we must be covering some ground because I know a lot about Mary. She's the eldest of five, from Cork originally but living in Dublin so long there's no trace of an accent.

'It comes out when I get excited, girl,' she says in a Cork accent. 'Ask Phil.'

We laugh.

Phil was her first real boyfriend. They're married twelve years and planned every child.

'It'd be nice to have a girl,' she says kind of wistfully.

Eventually we get to me.

I don't do detail. 'I'm on my own. It's just Charlie and me.'

She's silent for a moment. 'Is that OK?'

I do a half-nod, half-head-shake thingy. 'It's fine. It's the way I want it.'

'OK,' she says, nodding.

And when I don't volunteer any more information, she moves the conversation on with such ease I begin to question that there even was an awkwardness. She makes me laugh. Even her laugh makes me laugh. She's just one of those upbeat people who are good to be around.

We get back later than planned with a definite intention to do this again.

five

I'm taking up yoga. This time, I might actually stick it out. Mary seems to have enough motivation for two.

Charlie and I collect Debbie using our new system. She smiles as she walks to the car. Under her arm is a folder. *Homework, probably.*

'Hiya, Debbie,' Charlie says when she opens the car door.

'Hey, bud.'

'What's that?' he asks.

'A photo album I made. I thought you'd like to see my mom.'

'Can I see her now?'

'Sure.' She opens the book and holds it out to show him.

'Is that her?' Charlie asks, pointing.

'Yup. Isn't she pretty?'

'Who's that?'

'That's me.'

'No it isn't. That's a kid.'

'Me when I was a kid.'

'Did someone make you laugh?'

'My mom. She was always making me laugh,' she says with regret. 'That's my dad with my mom. I took that picture. It's my favourite.'

Charlie pats the back of her hand sympathetically.

'Cutie,' she says.

We pull up outside the house. Debbie closes the book.

'Jenny, can I leave this in the car so I don't forget it?'

'Of course.'

The community hall is not a temple of peace and tranquillity. Darkish, kind of chilly, and a faint whiff of socks. The instructor stands at the top of the room, lighting an incense stick. She moves fluidly to unroll a turquoise mat onto the floor. She glances around at us with a relaxed smile. When she introduces herself (Yvonne), her voice is like honey. She'll do.

The class is mixed, but only just. We have a token man. Poor guy. He looks like this is his first and last time. The rest of us come in a variety of shapes and sizes, many of them toned and tanned which is a little intimidating for someone who came in her pyjama bottoms. Grey and kind of tracksuity, I thought they'd look like the real thing. Proper yoga gear, I see now, is fitted and stretchy. Black is in. I do have a proper yoga mat though so all is not lost.

We spend an hour learning to relax, breathe, stretch and mould ourselves into positions named after animals. Mary turns out to be a giggler. Any excuse will do but when one unfortunate woman breaks wind, Mary fails to contain herself. I do only by turning away, holding my nose and avoiding eye contact with Mary for the rest of the class. I'm back at school on a Friday afternoon.

'That was great,' Mary says, walking down the steps of the community hall.

'You're terrible, you know that?'

She smiles. 'I don't know what came over me. Must have been the "tension leaving my body". '

I laugh.

'The peace was great, though, wasn't it? There wasn't a sound.'

'Apart from that one time.'

We burst out laughing. And I remember what it's like to have a friend.

Next day, I'm strapping Charlie into his car seat to head to school when I catch sight of Debbie's book on the back seat.

'Oh no.'

'What is it, Mum?'

'Deb left her book behind.'

'Oh God.'

'Don't say, "Oh God", Charlie.'

'You do.'

'Yeah. I shouldn't. Next time I say it, you can pinch me.'

'Really, can I? Cool.'

'Don't get too excited.'

'But we better give Debbie's book back to her.'

'Yeah, we will as soon she gets home from school.'

'Yay.'

I get back in the car after dropping Charlie off. The book is just sitting there on the front seat. I shouldn't open it, I know. But the people in it mean too much to me. Simon Grace changed my life. And how I feel about his family is: guilt. I can't *not* open it.

My heart pounds, like it knows I'm doing something wrong and will be caught any minute.

Oh God. There it is – the happy scene. He could be a different man. No sadness, just laughter in his eyes. She is beautiful, Alison. It could be an ad for engagement rings or honeymoons or anything involving happy couples - except for the fact that she's making bunny ears behind his head. *So much love in that one shot. Pity it wasn't shoved under my nose five years ago in a hotel room in Brussels.*

He answers the door.

I hide behind my hair, glasses, clothes.

He looks panicked. 'Debra isn't home yet. Is she babysitting today?'

'No, no.' I hold out the book. 'She left this behind last night.'

'Oh. Right.' He seems relieved. 'I'll see that she gets it.'

'Thanks.'

He's squinting at me, like something's bothering him. 'Have we met? You seem familiar.'

I feel the blush spread like a splash of paint. 'Eh, no. Don't think so. I've just one of those faces.'

'Sorry,' he says, like he's made a mistake. 'I see so many people in my line of work.'

'Sure. No problem.'

He holds up the book. 'Well, I'll give this to Debra. She'll be sorry she missed you.'

'We could wait,' Charlie says.

'No, Charlie. We have to go,' I say firmly.

'Aw, Mum, you're such a buzz-kill.'

Simon Grace does something I've never seen him do before. He smiles.

six

I wake. It's dark. Charlie's calling out in his sleep. I throw back the quilt. Chilly late-autumn air surrounds me. I pad into his room and find him crying, quilt half down where he's kicked it off. He is still asleep. I sit at the side of his bed and brush his hair back, over and over.

'It's OK. It's OK,' I whisper. 'Sh.'

He opens his eyes.

I smile. 'Hi,' I say quietly.

He looks at me with sleepy, teary eyes.

'You were having a bad dream, sweetie. But it's over now.'

'Mama?' He hasn't called me that in years. It makes me nervous.

'Yes, sweetie. I'm here. We're home. In your room. You were just having a dream. But you're awake now. It's OK.'

He sits up, rubs his eyes with two little fists and snuggles into me. I put my arm around him.

'You were gone,' he says. 'I couldn't find you.'

'I'm here now.'

I start to sing the one lullaby that always comforts him: *Hush Little Baby*. I change the words, like I always do. Mama's going to buy him a mocking bird, not Papa. With a finger, he twirls the hair at the side of his head, round and round. He doesn't take his sleepy eyes off me. With each blink, his lids become heavier. But he fights it, forcing them to stay open. His breathing becomes even and deep. His eyes finally close and I'm just beginning to think he has drifted off when he pats the bed with the flat of his hand, feeling around for me, making sure I'm still here.

He sleeps.

I stay with him till morning.

'I don't want you to go,' he says, looking at the ground. We're standing just inside the door of Charlie's classroom. We've hung up his coat, left his schoolbag at its dedicated spot, said our goodbyes.

'But you love school.'

'Don't leave me.'   .

'Charlie, we're blocking the doorway. And I have to go.' I start to walk out. He grabs my leg and clings to it.

'I want to stay with you,' he pleads.

'But what about Dara? He'll be lonely.'

'Don't go, Mama, don't go. I want to come with you.'

I want him to, too. But if I do, he'll be like this every day.

'Charlie,' I say, trying to be firm. 'Even if you come home, it'll just be boring. All I'll be doing is talking on the phone and writing on the computer. We won't be able to play. It'd be so boring.'

'Don't care. Want to be with you.'

This is killing me. 'Come on, Charlie. You love school. It's PE today. And treat day.'

Mary arrives with Dara. She grasps the situation immediately.

'Charlie, just the man I need,' she says. 'Dara's in trouble. Can you help?'

Charlie looks at her, then at Dara. She's got his attention. Now what?

'Come here. I want to show you something.'

He doesn't budge.

'Look.' She opens Dara's lunch box. 'I packed too much lunch today. Silly me – Dara won't be able to eat it all. Maybe you could help him with his treats. What do you think?' She smiles.

'No, thank you.'

Dara looks relieved.

'Nice try,' I whisper to her. 'I don't know what's wrong with him today.'

'Ah, they all have their off days. Just go. He'll be fine as soon as you're gone.'

'You think?'

'Sure. I'll stay with him for a while. He'll be grand.'

'Thanks so much, Mary.'

I bend down to Charlie, kiss his forehead. 'I'll see you later, sweetie.'

He starts to cry. He holds out his arms. 'Don't go,' he pleads.

And as I do go, I feel like the worst mother in the world.

Charlie wants to stay home rather than go to Dara's, as planned. This is despite the fact that it contains one father, three iPhones and a PlayStation. So, Dara comes to ours.

While I make spaghetti, they play Lego and chat about where babies come from. Dara has a new cousin. He's driving Mary crazy with questions.

'So, where does the seed come from?' Charlie asks the expert.

'It's in the body,' Dara says without looking up from the car he's making.

'But how does it get there?'

'It's just there but it takes years to turn into a baby.'

'Like a hundred years?'

'No! Cause then it'd be a granny.'

'Only if it was a girl.'

'Damn,' Dara says as a wheel flies off his car.

Later, Dara piles into the spaghetti. Charlie takes about three mouthfuls and stops.

'No ice cream till you finish.' This strategy always works.

'I'm full, Mama.'

'But you didn't finish your sandwiches at school. You must be hungry.'

'Do you call your mum, Mama?' Dara asks, apparently horrified.

Charlie looks down, doesn't answer.

'Sometimes he does,' I explain. 'What do you call your mum?'

'Mum.'

'Makes sense.' I smile. 'So what do you want to do now?'

'Football,' says Dara.

At the same time, Charlie says, 'Nothing.'

Dara looks at him. 'How could you want to do nothing?'

Charlie shrugs.

'Come on,' Dara pleads. 'You can be Ronaldo.'

'I'm tired.'

He must be very tired not to want to be his hero.

'Football will wake you up,' Dara says.

'My leg's sore.'

'Is it?' I ask.

He nods.

'Where?'

'Here.' He feels the upper part of his right thigh.

'Did you fall today?' I ask.

'No.'

'Bump into anything?'

'No.'

'Did someone kick you?'

'No.'

'I don't know. Pull down your trousers for a sec and let me have a look.'

He looks at Dara.

'It's OK, Charlie. Dara doesn't mind.'

'Nah, I see my brudders' butts all the time.'

'I have my undies on. You won't see my butt,' Charlie says.

'They're just white,' Dara says when he sees said undies. 'I've got *Star Wars* ones.'

Charlie's leg looks fine. 'It looks OK, Charlie,' I say, pulling back up his trousers.

'But it's sore.'

'Maybe it's a growing pain.'

'Yeah, I get them all the time,' says Dara. 'That's why I'm so big.'

'Would you like some Calpol?' I ask Charlie, sitting him up on the worktop and reaching up to the cupboard overhead for the bottle.

'Can I open it?' he asks.

'You can try,' I say, handing him the childproof container.

'It's broken,' he says eventually.

'Here let me try,' I say. I press down to disengage the lock then pour the pink, gloopy liquid onto a medicine spoon. 'Open Sesame.'

He opens Sesame.

'Why didn't it work for me?' he asks.

'The bottle's designed so that kids can't open it.'

'How does it know I'm a kid?'

I smile. 'It just does. Now, do you want to watch a movie till Dara's mum comes?'

Twenty minutes later, Charlie's asleep on the couch, Sausage snuggled up beside him. Dara's oblivious, hypnotised by the screen.

seven

'There's no such thing as daddies,' Charlie says, climbing into bed.

'Of course there is, Charlie,' I say, closing the curtains.

'No, Mum, there isn't. Only mummies. Not daddies.' He's sitting up, looking over at me, one hundred per cent sure.

I sit on the side of the bed and smile at him, trying to work out what I'm going to say. Where to start?

'A mummy's different from a zombie. They both are dead and come out of graves but they're different. Scooby and Shaggy are afraid of them, but I'm not.'

Oookaaay. 'Lie down, Charlie. Time to sleep.'

'I want to be a mummy for Halloween,' he says, flopping back onto the pillow, eyes still wide open.

'I thought you wanted to be a skeleton.' I've got the suit.

'No. A mummy.'

'Why?'

'Just do.'

'But skeletons are better.'

'Dara's going to be a mummy.'

Figures.

'Can I, Mum?'

Halloween is tomorrow. There's no way I'll find a mummy outfit, even if I had the time. I've an article to finish and an interview to do.

'We'll see. No go to sleep. Do you want the globe on?'

He nods tiredly.

I switch on his globe, a warm cosy football of turquoise and sand-coloured light, bought to help with his nightmares. It keeps the room from darkness and, if he wakes, it's familiar and he knows where he is.

'Lie down with me,' he says.

'Only if you go to sleep straight away.'

'OK.'

'OK.'

He sleeps instantly, almost as if it's a relief. *It must be school,* I think. *He's never been this tired before. I must get vitamins.*

I prise myself off the bed so as not to waken him. I stand gazing at my little angel with his blonde hair, determined little chin and cupid mouth. I kiss him gently on the forehead.

I go downstairs and ring Mary.

'How do you make a mummy?'

'You too?' she laughs.

'Afraid so.'

'Why don't you come over tomorrow? We'll work something out. Then you could come Trick or Treating with us. There are loads of houses in our estate and everyone's into Halloween. It's always fun.'

'You sure?'

'Of course. It'll be great.'

'Any of yours want to be a skeleton? I've a spare costume.'

'Probably too small. Sure bring it along. Someone might change their mind at the last second.'

'Never!'

Debbie wants to do Halloween with us because none of her friends want to do it anymore. Charlie thinks it's 'awesome'. She paints his face white, lips black and around his eyes red. Dara wants the same treatment. And he gets it. We wrap them both, head to toe, in bandages, giving them an instant excuse to ignore me.

'Can't hear you with the bandages.'

We start early, before dusk. Our reason: to get it over before they tire. Their reason: to get all the treats before other kids do. The older boys keep one house ahead of us, not wanting to 'hang out with the babies'. Debbie knocks on the doors with Charlie and Dara – two mummies and one giant skeleton.

'No one's in,' says Deb when she sees an outside light off.

'How do you know?' they ask, amazed by her psychic powers.

'I can feel it in my bones,' the skeleton says in a spooky voice.

She seems to enjoy a night off from being a teenager.

We drive to Killiney Hill to witness the illegal but brilliant firework display that happens here every Halloween. Rockets whizz, sizzle and pop to the sounds of ooh, wow and yahoo. Kids jump, hop, clap. Mary's second oldest, Alfie, the comedian, announces, 'zank you, zank you,' and bows flamboyantly. Luminous blue and white sparks light up the sky. We learn to judge how big an explosion will be by the noise the rocket makes on its way up. They keep the best till last – Catherine Wheels and Chinese Firecrackers impress so much we are silent. One firework escapes shooting along the ground, away from the crowd, then fizzling out. The kids gorge on their stash to the sound of U2's *Beautiful Day* on the car radio.

We go for chips in Dalkey. Charlie wants a whole packet but eats only four. He's too tired to walk so I piggyback him to the car. Less than a minute into the drive, he's asleep.

'He's such a sweetie,' says Debbie from the back.

'Yeah,' I say.

'He's so cute. Especially his little clothes.'

'Really?'

'The little shirts and chinos! He's such a dude.'

'He's going off them now. He wants Adidas hoodies.'

She laughs. 'He's a real little man, isn't he?'

I nod slowly. 'He's growing up so fast all of a sudden.'

'I guess you kind of have to when you start school.' There's something in her voice, like maybe regret? I think of her mum dying and how that must have made her grow up.

'Thanks for coming, tonight. It was amazing to have you here. He loves you, you know?'

'I so love him. The other day my dad, like, offered to increase my pocket money so I wouldn't have to babysit. But there's no way I'd stop babysitting Charlie. He's such fun.'

We pull up outside her house. I wait till she's safely inside before driving off, my mind racing. *Why would he do that, try to stop her? What's his problem? Does he think that I'm a bad influence, a single mum? Or has he finally recognised me? Do I remind him of his big mistake? He's not the one who suffered, though. I was the one who lost everything and had to start again.*

I head home, carry Charlie upstairs and stand outside the apartment, rummaging in my pocket for the keys. I find his toothbrush, which has been there since this morning, when I had to do a last-minute brush at the school gates. We've been so late for the last few days. Charlie is so slow to get started. He's just so tired. I let him sleep till the last minute. I put him to bed early. It doesn't make a difference. Maybe I should have waited till he was five to start school.

I settle him in, cover him up, switch on his globe and leave the door open. I wander back to the sitting room. Poor Sausage is hiding under the table. He hates Halloween. All those bangs and cracks. I light the candle in our pumpkin and admire the Muppet-like face we've sculpted – long, narrow nose, eyes too close together. He's lovely. I make a cup of tea, stirring the teabag with the toothbrush handle, too tired to look for a spoon. I slide onto the couch and kick off my shoes. I pat the cushion beside me and call Sausage. He looks unsure as to whether to stay cowering or take advantage of a rare offer. He goes for the rare offer.

We sit together, looking at the flickering light, as the noise

—
48

dies down outside, me rubbing his tummy absently. I'm thinking about Charlie and the battle I have with him every morning, to get him out of bed, to eat his porridge, to get him to stay at school. He really needs a break. *I* really need a break. Maybe we should take tomorrow off. Relax. Recover his energy reserves.

I wake at eleven to find him asleep in the bed beside me. It's such a treat to do nothing, so that's exactly what I do until he wakes. Instead of eating our usual breakfast, in our usual kitchen, I take him to the local coffee shop for croissants. I'm certain he'll eat all round him. But no. Half a croissant and not even a full glass of OJ.

Charlie wants to pay. He climbs down from his stool and walks ahead of me. I frown. *Is he limping?* It's hardly noticeable but he seems not to be pressing down fully on his right leg. *Is that the one he's been complaining about?* My stomach tightens. A sore leg is one thing, a limp another. I watch Charlie chat with the woman at the till and see how charmed she is. I do a quick mental calculation. It's not just the limp; it's the lack of energy, the loss of appetite, the fact that he has been really clingy – and worried. Almost as if he knows something's wrong. Maybe I'm overreacting. It's all pretty general and non-specific. He's probably just adjusting to school. Or having a growth spurt. Or missing having a dad. He's pale, though. And there's the limp. OK. I'm bringing him for a check-up.

The doctor has examined him. And found nothing. It doesn't help that the limp miraculously disappeared as soon as we walked into the surgery. The doctor is not worried but tells me to come back in a week if Charlie is still getting pains in his leg.

One week later, exactly, we're back. There has to be something wrong with his leg. He won't do PE. He won't play in the yard, afraid someone will bump into him. He doesn't complain every day. But most.

Again, Dr Finnegan finds nothing. The tiredness and 'pallor' she puts down to starting school and the fact that he hasn't been eating. Why he hasn't been eating she can't say but talks about 'non-specific viral infections' that are common when kids starts school. She recommends a tonic that I already have him on. She suggests an X-ray 'to be on the safe side', seeing as he has had the pain, on and off, for two weeks now. She writes a note for St Gabriel's Hospital, then pulls out a roll of stickers sponsored by some pharmaceutical company. Charlie picks two. A dinosaur and a shark.

Charlie has the X-ray and enjoys the experience. We're ready to go. Just waiting for the result. Unofficially, there's no break. Officially, they're waiting for some specialist to have a closer look. He doesn't seem in much of a hurry, though. Charlie is getting tired and cranky. I'm getting edgy and thinking of asking if we really need to stay for the result.

I stick my head out into the corridor to see if there is any news. Simon Grace is striding into the X-ray department, white coat flapping. I duck back into the waiting area.

I try to interest Charlie in a toy made of coloured, wooden counters that move over metal wires. He was interested – half an hour ago.

Someone behind us calls out Charlie's name.

'At last,' Charlie says.

I turn. It's Simon Grace. His eyes are scanning the room. He doesn't seem to notice he's calling my Charlie. He's holding a chart.

Wait. Hold on.

There must be some mistake. He must have the wrong chart. Simon Grace is an oncologist. We don't need an oncologist.

He calls the name again.

'It's me,' Charlie says.

Simon turns.

I stand up. Slowly.

Simon's face falls.

'Jenny,' he says slowly. Then he recovers, looking down at Charlie with a big smile. 'Hello, little man.'

'Hello. Can we go now?'

'I'm sorry,' I say to Simon. 'I think there's been a mistake. Charlie's just here for an X-ray.'

'Yes, I have it, here. I've been asked to look at it.'

'Why?' almost doesn't come out.

'Let's talk somewhere quieter.'

I follow him in terrified silence. Charlie's ahead, holding his hand and chatting about X-rays. We reach an office. I follow them in. He asks me to sit.

I don't feel like sitting. I feel like running. With my son. Out of here. But I sit, silently, with Charlie on my lap, my arms wrapped around him.

'Jenny.' He drags a swivel chair out from behind the desk and pulls it up to where Charlie and I are sitting. He smiles what he probably thinks is a reassuring smile. 'I've been asked to have a look at Charlie's X-ray...'

'Charlie's X-ray is fine. They told me. They just wanted to get a specialist to have a quick look at it.'

'Me.'

'You're an oncologist.'

He looks uncomfortable. 'Yes, I am. But my involvement at this stage is just a precaution. There's no reason for alarm. There are one or two things in Charlie's X-ray that require further investigation. There could be any number of reasons for them. We are just being thorough.'

'What other specialists are involved?'

'Well, none. At the moment. But, in fairness, that doesn't mean anything. This is a step-by-step process. I'll co-ordinate the tests, then we'll take it from there. I would like to examine Charlie, now, if that's all right with you?'

I turn Charlie so that he's facing me. 'Charlie, Simon wants to have a little look at you, OK?'

'OK,' Charlie says cheerfully.

Simon walks over to an examination bench that is covered in disposable paper. He pats it.

'Do you think you could climb up here? Only really clever boys – and monkeys – can get up here.'

Charlie gets down from my lap, guarding his leg. 'I can get up there.' He climbs the portable steps. 'See?'

'Hmm. You are smart,' Simon says.

'No. I'm a monkey. Ooh, ooh,' Charlie says, lifting his arms and pretending to scratch under them. He beats his chest.

We laugh. But I don't mean it.

'So. How are you, Charlie?' asks Simon.

'Ooh, ooh,' Charlie chirps.

Oh no.

Simon just smiles. 'Can you be a boy again for a minute?'

'Can I be a doctor, like you?'

'You can. Would you like to examine me?' asks Simon. 'This is a stethoscope. Do you want to listen to my heart?'

Charlie takes it. 'Nifty.'

Simon laughs.

'Breathe in,' says Charlie, putting the stethoscope to Simon's chest, frowning and turning his eyes towards his left ear as though listening with them. There is something unnerving about the two of them being so close together.

'Again,' instructs Charlie.

Simon breathes in.

'Again.'

Simon inhales.

'Again.'

He obeys. Then says, 'Now, my turn.'

I examine him examining my son – throat, ears, eyes – the usual drill.

'I'm just checking for swollen lymph glands,' he explains to me when he starts to feel Charlie's neck.

Lymph glands. Why lymph glands? I'm trying to remember all the articles I've written, all the conferences I've attended. *Lymphoma?* I panic.

'They're fine.'

Thank God. I breathe out.

'Now I'm checking his liver.'

Liver? Why liver?

'Fine.'

It's OK. Everything's going to be OK.

'Now I'm checking to see if I can feel Charlie's spleen.' He stops, shifts position. Presses around a bit more. 'I can feel the tip ever so slightly.'

So? What does that mean? I'm afraid to ask.

'How has he been?'

I list the symptoms. They sound so familiar, having called them out so many times, to so many people, including myself. I feel like a suspect in a murder enquiry.

'How long has he been feeling like this?'

'About two weeks. Though, he's been pale for longer.'

'I see.'

'I've been to the GP. Twice. She said Charlie's fine. The X-ray is just a precaution.'

He nods. 'I'd like to run a few blood tests, if that's all right with you.'

'What tests?'

'A Full Blood Count to check for anaemia, to see why Charlie is so pale. And a test to check for inflammation, to see why his spleen might be swollen.'

Swollen? You didn't say swollen. You said tip. Not swollen.

'We'll know more when we have the results. I'll organise someone to take them now, if that's all right with you?'

I nod.

'I'll need you to sign a consent form. It's just a formality to say you agree with tests being carried out.'

I nod again.

'Have you had a cup of tea?'

'We're fine, thanks.' We'll be going home soon.

'I'm thirsty,' Charlie insists.

I pull a carton of apple juice from my satchel.

Simon smiles, then gets up, looking a bit weary. 'I'll just sort out the paperwork.'

eight

A woman in blue arrives with news that she will be relieving my son of blood. She taps his arm, 'looking for a suitable vein', then rubs 'magic cream' onto two areas – the back of his hand and the area where his arm flexes. It's an anaesthetic she explains. Then she covers the cream with something like Cling Film. It will take forty-five minutes to work. That's when she'll be back for the real action.

I distract Charlie by taking him to look for the canteen. We stop a man to ask for directions. He has two children with him, one in pyjamas – he knows his way round.

'Go up that ramp, turn left and down the stairs,' he says.

'Thanks.'

'I wouldn't touch the coffee, though.'

I smile.

Charlie finishes his apple juice and doesn't want anything to eat. I risk the coffee and survive. We kill ten minutes, then get restless, so it's on to the hospital shop to buy colouring books, crayons and a toy Ernie that sings and wiggles his bum. Enough, I hope, to distract Charlie from Dracula.

She's there when we get back. Waiting. Like a bird of prey. She smiles. Charlie doesn't notice her, too busy checking to see what colour crayons he has. He doesn't want the pink.

'We'll just pop in here for a second, love,' she says cheerfully, heading for the room we were in earlier. I wonder is it the Bad Luck Room or even the Bad News Room. Either way, I don't like it. But I'm the adult. Agreeable. Co-operative. Calm.

I follow her.

In five seconds flat, she has me in a chair with Charlie sitting crossways on my lap, just so. I wonder how many times she does this in an average day.

'Now, sweetheart,' she says, quickly applying a tourniquet to Charlie's arm. 'I just have to give your arm a little squeeze for a moment. You look at your mum, pet. I think she's got something she wants to show you.' She gives me a meaningful look.

'Oh, Charlie, look – Ernie sings.'

'I know,' he says, eyeing Dracula.

'Let's see what he says,' I try.

'You ain't nothing but a hound dog,' says Charlie. 'I know. Dara's got a singing Ernie. What are you doing?' he asks the Count just as she produces a needle.

'It won't hurt, love, because you've got the magic cream on.' She doesn't give him a chance to argue. In the needle goes. Charlie screams, 'It's sore, it's sore, take it out.'

'I just need to keep it in for a little bit longer, pet. Then it'll be all over.'

She lets my son's blood drip into three test tubes, each with a different coloured rubber top.

'Now, Charlie, I want you to meet Freddie,' she says, and to me: 'It's a cannula that stays in his vein in case he needs medicine intravenously.' She seesaws back to Charlie. 'We'll just put on his little green hat.'

'Take it out. Take it out. I don't want it.'

I hug him tighter and kiss the top of his head.

'Charlie,' she says. 'You need Freddie. He's going to stay in your arm for a little while.'

'Dr Grace didn't mention this,' I say to her. 'He just said about the blood test. We're not staying.'

'It's probably just a precaution. We do it all the time if we're taking blood. It saves the child having to have another jab later if he needs intravenous medication.'

What intravenous medication?

'Don't want Freddie. Don't like Freddie. Take him out.' Charlie's crying now, his little face contorted and red. I want to stick a needle in her arm so she can see just how unmagic her cream is.

'Freddie is just a straw,' she says. 'He's not a needle. I took the needle out, Charlie. Freddie is just a tiny little straw. He's all bendy. He doesn't hurt. I think he wants a little drink. Will we give him a drink?'

'No. Freddie's not thirsty. Leave Freddie alone.'

'Just a little tiny bit of 7Up. It won't hurt.'

'You said that before. And it did hurt.'

'Charlie,' I say. 'If you just let Freddie have a little drink, this nice lady will go away and maybe then we can play soldiers, OK?'

'But you didn't get the soldiers.'

'I will. We'll go back to the shop and get them.'

He looks down. Frowns. 'OOOOK,' he says at last.

It's over very quickly. She starts to pack up her things. Charlie climbs down off my lap and starts to poke at her box of tricks. It's like a plastic toolbox and I can see the attraction to child eyes – lots of nooks and crannies and interesting unfamiliar objects. She looks at me as if to say, hel-*lo,* these are sterile.

'Charlie, stop, love. Leave the lady's things alone.'

'Can we get the soldiers now?'

'In a sec.' I turn to the phlebotomist who is snapping her toolbox closed and lifting it up by the handle. 'How long will the results take?

'There's a rush on these, so we should have them in a couple of hours.'

'Hours?'

Simon arrives. She smiles hello to him and bye to me. Then off she hurries to puncture someone else.

'The results will take hours,' I tell him. Stupidly. He, of all people, must know that.

'I'm afraid that's the quickest we can get them, Jenny.'

'Maybe we could go home and ring in for them, rather than waiting?'

'I'd prefer you to wait, if you don't mind.' He pauses, looks at me directly and says, slowly, clearly. 'There is a possibility we might need to admit Charlie for further investigation. Maybe there's someone who could come in and keep you company?'

I shut down my brain. I, will, not, think. I, will, not, panic. 'We're fine, thank you. We're fine.' I fold my arms. Because we won't need anyone. We're going home.

He looks at Charlie, then back at me, his face full of meaning. 'It might be an idea.'

My stomach whooshes towards my chest and the thoughts break through. *It's cancer. It's cancer.*

'A family member, friend?'

I look at Charlie, his face all innocent and light. He's banging the 'I've been brave' sticker the phlebotomist gave him onto his chest. I feel like bursting into tears but know that it's me who must be brave now.

'I have a friend. Mary. I need to call Mary.'

'Good. Good. Maybe, while you do that, I could bring Charlie off to show him his X-ray? As he's going to be a doctor.' He stoops down to my son. 'How about it? Would you like to see your X-ray, Charlie?'

'Cool. Wow.' He rushes over to Simon and takes his hand. He gives a little excited jump. *My baby; don't take my baby.*

'We're just going to the room opposite. We'll be back in three or four minutes. Give you a moment to talk.'

'See you in a minute, Mum,' says Charlie, his energy suddenly recharged just when I'm about to be told there's something wrong.

Charlie returns with an impressive vocabulary of radiology banter. Simon has a few things to do but promises to be back as soon as he has news. We go for the soldiers, then wander round the hospital. I'm distracting myself as much as Charlie. The corridors are busy. So many people. So many uniforms. I pretend I care which is which. Who wears the white tops and navy trousers? Nurses? What about the green tops and navy trousers? Physios? The phlebotomists are blue; *that* I know. Doctors are identifiable as much by their attitude of cosy superiority as by their customary white coats and stethoscopes. People in scrub gear remind me of *Grey's Anatomy*.

The people keep coming. Children in pyjamas and slippers. Some in dressing gowns, others not. Parents, brothers, sisters dressed for the outside world, some looking displaced, confused, others sadly familiar with the place. Every now and then a really sick-looking child passes, wearing a hospital mask, or in a wheelchair, or attached to a drip. Or all three. You think the boy with the sling is lucky that all he has is a broken bone, then you think again – maybe there's more to it. One thing is obvious: the lack of smiles. The worry.

The walls are the colour of strawberry cheesecake, decorated at regular intervals with cartoon murals – *Bear in the Big Blue House*, *Peppa Pig* and quite possibly every Disney character ever created. We end up back at X-ray and decide to stay put.

Charlie needs to use the toilet.

We find a single one.

As requested, I stand guard outside the unlocked door. That's when I see Mary, coming through the doors of X-ray, looking around for us.

I wave. She looks relieved to see me. I'm relieved to see her.

We hug. Cool outdoor air clings to her like a healthy aura. Fresh and crisp. I try to suck in its energy.

'There's something wrong, Mary,' I say, pulling back and looking at her. 'It's, it's... There is an oncologist doing tests.'

'Have they said anything definite?'

'No but why else would they ask me to bring someone in?'

'Maybe they just want to talk to you without Charlie there.'

'They wouldn't need to do that if the news was good.'

'Just wait and see, Jenny. Whatever happens, I'm here. OK?'

'Hi, Mary,' chirps a little voice. 'What are you doing here?'

I switch on my happy face.

'Just popped in to say hi,' she says, smiling.

'Hi!'

'Hi, Charlie.' She bends down. 'How're you doing?'

'Great. I got soldiers.' He holds them up. 'Can I play with them now, Mum?'

'Course you can, sweetie. Let's go in here.'

We sit in the waiting room. And wait.

The moment I've been simultaneously waiting for and dreading arrives. Dr Grace, the man who messed up my life once, is here to do it again.

Charlie's so busy he doesn't take much notice.

'Charlie, do you mind if I have a chat with your mum in my office?'

He looks up, suddenly alert.

Mary roots in her bag. 'Charlie look what I got.' It's Dara's Nintendo DS.

'Cool! Can I've a go?'

'Sure. It's *Scooby Doo*.'

'Aw, deadly.'

I rub his hair when really I want to scoop him up and run. 'See you in a minute, bud.'

nine

He offers me a chair, then sits himself.

'How are you?' he asks.

'Fine thank you.'

'Did you get a cup of tea?'

'Yes, thanks.'

'Good. I'm sorry to have held you up, Jenny, but we have a preliminary result.'

Three things tell me it's not good. One: he asked me to sit. Two: his face. Three: his voice. I hold my breath.

'Charlie is anaemic.'

Anaemic? That's not bad.

'Have you any idea why that might be?'

I remember what Dr Finnegan said. 'He hasn't been eating?'

'Yes, it could be that. Though it's quite marked. His White Cell Count is quite low, too.' It's the way he says it.

'What are you trying to tell me, Simon? Please just come out and say it.'

'Jenny. There are a few things it could be. Charlie has anaemia, a low White Cell Count, combined with tiredness, pallor and loss of appetite.'

I think of Great, who had all those symptoms. But it couldn't be. Not Charlie. Not again.

'It's not leukaemia, Simon. Please tell me it's not leukaemia,' I whisper, afraid to look up. Because I couldn't take it.

It's very quiet.

I have to look up. I have to know.

He seems to be making a point of looking straight into my eyes. 'I'm considering a few things, Jenny. But, in fairness, leukaemia is one of them.'

'Oh God.' I bite the back of my hand. Hard.

'We need to do a bone marrow biopsy. That will give us a clearer picture.' He pauses. 'Do you know what a bone marrow biopsy is?'

'Yes. My grandmother died of leukaemia.' I feel heat at the back of my throat, my eyes beginning to smart.

'We don't have a diagnosis yet, Jenny. I know this is a very worrying time for you, but try not to think of the worst, not yet.'

'How can you say that?'

'Children are very sensitive to their parents. You mightn't realise it, but Charlie can read you better than anyone. You don't want him picking up on your anxieties.'

I fill my lungs to give me strength. The ribs in my back expand and rise.

'With children, we do bone marrow biopsies under anaesthetic because they can be quite sore. But it's a very straightforward procedure and over quickly. Charlie would need to be fasting for six hours, though, so he would need to be admitted overnight. I've checked with theatre and they can fit us in tomorrow.'

Slow down. Slow down. Stop!

'I'll need you to sign another consent form to say that you agree to his being admitted and to any tests that are needed,' he says, eyebrows raised as if in permission.

I close my eyes and nod.

'I'd like to get Charlie up to the ward now and settle him in. He should have something to eat. It's been a long day. I need to confirm some things with the ward and get that consent form. That will give you time to arrange things.'

I sit, unable to move.

He must have said something because he's looking at me like he's waiting for an answer.

'Can I just sit here for a few minutes?'

'Of course. Take all the time you need. Do you want me to stay?'

'No. I just need a few minutes before going back to Charlie.'

'Would you like me to get a nurse?'

'No. No, thanks.'

'I'll be back soon.' He puts a hand on my shoulder on the way out.

I don't like asking Mary to get the few things we need. And I don't have to. She offers before I can ask. Not only that but she reminds me that we have a dog that needs to be fed and walked, remembers to ask for the key to the apartment and the alarm code. She thinks of getting Charlie's pillow so he'll sleep. She even knows to ask where things are. My brain has shut down, my thoughts telescoped into Charlie and this.

Mary goes, reminding me that she has her mobile if I think of anything else we need. Simon returns and walks us to the ward, carrying Ernie, the soldiers and the colouring paraphernalia. I think it strange for a doctor to volunteer his arms in such a way but mine are full, carrying a very tired little boy. We were offered a wheelchair but No Thank You.

The ward looms ahead of us, at the end of a long, long corridor.

'St Anne's,' says a big yellow placard. 'Haematology/Oncology/Bone Marrow Transplant,' declares another. *What are they trying to do, terrify us?* There are so many signs, I can't take them all in. 'Please Switch Off Mobile Phones Now.' 'Parents Only Allowed On Ward.' 'Please Keep Door Closed.' 'Door Locked after 7.30pm.'

We all go quiet. Even Charlie.

We're about fifty yards away when one of the doors opens out. A lone girl emerges, quiet and slow. From her height, I reckon she must be in her early teens. Otherwise, she is ageless – hair gone, replaced by a vague coconut-type fuzz of frosted light brown. Her head is big in comparison with her body, which seems shrunken behind a pale pink dressing gown. Her ankles are thin.

I think of Belsen, Auschwitz.

She glides forward, head erect, nothing moving apart from her legs. Her feet make their way slowly, silently, along the Marmoleum floor yet she seems to float. Like a ghost. The full force of what is happening to us hits me and I feel like throwing up. I start to turn away but realise that the girl might think I can't look at her. So I face her, smiling as if to say, 'Hello, you look perfectly normal and aren't scaring me to death.'

She smiles back. *She is only a child. How can she be so calm, so serene, so confident? How can she not be panicking?* She waves at Charlie.

'Why doesn't she have hair, Mum?' He asks at the top of his voice as she passes by. He says it innocently, happily, as if it's a personal choice she's made.

'I'll tell you later,' I whisper, which of course I won't.

'But I want to know now.'

'Later, Charlie.'

Simon holds the door open.

The ward is cheerful. Too cheerful. Primary colours everywhere, bright posters with happy faces, natural light pouring in through skylights and large windows. Everything looks clean, fresh, modern. A woman in green is coming towards us, smiling. I want to turn and run my baby out of here.

'You must be Charlie.' He gets a special smile reserved for small sick people. 'I've been waiting for you. My name is Anne. See?'

She shows him a smiley badge pinned to the pocket of her uniform. 'How are you?'

Suddenly shy, Charlie hides his face in my chest.

She smiles at me.

'I'll leave you to settle in,' says Simon. 'I'll call in to see you before I leave.' He ruffles Charlie's hair. 'All right, son?' It's an innocent expression. That makes me catch my breath.

'He's a wonderful doctor,' sighs Anne, as we watch his back disappear down the corridor and into a room marked Oncologist. 'He's in charge here, but you'd never know it. We're a team. I'm the sister, which officially means I'm the nurse in charge, but, as I say, we're a team. If you need anything at all while you're here, please, just ask. And I'll introduce you to everybody else...'

'Thanks, Anne. But we should be gone tomorrow.'

'Yes, yes, of course. Maybe I'll show you Charlie's bed now? He looks tired. And must be hungry. You're just in time for tea, Charlie.' Her voice starts to sing. 'Do you like chips?'

He doesn't answer.

'He hasn't been eating much, but he might try a few chips,' I say, passing a large metal trolley with meals on it. The smell of hospital food reminds me of Great and I feel sick again.

We get to a room with six beds. Children and parents go about their business. I don't take in detail, apart from three things – a little bald boy scooting around in a yellow and orange toy car, a tube coming from his nose; an empty cot; and a teenage boy sitting cross-legged on his bed, wearing a grey hoodie. The hood is up. I can guess why. His head is down. He is concentrating on an iPhone that he's tilting from side to side. He's chewing gum – fast. His headboard is covered with cards. His locker is full of drinks and sweets and his bed is strewn with clothes, books and sweet wrappers.

'Damn,' he says and looks up. He sees us. 'Hey,' he says to Charlie.

'Hey,' Charlie says. 'What're you playing?' He goes over for a look.

'Well, I *was* playing Doodle Jump but I just lost.'

I'm aware of Anne waiting. 'Come on, Charlie, we better go.'

'But I'm talking to this guy.'

The boy smiles. 'Mark.'

'I'm talking to Mark.'

'Well, maybe you can talk to Mark later because we have to check out your bed now.'

He sighs dramatically. 'OooKaay.'

I take his hand and, as we walk away, he keeps looking backwards.

We reach his bed. It looks clinical and bare.

'I want a bed like Mark.'

'It takes a while to make your bed like that.'

'Where's everyone's hair?' he asks, quieter this time.

'Their hair has fallen out, Charlie, because of the medicine they're taking. But it will grow back,' says Anne.

'Everyone looks sick, Mama.'

'They are sick, Charlie. That's why they're in hospital,' I say, trying to be as honest as Anne.

'But I'm not sick, sure I'm not?'

Anne answers for me. Luckily. 'Charlie, the doctors need to check out why you haven't been feeling well.' She sits on the bed with us and explains in child terms what a bone marrow biopsy is. Charlie has no difficulty grasping the concept of taking a teeny tiny piece of bone so the doctors can have a look at it under a microscope. He has a question, though:

'Will it hurt?'

'No, Charlie, you will be asleep.'

'How do you know?'

'The doctors will give you medicine to make you sleep.'

'Will that hurt?'

'No.'

'Are my bones like the ones that Sausage eats?'

'Sausage is our dog,' I explain.

'No, pet,' Anne says. Our bones are a little bit different.'

The conversation continues for another few minutes before Charlie starts to wilt. Anne leaves and I take off his runners to put them into an otherwise empty locker. I bang them together to make the lights flash. I make a wish.

ten

Mary arrives, globe in one hand, my case in the other.

I laugh. 'Where did you dig that out?' The case is gigantic, bought when I was moving in with Great.

'It was either that or a bin bag,' she says smiling. 'I'm thinking of your image, here.'

'Are we going on holidays?' asks Charlie.

'No, handsome,' Mary says. 'I've just got a few of your things in here.' She heaves it on the bed, then opens it up.

'You're like Mary Poppins,' Charlie says.

'Practically perfect in every way?'

'No. The way you're pulling stuff out. Mary Poppins does that. Have you got a lamp in there, too?' Charlie kneels up beside the case, holding on to the edge, peering in. 'What have you got?'

Two pillows, PJs, Cookie Monster, towels, hair gel, toothbrushes and paste, my mobile phone charger, even the cool yoga gear I was intimidated into buying by the yoga babes.

'For sleeping in,' she tells me.

'Brilliant.' Because it would have felt weird wearing pyjamas.

'How's Sausage?' Charlie asks, holding Cookie Monster to his chest.

'He's fine, Charlie. Dara, his dad and the boys are taking him for a walk on Killiney Hill. They had a fight about who'd feed him.

'Who won?'

'Dara.'

'Yes!' Charlie punches the air. 'Go, Dara.'

'Alfie got to hold his lead.'

'You don't need a lead on Killiney Hill, Mary,' says Charlie who's been given a mood boost by the sight of his favourite books, jigsaws and trucks.

'I'll let them know, Charlie. Come here. Have you got a hug for me?'

'I'm not a hug man, Mary.'

'Is that right?' She looks at me and mouths, 'so cute.' Then she hands me a packet.

'What's this?'

'Earplugs. You'll need them. I'll never forget the noise when Dara had his tonsils out. Drips bleeping, kids crying, other parents snoring. Nightmare. Anyway, with these little babies, you won't hear a thing. Now go get your mattress before all the good ones are gone.'

'What mattress?'

'A mattress for you to sleep on. Where did you think you were going to sleep?'

'Hadn't got that far.'

'Beside your son on the floor. Here, I'll get one for you. They leave them outside on the corridor usually. I'll get some blankets in the linen cupboard. They're a bit tight with them so I'll sneak as many as I can. You'd be surprised how cold it gets at night.'

'Mary, they don't strike me as being like that. They seem very nice so far.'

'You're lucky. There were a few cows looking after Dara.'

Charlie's head pops up. 'Were there *cows* looking after Dara when he was in hospital?'

'No, sweetie. Mary was joking.'

Mary winks at him. 'Now, let's see,' she says to me. 'Is there anything else you should know? Food. Yes. Well, you'll have to look after yourself on that front. Pop down to the canteen and collect something and bring it back to the ward. There's usually a sitting room where parents can eat. There's a kitchen too with a microwave, fridge and water dispenser. Some of the staff don't like you going in and helping yourself. Others don't mind. Play it by ear. Now, have you money for food?'

God, she thinks of everything. 'Yeah, I think I'm OK, thanks.' I check my wallet to be sure. 'Yeah, I'm grand, thanks.'

'OK well let me know when you need more and I can get it for you.'

'Mary, we're only staying a night.'

'Oh yeah.' She laughs. 'Got a bit carried away. OK, look, I'd better go. I'll call, in the morning. Are you sure you're all right, now? Nothing else I can do?'

'No. You've been amazing, thanks. And you don't have to come in tomorrow. You've loads to do.'

'It's fine. The boys will be at school. Free agent.'

'School! I better tell them.'

'I'll tell them, if you like.'

'God, Mary, that'd be great. I'm not supposed to use the mobile. It affects the machines or something.'

'I know, yeah, but everyone does. Anyway I'll tell Ms Ford.'

'Thanks.'

As she leaves, a nurse we haven't seen before walks onto the ward and over to the boy in the tracksuit.

'Is that the pig?'

'What?'

'The pig who was looking after Dara?'

'Charlie, shh. There were no animals looking after Dara. Just people, OK?'

'OK, Mum, but Mary said...'

'Mary was joking. Now come on – let's get you dressed for bed.'

71

He slides onto the floor and starts to take off his trousers. I watch in amazement.

'Good boy! You're dressing yourself! Wow!'

'Dara does.'

'Does he now?' I say, impressed.

'Yup.' He holds his pyjama bottoms up too high, then tries to get his leg into them. I'm about to come to the rescue when he falls over.

'You OK?'

'Yeah. Dara falls over all the time. He says you're supposed to.'

'I see. Here, I'll hold them – now you step in. Great. Now sit up here and we'll take off your top.'

He holds his arms up. I pull the jumper over his head.

'Ow. What was that?' he asks.

'I think we must have given each other a little shock.'

'Why?'

'It's static electricity. It's probably because the air is so dry in here.' I pat down his hair, which is still sticking straight up. His skin looks like it's never seen sunlight and his ribs stick out. I hurry to put on his comfy white cotton top with long sleeves. Then give him a hug.

At nine, Charlie's asleep and I'm getting my own 'bed' ready, dragging the mattress into position, when Simon appears so quietly, I don't realise he's there for a moment.

'Oh, hi,' I say, leaning the mattress against the side of the bed and rubbing my hands together.

He looks at Charlie and smiles. 'Did he settle in all right?'

'Once he got his toys and pillow.'

'And you? How are you?' He sits on the wooden arm of the standard-issue, wipe-clean armchair beside Charlie's bed. I take it as a signal and sit at the edge of the bed.

'I'm fine. Thanks.'

'Not an easy time,' he says quietly.

'No.'

'You know, Jenny, family can be a great support at times like this.'

I think of my mum. Say nothing.

'Do you have family?'

'We're not close.'

'Anyone outside of your friend...?'

'Mary?' I think of Jack. But Jack's my boss. 'Not really, no.'

'No one at work?' He looks at me. *Does he know? Has he remembered?*

'Charlie and I, we look after ourselves.'

He nods slowly. 'Well, if you need it, you'll find a lot of support here.'

'No offense but I'm hoping we won't need it.'

'Jenny. We'll get a preliminary result while Charlie is in theatre tomorrow.' My stomach contracts. 'Depending on what we find, I need your permission to insert a permanent cannula into a vein in Charlie's chest. It's a better way of giving medication than the Freddies in peripheral veins, which don't last and need to be replaced constantly. We can also take blood samples this way. It's much more convenient for the children.'

Every time he talks, he seems more and more certain of what he'll find. If Charlie comes back with something in his chest, I'll know.

'Try to get some rest,' he says. 'I'll bring a consent form in the morning and talk to Charlie about the Freddie.' He looks at him. 'He's a lovely little fellow.'

'I know,' is my hoarse reply.

The mattress is a child's one – wafer thin and about the same dimensions. My feet overshoot it. I have to put my pillow onto the floor. My feet still stick out. I try sticking my bum out and pointing my legs forward to the opposite corner. Better. Temporarily. I turn over and adopt the foetal position. My direct line of vision is under Charlie's bed. My eyes adjust in time to see a spider of tarantulan proportions crawling stealthily towards me. I spring up, impressively silent, and kick the mattress out of the way. I imagine it crawling into my ear or hair while asleep (if I ever do) and think about killing it. But I can't go near it. All I can do is stand watching it continue on its hairy way under the next bed towards a sleeping mother with an open mouth. Which is another problem. She snores. Loudly. The earplugs take the edge off but now that I've become familiar with the timing of the honks, I'm waiting for the next, like a dripping tap.

Three things stop me from lying back down. Arachnophobia, snoring and stiffness. I stretch, circle my shoulders, let my head fall forward, then backwards. A walk might help. I check that Charlie is sleeping soundly, take out the earplugs, (they're pushing against the walls of my ear), slide my feet into my slippers. Head muzzy, eyelids heavy, I walk along the corridor.

From somewhere near the nurses' station comes the inconsolable, unformed cry of a very young baby. *Surely, you can't get cancer that early? Why else would it be here? And what are they doing to make it cry like that?* I turn and walk in the opposite direction, try to blank it from my mind. What I need to do is remember. Everything I've ever heard, read or written about leukaemia. I think about Great and how it affected her. But I can't do it. Not in a detached way. Not without getting upset.

I think of a woman I interviewed from Dun Laoghaire. Her daughter had leukaemia. I remember how brave she was, how well she seemed to cope. It came on quickly, I remember that. Her daughter – what was her name? God, I can't remember. Too many interviews between then and now. I remember her face, though. So clearly. She started getting infections. One after the other. Charlie hasn't had that. Her blood count was like Charlie's. Everything down. She had Acute Lymphoblastic Leukaemia. She was doing very well on chemo. If she stayed in remission for five years, her prognosis would be excellent. I wonder how she's doing. And can't believe I've forgotten her. When I get out of here, I'll look her mother up.

I hear the sound of vomiting and hurry back to the room. It's not Charlie. It's not anyone in this room. My boy is in a happy restful sleep. I move a strand of hair from his face. My little angel.

I wander over to the window, pull back the blind with a finger and peep out at the clear night sky. The full moon looks like a poppadum. The stars wink at it – 'come on, don't hang there all night, taking everything so seriously; come play.'

I try to think of anything else it could possibly be – something with the same symptoms, something that needs a quick course of antibiotics and a little rest. I look over at my baby. Then back to the sky. I ask whoever's up there why he should have to go through this. If he does. But in my heart I know he does. Why else would I be standing here in a cancer ward at three in the morning looking up at the stars?

eleven

A man stands in front of you, a shotgun pointed at your stomach. He squeezes the trigger. You get the full blast and reel back against the wall. Your insides are blown out. You can't breathe. An animal wails. But it's not an animal – it's you. You slide down along the wall to the ground, wrapping your arms around your legs, pressing your face into your thighs, hands over the back of your head, eyes shut. You can't speak, react, move. You just crouch there like a fool. That is what it's like to be told that your child has leukaemia. At least, that's what it's like for me.

I'm sitting in the chair opposite him now, Mary beside me. I don't know what he's saying. And Mary might as well not be here. I ignore them and cling, like a spider at the edge of a drain, to the possibility that it's a mistake. *Preliminary results, he said – not final, not definite. Charlie has anaemia, nothing more. The other thing is a mistake. It has to be. What are the chances that the two people you loved most in the world would get the same disease? Tiny. Miniscule. Impossible. It just couldn't happen.*

Why won't he shut up? Can't he see I'm not taking any of this in? Why doesn't he leave me alone?

He is only four. HE IS ONLY FOUR.

I'm supposed to be next, not Charlie. He has another eighty years. Let this be a mistake. Please God, let him be OK. I'll do anything. Be a better mum. Be a better person. Whatever it takes.

I hear the words, 'cure rate'. Eighty to eighty-five per cent. 'That's-really-good,' Mary's face says, eyebrows up, head nodding. She doesn't know that I've watched the person who'd been my mother all my life being eaten away by this disease. I looked on the positive side then. It didn't work.

I can't go through this again. I can't.

I should have known something was wrong. Charlie knew. He was worried. He didn't want to be away from me. He knew. Why didn't I? What kind of mother am I?

There will be a cannula in his chest now, my little man, lying unconscious, in the recovery room, oblivious to the cancer cells attacking his bone marrow, suffocating the good cells. I want them to start treatment. Now. This minute. Don't wait another second. But what will I tell Charlie? I can't tell him he has leukaemia. He knows what that means.

'I can't tell him,' I say, my head jerking up and swinging in panic from Mary to Simon. 'I can't tell him he has leukaemia.'

Mary looks from me to Simon, eyes wide. But he is calm, unruffled.

'Would it be easier if I told him?' he asks.

'No! He's my son. My responsibility. I'll tell him.' But I'm stuck. 'I just can't say it's leukaemia. His great-granny died of it. He was mad about her. He'd be terrified. He'd think he was going to die.' I'm up from the chair, standing with a hand on either side of my face.

Simon gets up and comes around the desk to me. He puts an arm loosely behind my back and leads me back to the chair. Then he goes to the water cooler. He hands me a plastic cup. My hands are shaking so much I'm afraid it'll spill. I reach forward and put it on his desk. I knock it over. Water oozes out all over his desk. I watch, hypnotised by it. Mary starts to mop it up with hankies. Her rapid movements bring me to attention. I look at Simon.

'I actually can't tell him. I can't do it to him.'

'Jenny, I'm so sorry about Charlie's great-granny. In fairness, though, childhood leukaemia has a significantly better prognosis than adult. You could almost consider them different diseases.'

The relief when he says that. Two different diseases.

'In terms of explaining things to Charlie, in my experience, you can be honest with children without frightening them.' He pauses. 'And it is best to be as honest as you can. You would be surprised how sensitive they are to their parents. If you are worried, they'll know, and they'll worry too. If you're not open with Charlie, he'll hide his feelings from you so as not to upset you further. But he *will* worry.'

'But he's only four.'

'At that age, instinct is very strong. And you must remember that there is an especially strong bond between you and Charlie because it's just the two of you. You are the most important person in his world. He is highly sensitive to you. There's another issue. If you're not open with him, when he goes back to school – and he will, Jenny – other children will know that he has leukaemia. News travels. Being children, they'll say it to him. He needs to be prepared for that.'

'Telling him he has leukaemia would be like telling he's going to die. That's what he'd think.'

'In fairness, we could explain that his great-granny...'

'Great.'

'Sorry?'

'Great. We called her 'Great'. You should know that in case you're ever talking to him about her.'

He nods. 'Thank you. I think it's important that we explain that Great had a different type of leukaemia; the type that children get is much easier to fix. Then, if he's confronted with it, he won't be afraid. He'll have an answer for himself as well as for them.' He pauses, then says, 'Would you like me to stay with you while you're telling him – just in case?'

'I don't know...yes...maybe...I should tell him though.'

He nods.

'Can I though? Look at the state of me.' I look into his eyes. 'Do we have to tell him today?'

'No.' A pause. 'Not until you're ready. But he will sense that something is wrong and he will worry, so we can't leave it too long. Maybe this evening, when he has recovered from the anaesthetic. I'll be around.'

His bleep goes off. He fishes it out of his pocket, squints at the number, picks up the phone and dials.

'Simon Grace.' He listens, then says, 'Thank you. We're on our way,' he says, looking directly at me. He replaces the receiver and smiles when he says, 'Charlie's awake. He'll be coming out of the recovery room in a few minutes. Let's go up to meet him.'

I stand up immediately. My head spins. I reach forward to steady myself with the desk. I close my eyes to stop the spinning. I feel an arm around my back.

'Sit back down, for a second, Jenny,' he says. 'Catch your breath.'

'I'm fine. I'll be OK.' I have to be. For Charlie. But I've started crying. Of all times.

'Sit for a moment. You got up too quickly. Wait for your blood pressure to adjust. Sit.'

'I don't want Charlie to find me not there.'

Mary hands me a hankie.

I blow hard, shove the hankie in my pocket then wipe each eye with the heel of a hand. I take a deep breath and hold it, pushing myself up using the arms of the chair.

'Let's go.'

Simon leads the way. He asks us to wait at the entrance to the theatre. He continues on and disappears. Mary takes hold of my hand and gives it a squeeze. I'm embarrassed because mine is soggy. She smiles. I notice for the first time that I'm not the only one who's been crying. Poor Mary – she's doing her best.

'Thanks, Mary,' I say. 'Sorry for being such a wimp.'

'You're not a wimp. You're great. I don't know what I'd do...'

Her voice breaks and she wells up. 'Oh, for God's sake,' she says crossly and then we laugh. 'It'll be OK,' she says, though we both know it won't.

The end of a trolley appears out from one of the doors. Two people in scrub gear arrive with the rest of it. *Is it Charlie?*

The emergence of Simon answers my question. To hell with the rules. I walk towards my son.

No one stops me.

As I get closer, I see that he's lying on his side, behind bars to stop him falling off. I'd forgotten how small they are at four, still babies. He looks so delicate, like a pale little Lladro. *Was he really that thin and weak-looking when he went in?*

His eyes open.

'Mama,' he cries and stretches his arms out to me, through the bars.

I plaster a smile on my face. 'It's OK, Charlie. I'm here.' I rub his cheek with the back of my finger. My eyes burn. *Don't cry.*

'We're just going to transfer Charlie to the ward now, Mrs Dempsey,' one of the people in scrub gear says. I catch Mary's eye and throw mine to heaven. She gives me a be-patient-they're-only-doing-their-job look. They start to move the trolley and I walk beside Charlie, holding his hand. It feels tiny in mine.

We reach the ward and Anne leads us to Charlie's bed. It has been pumped up so that it's level with the trolley.

'Mama. I'm cold.'

'OK, sweetie. We'll sort you out now. The doctors are going to put you back in your own bed, OK?' I let go of his hand as they lift his light, limp body across. Some paper from the trolley comes with him. There's dried blood and orange staining on it. A thin blanket covers Charlie's hospital gown. It wasn't designed for heat. Charlie's shaking all over. His teeth are chattering. He moans when they land him gently on the bed.

I hurry to his locker and yank it open, grabbing the little quilt he had when he was a baby. One of his runners falls out and disappears under the bed. The light flashes as it bounces along the floor.

I cover Charlie with the quilt, up to his neck. I pull his blankets over it, brush back his hair and kiss his forehead.

Anne is taking a report from the theatre staff. Mary is speaking quietly with Simon. I notice that she is holding the runner.

I take it from her and try to be polite when I ask them both to leave. I want to be alone with Charlie now. Simon looks like he's about to say something but changes his mind.

'We'll talk later,' he says and leaves with Anne.

Mary hugs me goodbye and says she'll call in later.

'I'd prefer if you didn't.'

She looks hurt.

'I'm sorry, Mary. You've been amazing. But I just need to sort this out in my head. OK?'

She nods. 'Of course. See you tomorrow.'

We hug again.

'Thanks so much for everything.'

As soon as they're gone, I pull a chair level with Charlie's face. I sit on the arm to get closer to him. I rub his cheek with the back of my finger.

He opens his eyes. 'I was scared, Mama. I couldn't find you.'

'I'm sorry, sweetheart. I'm here now.' I put my face right up to his, noses touching, gazing into his eyes. We do that sometimes.

His eyes well up. 'I thought I was in a spaceship.'

All those bright lights. All that equipment.

'I thought they were taking me away.'

'That was just a nightmare. You're here with me now. See?' I rub his nose with mine.

'Want to go home.'

I sit up. 'Charlie, pet, you've had a test. You need to rest for a while, OK?'

'I'll rest at home. Come on, Mama. Let's go.' He makes an attempt to get up but, he's so groggy, he falls back onto the pillow.

'Mama,' he panics. 'What's this?' He touches the bandage on his chest.

'It's the new Freddie, sweetheart.'

'Don't want a Freddie. Don't like Freddies.' His face has gone from sad to mad.

'This one's different, Charlie. This one's cool. D'you want me to show you?'

'No. I don't want a Freddie. I want to go home now.' He starts to cry. He turns his head away. *Oh, that frown. I've always loved it.* I want to reach out and flatten it with a finger.

'D'you remember what Simon was telling you? This is a proper Freddie,' I try to explain. 'The ones in your arm aren't the real thing. Just copy cats. This is a real Freddie.'

'Don't care. Don't want it.'

'Hey, Charlie,' comes a voice behind me.

I turn.

It's Mark, the teenager that Charlie thinks is God. 'Freddies are actually OK. I've one.'

'Really? You've a Freddie?'

Mark nods. Then he pulls up his T-shirt. 'They're pretty cool.'

'Oh. OK.'

I smile at Mark and mouth, 'thank you.'

'You should probably have a little rest now. Bet you're tired.'

Charlie nods sleepily.

'Maybe later we can hang out.'

Charlie falls asleep with a smile on his face.

twelve

Rain is coming down in shafts, slamming into concrete, merging into muddy puddles. It's day but dark, the fluorescent lights of the ward reminding me of school in winter. Mark's TV, tuned to Sky News, zooms in on a woman knee-deep in tea-coloured water. Reports of flooding have newscasters excited. 'More to come,' warn the words that slow-train across the bottom of the screen. The woman wades into her home, anxious to show the world the full extent of the damage – everything that couldn't be moved upstairs, ruined.

Swap, I think. I turn to see Simon coming. With him is a pretty brunette.

Siobhan is a play therapist. Her job, she explains, is to use play to keep children's spirits up, explain things and distract them from difficult procedures. *How many of them are we going to need?* She has an iPad, which makes her an instant hit with Charlie. And she does seem genuinely friendly and helpful. I'll like her, provisionally.

They settle into a game. Simon says he'd like a 'chat', expanding Siobhan's job description to include: occupying mums while doctors break more bad news. Despite my cynicism, I could do with the chat. There's so much I need to know: What's going to happen? How soon can they start? What treatments are planned? What can I do?

And as I follow him into his office, I worry that I won't take it all in. It's a problem I'm having.

I do all right. The bad news, I pretty much knew already. Charlie has Acute Lymphoblastic Leukaemia, the most common cancer in children, more common in boys. Cells called lymphoblasts are attacking his bone marrow, suffocating his blood cells, snuffing them out, making him anaemic, prone to infection and bleeding. There is good news. The cure rate is high. And more bad news. The drugs are strong. They will depress his immune system, making him even more prone to infection, anaemia and bleeding. Regular blood tests will keep tabs on the cell levels and they will intervene with transfusions or antibiotics to prevent 'events'. The medicine might make Charlie sick but anti-nausea treatments are 'very advanced' now and should prevent this from happening. His hair will fall out. Soon.

Treatment will begin once Charlie has had a blood transfusion. He will get a short, sharp blast of chemotherapy – their version of short, sharp being ten to fourteen days. They hope this will induce remission. If we are lucky and it does, Charlie will start an intensification phase – intense chemo for months. He will be on oral therapy at home and will need to come back to hospital, once a week, for chemo and blood tests. Then it's on to 'maintenance therapy', which he can have at home.

One step at a time. Remission. Just aim for that. The rest can wait.

Simon's approach is straightforward. This is what we have to do – let's do it. No pity. I'm grateful for that. I tell myself I'm not afraid. Of the treatments. Of blood transfusions and their risks. Of coping alone, especially at home. Of the looks Charlie will get when his hair falls out. Of the fact that despite everything they do, every horrible treatment I let them inflict, my little boy might die anyway. Like his great-grandmother. Who was my real mother.

'Do all parents feel this useless?' I ask.

He leans forward, puts a hand on mine and looks at me directly. 'You will be anything but useless.' He lets go, sits back. 'I've worked on this ward for ten years and one thing I've learned is that parents, especially mothers, are amazing. Amazing.' He shakes his head, in wonder. 'They have, without doubt, the most important role on this ward.' When he sees the disbelief on my face, he adds. 'It's the parents who make sure that medicine gets taken, that spirits are kept high, that boredom is kept at bay, that difficult tests go ahead smoothly. You couldn't pay parents for what they do. Nurses don't have the time to give the constant attention that parents give – the jumping up and down to get drinks, the constant monitoring of the children. Think of how lonely kids would be without their parents in hospital. It simply wouldn't work. The whole system would break down. While you are in here, expect to be overworked, but don't ever expect to be useless.'

'Sounds like I'll be busy,' I say, my spirits beginning to lift.

'You won't be alone, Jenny. You'll have me; Anne; Siobhan; the other nurses; Pat, the psychologist; Mairead, the social worker; Sheila, the nurse specialist...' He must see my what's-that face because he adds, 'She explains all about the disease, the tests, the results...'

'You seem to have everything,' I say. *Except a guarantee.*

We get back to Charlie. He and Siobhan are playing doctor. Cookie Monster is the patient, Charlie the doctor, complete with stethoscope.

'It's good practice for when I'm big,' he says. And I wonder how many times I have taken for granted simple statements like that. 'When I'm big,' claps in the air, a cheeky, thunderous presumption.

'Cookie Monster has a Freddie, Mum, see? I'm just going to give him a little rejection.' He squirts air into a Freddie that has been bandaged to Cookie Monster's chest. He carries out the task with the efficiency of someone who has been at this for a good ten minutes.

'How is Cookie Monster?' Simon asks Little Doc.

'Not great,' says Charlie, frowning, one doctor to another.

'Oh?'

'He's really tired. His tummy is always full and his leg is sore.'

'Like you,' says Simon, sitting on the bed beside him.

'Yeah. But Cookie Monster's sick.'

Oh my God. He's going to tell him. Wait! Not yet.

'Charlie, do you know the way your leg has been sore?'

'What?' he asks, disconnecting the syringe from the Freddie. 'That's it,' he says to Cookie Monster.

'Do you know the way your leg has been sore?' Simon repeats, patiently.

Charlie is too busy screwing Freddie's cap back on to listen.

I squat down in front of him, put my hand on the knee of his good leg. 'Charlie,' I say, gently. 'Listen to Simon, love.'

He looks at Simon.

'You know the way your leg has been sore, Charlie?'

'Yeah.'

'And the way you've been tired a lot?'

'Yeah.'

Normally, I'd tell Charlie to say 'yes' not 'yeah'.

'Well, there's a reason for that,' Simon continues.

Charlie looks at him.

'You're sick, Charlie...'

'Am I?' He looks at me for confirmation.

I nod.

'You have leukaemia,' Simon continues.

Full attention now. Big, big eyes. He looks at me in panic. 'Like Great?'

I shake my head. No, it says. No, definitely not.

Simon continues, 'You have a different kind of leukaemia from Great. A kind that children get.'

'Will I go to heaven too?'

'No, sweetheart!' I don't care what I'm supposed to say or not say; I'm not going to have him thinking that. I get up and sit on Charlie's other side, then lift him onto my lap so that he's facing Simon. His feet touch the doctor's legs. Simon cups them in his hands.

'Charlie,' he says. 'The leukaemia that Great had is not at all like what you have. The leukaemia you have is much easier to fix.'

Charlie looks at me.

I nod, yes, yes, absolutely.

Simon continues. 'What's happening is that in your body.... Siobhan, do you have that book? Thanks. Here, I'll show you in this book.' He hooches up closer to my son, lifting his little feet and settling them on his lap. 'Look, see these guys,' he says, pointing. 'They're good guys. They're called cells. Now, you need them in your body to stay healthy and full of energy. And see these guys? These are the bad cells. They've moved into your bones and are taking up all the space that the good cells need, squashing them. Now, what we need to do is get rid of the...' His voice goes up. He pauses, so that Charlie can finish.

'Bad guys,' Charlie says, like it's a game.

'Exactly.'

'Will we shoot them?'

'Yes. Just not with guns.'

'Oh,' Charlie says, disappointed.

'With medicine.'

'Oh.' Even more deflated.

'We'll give you medicine into your Freddie. And that will kill the bad guys.'

Silence.

'You and your mum are going to stay here for a few days with Siobhan and myself and Anne and the other kids. Have you met the other kids?'

He doesn't answer.

'And after a while, you can go home to your own friends.'

'When?' Charlie asks.

'Two weeks, maybe.'

'Is that before Christmas?'

'Long before Christmas.'

'What about Sausage?'

Simon looks at me, his face a question.

'His dog. I presume they're not allowed?'

'Not in the hospital, no. But there won't be a problem when Charlie goes home, as long as...Sausage...is wormed.'

Simon spends a lot of time explaining to Charlie about leukaemia. He says that nothing we did or didn't do caused it. 'Being bold doesn't make you get leukaemia or not tidying your room, or anything like that. It just happens. And it happens to lots of kids, not just you.' He explains about the blood transfusion and chemotherapy. Charlie believes everything he is told, unquestioningly, the way he believes in Santa Claus. He believes he will get better.

thirteen

I'm sitting by the bed. Charlie's lying flat on his stomach, propped up on his elbows, knees bent, legs swinging. But really, we are in the jungle with the armadillos and David Attenborough. One armadillo climbs up on the other. *Oh, oh.*

'What's he doing, Mum?'

'Eh, must be giving him a piggyback. Actually, Charlie it's time for bed, sweetheart.'

'Aw, can we just finish this programme? It's good. Can you give me a piggyback later? You haven't given me one in ages.'

'Eh, OK.' I try to think of something else to say to distract him from the screen. But it's OK – the armadillo is getting off. That was quick.

'...coitus complete, the armadillo...'

I let Charlie watch it to the end, then it really is time for bed. Not easy to convince Charlie, though, when the ward around him is buzzing with noise and activity. Visitors in and out. Voices raised. The shock of sudden laughter. Television blaring. Nurses rattling around with drips and medicine trolleys. I give in to a piggyback. Then start the bedtime routine: collecting his toys and putting them at the foot of his bed, slotting his crayons back into their now tatty cardboard box, tidying away as many games as will fit into the second drawer of his wooden locker. I pull down the white, blackout blinds and turn off his TV. I do this every night so that he learns to associate it with settling down. I go about it quietly, determinedly, sending a signal without fuss. It does tend to work. Now, in the bottom part of his locker, a cupboard with two shelves, I find a change of pyjamas and his baby quilt. I look for his toothbrush and a fresh facecloth in the top drawer.

'Is this your book?' Charlie asks.

'Hmm?' I say, rummaging for toothpaste.

'I'm just drawing circles on the front.'

'OK,' I say, not looking up.

'These are shells.'

I check to see what he's at. Happily drawing on the cover of...*Oh God*...The Children With Cancer booklet that Siobhan left.

'I'm tracing this guy,' he says matter-of-factly.

I freeze. It's like he's tempting fate, playing with cancer. I want to snatch it from him. But don't want to overreact. Frighten him.

'Good boy,' I manage. 'Now, let's go wash your teeth and face.' I slowly slip it from his hand, then fling it to the end of the bed, afraid to touch it myself.

He sleeps. I eye the booklet, lying discarded. I pick it up, put it down. I sit looking at the cover. A family on a beach – Mum, Dad, two kids. Nice, neat, nuclear family. Which one has cancer? I pick up the booklet as though it's carcinogenic, holding it with the tips of my fingers. Paper and ink – that's all it is. I open it. It's supposed to help.

I start to read it in a detached, this-has-nothing-to-do-with-me way. And some of it doesn't. Statements like 'two heads are better than one', 'work together,' and 'share the burden,' are designed for the family on the cover. There's a small section for people like me – single parents. The main message is to 'try not to make your sick child the centre of your world'. Too late. He is my entire world. And I'm going to be here for him one hundred percent. I know I'm lucky that, thanks to the rental income and the fact that hospital care is free, I can do that. Earlier, I called Jack and told him not to expect his health page. Not this week. Not ever. He asked why. I told him the truth, though I'd promised myself I wouldn't let it out. After everything he's done for me, I owed him honesty at least. So that's what he got. His words didn't form sentences. He kept repeating 'little Charlie' and 'poor little fella'. Kept asking what he could do. I said, give the health page to someone else. But he didn't seem to grasp that I was quitting for good. He just kept saying, 'Take as much time as you want.'

I snapped. 'It's not a cold, Jack.'

He went quiet.

I was sorry but all I could say was, 'Look, I've got to go.'

To the principal in Charlie's school, I divulged, out of necessity that Charlie was 'sick'. I even admitted that he was in hospital. But instead of leukaemia, I spoke about blood tests and investigations. She bombarded me with sympathy and questions, promised to get a Mass said, reassured me that the children would make cards and visit when Charlie's up to it. I told her I'd let her know, then warned Mary not to give her details.

They've started treatment, most of which is given through Freddie. Charlie 'tolerates it well' but hates the one medicine he has to swallow, and is very fussy about how he takes it. I have to give it to him. In a syringe. Millilitre by millilitre. Our system is as follows: start with a crisp – not just any crisp, a Snax. This gives him a taste in his mouth. Then squirt in one millilitre, then a drink (7Up only acceptable, with ice and a straw, in his Mickey Mouse cup), followed immediately by another Snax. This is repeated until five millilitres are taken. The routine averages fifteen minutes and has to be followed with a sweet. Mint Toffo. They tell us not to spoil our children. This, I assume, breaks that rule. But, at least, he takes it and that, surely, is the point? Or so I tell myself, while monitoring how quickly he'd down it for someone who wouldn't tolerate nonsense. My mother, for example. Someone I've never exposed Charlie to.

He is tired and rests without being asked to. It may be the treatment or the disease or the lack of fresh air, exercise or appetite. It may be all of the above. But, overall, his form is good, thanks mainly to the fact that he has 'made friends' with his superhero, Mark. Together, usually sitting on Mark's bed, they battle alien invaders and enemy star ships. They fight each other on game boards too. Mark has taught him Ludo and draughts. He's been known to let Charlie win more often than occasionally.

'I've a brother who's four,' Mark says, shaking the dice, one day.

'Do you?' Charlie looks up at him in wonder. He could have said, 'blah, blah, blah,' and it would still be amazing to Charlie.

'Yeah. His name is James.'

'Where is he?'

'At home.'

'Why doesn't he come to see you?'

'We don't live near the hospital, Charlie,' he says counting to six and shaking the dice again.

'Where do you live?'

'Donegal.'

'Where?'

'It's a place that's very far away.'

'Where's your mum? Why isn't she here with you?'

'She has to mind my brothers but she comes to see me once a week.'

'Do you've a dad?'

'Yeah.'

'Does he come?'

'No,' says Mark, looking out the window.

'Is he too busy?'

'Yeah. He's too busy.'

'My dad's too busy, too. Dads work too hard, don't they?'

'Yeah.'

And maybe that's why Mark decides to adopt Charlie, spending time with him, teaching him games, playing with him, listening to him, explaining things, calming him down when he's worried or upset. He misses his own brother. Or is lonely. Or maybe he feels a bond because both of them are missing fathers. Or both are sick and in here. Or maybe he just likes my son. Whatever reason, it's a gift, giving Charlie something to focus on, something to get excited about, something to distract him from treatments, tests and the boredom of hospital.

After three days, I'm beginning to know my way around. The bendy straws and ice machine (lifesavers, both) are in the kitchen, the ice machine donated by a boy and his family. I look at the plaque and wonder if the boy made it, survived. And whether Charlie and I will be donating something in the future. And if so, what?

I know the pattern to Charlie's medication, hospital meals, doctors' rounds. I know the television schedules and how to put on a DVD. I know who wears what uniform. I know where X-ray is, the playroom, the nurses' station, and I know what time the play volunteers arrive. I know the nurses by name. I know all the children in our room and their parents. I've discovered that hospital food lives down to its reputation and have found ways around it – Mary, primarily, who brings an endless supply of healthy options. I keep thanking her and reassuring her that we'll be home in two weeks. I've become used to the expression, 'Don't worry about it.' She has even wormed the dog.

I know where the chapel is. And I've remembered how to pray.

I learn to bath Charlie without wetting his Freddie. I learn how to keep him entertained and upbeat (Mary's DS when he's feeling down or bored; DVDs when he's tired; good old-fashioned stories when he needs attention or a cuddle; and playing with other kids when he's feeling energetic). I learn what upsets him and try to avoid these situations or distract him when they're happening.

I've developed habits like banging his runners together to make them light up, every night before going to bed, well, mattress. I've taken to brushing his teeth with great precision because he is going to make it, and he'll need them. I run my hands through his hair rather than brush it, in an attempt to delay the inevitable. I devour Cornflakes in the kitchen during the night, when hunger pangs finally remind me to eat. I forget to taste.

Mairead, the social worker, and Mary keep trying to get me to take 'little breaks', but really I don't want them. I do give in, once, and go across the road to the shopping centre where I stock up on multivitamins that I hope they'll let me give Charlie. I buy his favourite foods, Lego, colouring books and jigsaws. I wander into a computer shop but don't know where to start. The sales assistant could pass as a Gallagher brother. He tells me the iPad is 'the business,' and I guess that's all I need to know.

I'm cleaned out but at least I'm, 'the best mum in the world.' I feed Charlie yoghurt while he plays on the iPad.

'Get me out of here, get me out of here. Quick, Mum, I'm going to get killed.' He is shoving the iPad at me.

'Charlie, I don't know how to play.'

'Quick, Mum. Oh my God, here they come.'

'Here, give it to me. Where does he have to go?'

'Through the door, quick, through the door.' Charlie's hopping up and down on the bed beside me.

'Sit down, sit down. Is this how you move him?'

'Yeah, yeah, quick or you'll get killed. I've only one life left.'

'OK, there. Saved you.'

'Phew,' he says, taking it back.

If only saving lives were that easy.

fourteen

I'm not superstitious. But... some people are bad luck. Simon Grace is bad luck. Once wasn't enough for him to collide with my life and send it into a spin. Twice even. He's going for a record. Sitting opposite me (always beware the sitting doctor), grim-faced, talking about the results of the blood tests, about a chromosome called Philadelphia. Which Charlie has. Which changes everything, altering the treatment course, hammering his prognosis. He sits there and tells me that Charlie won't survive without a bone marrow transplant.

I don't understand. What? What is he talking about? What test? I didn't know he was doing a test. It's standard,' he says. Maybe, but this is too much to take in. I need him to repeat everything. Say it all again. Try to understand. And when I do, I want to lash out. Physically. Verbally. Why is he doing this to us? And why now? Did he know sooner? Is he trying to break it in stages as if I'm some sort of fragile flower? It's like going over the diagnosis all over again. Only worse. Because I'd bent down, gathered my hopes and dreams back up off the floor and started again with the new hand that I'd been dealt. I'd begun to get going again after everything had stopped so terrifyingly. But, now. Now, I'm flattened.

They have to find a donor. Where, though? And will they? How quickly and in time? It is too much. Too much. They roll out the psychologist, then the social worker. But they're trying to reassure a catatonic. I'm numb, not listening, useless, stupid.

They take over, arranging for someone to stay with Charlie and for Mary to take me home for a while. I don't want to leave him but don't want him seeing me like this either. Mary is decisive. And I find myself wishing I had a mother like her, a mother who'd care enough to be firm like she is being, a mother who'd be here with us now, fussing over Charlie, insisting that we do rosters. Not painting on a plastic smile and walking out the door.

Charlie, glued to the iPad, hardly notices when I kiss him goodbye.

'Bye, Charlie,' I say to make sure it's registering with him that I'm leaving, so he won't be looking for me as soon as the game is over.

'Bye, Mum,' he says, without taking his eyes off the screen.

The tears start as soon as I turn to go. This time, I don't try to stop them. This time, I don't care. Out in the fresh air, I squint in the glare of natural light and wrap my jacket around me. My head is fuzzy. I lower it and close my eyes as much as I can without bumping into something, as I walk with Mary to the car park. I could fall asleep walking. The hum of traffic and the movement of cars passing remind me that people are getting on with their lives – no worries, going to work, school, whatever. Carrying on. While we are stuck. Not moving. Left behind.

We find Mary's car and I don't notice the journey home.

I don't want her to come in. And she seems to understand that I need to be alone. To think, to sleep.

I let myself in. It's silent, still, cold. Sausage hasn't come to the door.

I find him, nose to the window, staring out as though waiting for us to return. The first time he has ever acted as a watchdog. He turns to look at me, then away again in a sulk. I call him. He ignores me. I go over and sit beside him.

'I'm sorry, Sausage.' I rub his head and pull him to me. 'Charlie's sick,' I say and I'm crying again.

He looks up at me with sad chocolate eyes, then around the room as if to say, 'Where is he?' He whimpers.

I lift him onto my lap and cuddle him. Feel his heart. Ka thunk. Ka thunk. I carry him over to the couch. He snuggles into me. I am forgiven.

I'm home. But it doesn't feel like home. Just a shell. Everything is as we left it, four days ago. Charlie's half-eaten melon slice on the worktop, his pyjamas in a heap on the floor, his 'proper shoes' he refuses to wear, clean and tidy on the shoe rack inside the door. Everything the same. But not. By body jerks involuntarily and I let loose a wail that has been building inside me for days. The dog jumps out of my arms and scurries under the coffee table. I wrap my arms across my stomach, fold forward, then rock. Another quieter wail, then unchecked crying. Nobody to hear, now. No need to hide.

Sausage's wet nose nudges my hand. I pick him up and put him on my lap.

'What will we do?' I wail into his head. He tilts it back and looks at me upside down. He's a dog. *Why are you asking a dog? What is he going to do? Oh God. Why didn't I stay with Dave? What was I thinking? I wasn't. I was a fool to let him go. If he'd stayed, he'd be here now with his chest to lean in to, his arms to wrap around me, his shoulders to soak with tears. He'd hold me. And be strong. And I wouldn't have to be. For five minutes. Just for five minutes.*

I have to get up or I'll drown the dog. Already his hairs are sticking to my hands, coming off on them. At the sink, I wash them off. The water's cold. I splash it on my face. I reach for the kitchen paper, knocking over a framed photo of Charlie. It smacks off the worktop. I snatch it up, hold it between my wet hands and gaze at my little boy. He beams back at me. Sparkling, dancing eyes. Gleaming rows of white teeth. Tanned and freckled summer skin. His hair highlighted by the sun. The picture breathes life, health. And I'm off again.

'Stop!' I say, aloud.

Sausage looks up from the tiled floor reminding me that I've people depending on me. I have to be strong.

'Right!' I grab a black plastic bag and tear around, dumping stuff in – the melon peel, gone-off milk from the fridge, bread, fruit, the contents of the pedal bin and the one in the bathroom. I leave the black plastic bag outside Louis's door with a quickly scribbled note. Louis being Louis, he will need instructions.

Sausage, constantly at my heels, follows me back into the apartment. I turn on the heat and climb into my unmade bed, the bed I've taken for granted. The dog, ever the opportunist, steals up and snuggles in beside me. I let him and fall asleep, my hand resting on his warm tummy.

When the alarm goes off, I drag myself out of a near coma. Eyes still closed, I feel my way to the shower. I turn it on full blast. Water pounds onto my scalp massaging it. I let my head drop forward, directing the cascade onto the back of my neck. After a few minutes, I move the blast onto my shoulders. It hardly touches the tension that has built up there. I let my head fall back now. Something clicks inside, loosens. Water smashes against the tight elastic bands that have formed on my forehead. I circle my shoulders, turn my neck from side to side, bend down with straight legs to retrieve the soap. Stretching, loosening.

'You can only do your best,' I hear Great whisper. Or is it just the sound of the spray? You can only do your best – the phrase she repeated time and again to a little girl who spent too much time trying to impress a mother who didn't notice. 'You can only do your best, Jen.'

I stay in the shower until it starts to go cold. Rub myself briskly with a towel as though it'll help me come back to life. Oddly, I want to wear something very specific – something soft, cosy, pale pink. I've nothing to fit that description so opt for an old baby blue, cashmere hoodie that always feels like a hug. My denims hang off me, reminding me I need to start eating again. I blast my hair with the dryer, anxious to get back to the hospital before dark. I call Mary to tell her I'll take a taxi. She says she's already on her way. She arrives in minutes.

'Have you eaten?' she asks.

'I'll get something in there.'

'Right. I'm ringing the hospital to see if he's OK. If he is, then you're eating. It'll take fifteen minutes.'

She makes the call.

'He's fine. Asleep.'

'Oh good. Did he have a good afternoon?'

'Great. Now, sit.'

Both Sausage and I obey.

She laughs at the dog. 'Good boy.' She marches over to the fridge, opens it and starts to check expiry dates on what's left of the food. She selects cheese and a tomato, cutting the edges off the cheese. She checks the freezer and takes out a frozen sliced pan.

'Have you a toasted sandwich maker?'

I start to get up.

'Sit,' she orders. 'Just tell me where it is.'

'In the cupboard beside the fridge.'

She yanks it out, gets busy. Puts on the kettle.

'There's no milk,' I say.

'Right, juice then. Better anyway.' She pours orange juice, leaves it on the counter, feeds the dog and puts out fresh water for him. She washes her hands then puts the sandwich and juice in front of me. She sits opposite me with a glass of juice.

'Eat.'

I look at her. 'Thanks, Mary. For everything.'

She waves it away as nothing.

'I don't know what I'd do without you.' I start to get teary. Because it's true. What would I do without her?

'Did you sleep?'

I nod. And bite into the sandwich because I know she won't let me go without eating it.

'You look a bit better.'

I smile. For her.

'Jenny, I've been thinking. All afternoon. I want to ask you something. And I hope you don't think I'm being nosy because I'm not. I'm just trying to help, OK?'

'OK,' I say, warily.

'Is Charlie's father alive?'

'Why?'

'Well, if he is, don't you think he should know?'

I take a deep breath and let it out very slowly.

'Look at it another way. If you're going to need donors, don't you think Charlie's father might be an option?'

My head is throbbing. I hold it between my hands. 'It's not that easy. It's not as easy as going up to a person and saying, "Your son is in trouble."'

'Why not?'

'Because, for one thing, I don't know who he is,' I say, too loudly.

That's stopped her.

'I don't know who he is, OK?' I say more calmly.

'OK.'

'It's not like there are hundreds of options out there. Just two. I'm not a slag, if that's what you're thinking.'

'Jenny, I'd never think that,' she says, reaching out for my hand and holding it. 'But if there are only two options, couldn't you approach both?'

'No.'

'Why not?'

'Because one of them is in the US getting on with his life and one of them is Charlie's doctor,' I say, finally giving in, admitting it. I don't look at her when I say, 'And he doesn't know.'

'His doctor? Who? Simon? Simon Grace? Dr Grace?'

I nod. I concentrate on the cheese oozing from the sandwich.

'I don't believe it.'

I shrug.

'What are the chances of that happening, that you would end up with him as a doctor?'

'I don't know Mary.' Even to me I sound tired. 'He's the chief oncologist in Ireland's only cancer centre for children. Charlie has cancer.'

'And he doesn't know about Charlie?'

I shake my head. The pressure in the silence builds. And builds. Until I have to tell her. I can't keep it all in any more. I can't do everything on my own any more. I have to let someone in.

'Five years ago, I was engaged...'

'To Simon?'

'No, Mary. Can you just listen?'

'Sorry.'

'I was engaged to a guy called Dave. He's a journalist. We'd met through work and had been going out two years, engaged six months. We were happy. He was my best friend. I was sent on a work assignment. It was a big international medical conference in Brussels. Simon was a speaker. I had to interview him. Only he didn't show up for the interview. I had to file the piece that evening. I rang his room. He answered but only because he thought it was his wife. He said he couldn't do the interview. I didn't ask why. I didn't care. All I could think about was my stupid deadline. I lied. Told him I'd lose my job. I wouldn't let it go. I was so ambitious. He said he'd give me five minutes in his room. As soon as I saw him, I knew something was wrong. He looked terrible. Red eyes, hair all over the place, so pale. He was trying to put up a front, pretend everything was fine. He offered me a drink and poured one before I could answer. His hand was shaking so much, the bottle kept hitting the glass. I pretended I didn't notice. I started the interview. We didn't get far. It was about cancer – well, obviously. About five questions in, he couldn't go on. That's when he told me, his wife had been diagnosed with lung cancer just before he'd left for the conference. He'd wanted to drop out. She had insisted he go. He'd managed to hold everything together until he'd done his presentation. Then, back in his room, he broke down. I walked in on that.'

Suddenly, I'm in that room. Just him and me. I sit him down on the neat hotel bed, stay beside him, stay close. I match him, drink for drink. Listen as he talks. There is little hope, he says. The cancer is an aggressive one. She doesn't know how aggressive. She doesn't know what it will do to her. How quickly it will win. I don't know how to calm him. He's crying. I'm desperate to help. I hold his hand. And that's how it starts, with that simple touch. Before I know it, we're kissing. His mouth is on mine, hungry, searching for comfort. I know he's losing himself, forgetting. And I don't know whether it's the drink or the pity but I don't stop it. When it's over, he's even more distressed, realising what we've done. He's telling me over and over, as I hurry to dress, that he loves his wife. He loves Alison. He's saying he's sorry but he can't get me out of that room fast enough. Which makes me feel dirty, wrong, at fault. It's weird. Like a nightmare. Happening so suddenly, so fast that I find myself back in my room wondering if it really happened.

'So many times, I've told myself I should have walked out of that room as soon as I saw him. So many times.'

'Did you tell Dave?'

'Not at first. I thought about it. I thought about nothing else. But I didn't want to risk what we had. It had nothing to do with my life or our relationship or future. I didn't even know Simon Grace, apart from the fact that he was an oncologist who could give a good talk and had a sick wife. I wanted to forget what happened. But I became pregnant. And I couldn't be sure. I had to tell Dave.'

'So he ended it?'

'No, Mary, he didn't. He was gutted. Really, hurt. The way he looked at me. As if he couldn't believe what I'd done. We seemed so separate, suddenly. I knew then that what had happened did affect our relationship. Because it affected the way he looked at me. He took leave, went away for two weeks. And I thought it was over. But he came back, told me he loved me and had forgiven me, and that he wanted us to pick things up and carry on, the way we were before, as if nothing had happened. I should have been happy. I should have been relieved – everything back to normal. Only it wasn't. I couldn't stop thinking, *What if the baby isn't*

Dave's? I couldn't get it out of my head. I couldn't expect him to take it on. It wouldn't work. He'd always be wondering, thinking... So I ended it.'

'But what if he was the father?'

I shrug.

'Jenny! Couldn't you have done a paternity test?'

'Of course. But think about it. We do the test, what then? If Dave's the father, I marry him; if not, forget it?'

'But you loved him, Jen.'

'Yes.'

'And he forgave you.'

'He said he did. But did he really, Mary?'

'I don't know. He sounded like he did – or at least wanted to.'

'It's easy to pretend everything will be happy ever after. But it's not easy to make it that way. It had happened. There would always be that niggle. That niggle would grow to resentment. I'd ruined it. It was never going to be the same.'

'How pregnant were you then?'

'Ten weeks.'

'And you never thought of...'

'No!'

'So Dave just accepted that it was over? That was it.'

'No. He tried to convince me it didn't matter. But the more he tried, the more sure I became that it would be unfair on him. In the end, he got tired of trying or tired of me. He left. A post came up in the States with a sister newspaper. He applied and got it.'

'Didn't you miss him? You were together for two years. You were going to be married.'

'Yes, I missed him. I missed him so much I almost went after him. But I got sense.'

'You got sense,' she repeats, incredulously.

'It's hard to explain. I knew that if he came back, I'd start feeling the same again – like we were making a mistake.'

'What happened with Simon?'

'Nothing. I never told him.'

'Why not?'

'I wasn't sure the baby was his. We didn't know each other. His wife had cancer.'

'It must be awkward for you, now. I must be blind. I never noticed any tension between you.'

'He doesn't remember me.'

'What? He ruined your life and he doesn't even remember you?'

'Mary it was five years ago. He was in a state when I got there. It was over in minutes.'

'Still, I...'

'He loved his wife – it's not something he'd *want* to remember. And there are other reasons, practical reasons – he knew me as Jennifer Grey, the name I use for the paper. My hair is different now; I wear glasses. I'm a mum with a completely different attitude to life. I dress differently. I am *actually* a different person.'

'Why d'you write under a false name?'

'To dissociate myself from my mother, Kathleen Dempsey.'

'The politician?'

I sigh. 'My views aren't hers. I didn't want us linked. Grey was Great's surname. And it was nice to be able to call myself after the person who treated me like my mother should have.'

'Wow.'

'There's another reason he hasn't recognised me. He's a man.'

'Ah, you see, *now* you've convinced me.' She smiles.

Then I remember. 'He did say I looked familiar, once. But I talked him out of it.'

'So you've brought Charlie up on your own.'

'And sometimes, like now, I think I've made the biggest mistake of my life. Charlie could have had a father, maybe not his real father, but a father. Do you know how much he'd love that?' I'm starting to get upset. 'Do you know how often he mentions his father? Especially since he started school. And what if Dave *is* Charlie's father and I've stopped them being together?'

'Call him. Tell him what's happened. I'm sure he'd help.'

'I sent him away, Mary. How can I expect him to come running back as soon as we get into trouble?'

'Maybe you don't have a choice.'

'Maybe I'll be the match. Then I won't have to tell anyone. Not Dave, not Simon. And I can just keep going. Get through this.'

She squeezes my hand. 'I'm here. You know that, don't you?'

I nod. 'Thank you.'

'Everything will work out. I know it will.'

'Yeah.'

'Anyway, come on. We'd better go. I'll clean this up later.'

Sausage wants to come with us. He whimpers from the other side of the door as I lock it. And I walk wearily down the corridor.

fifteen

On our way back, my mobile rings. Automatically, I think it's the hospital and my stomach jumps. It's the school, looking for an update. I keep it brief and vague. It rings again. Jack.

'Can I do anything?' he asks.

'I think I'm OK, Jack, thanks.'

'Are visitors allowed?'

'Only a small number.'

'Are you getting many?'

After a pause, I admit. 'Not really, no. I haven't told anyone outside of you and a friend.'

'Oh,' he says, then is quiet for a second. 'Could I come in, d'you think?'

'Maybe in a day or two, Jack. Today isn't good.'

'D'you want me to come in at all?'

'No, yes, I mean, yes of course – that would be fine.'

We pass a woman in a dark, wintry coat, hunched over an

ancient, black penny-farthing bicycle, her flat, rubber-soled shoes and thick calves circling slowly as though she's going uphill. The road is flat. She is old. Strapped onto the back carrier of her bicycle is a white jumbo box of Special K. It's surreal.

Jack has asked me something.

'Sorry?'

'Is there anything I can bring in?'

'No. No thanks, Jack.'

'Can I do anything?'

'No, I'm fine. Honestly.'

'What about the internet? Do you want me to look anything up?'

'Actually, yes! How did you think of that? There *is* something. Could you Google the Philadelphia Chromosome?'

'The what?'

'The Philadelphia Chromosome. Philadelphia, as in the city. Chromosome as in genes.'

'Grand, yeah, OK.' He doesn't ask what it is, though I know he hasn't a clue. 'When do you want it?'

'Always the deadline, Jack.' I smile. It's good to be talking to him.

'You know me.'

'There's no rush.'

'I'll call in a day or two and bring it with me. Would that do?'

'That'd be great.' I might be ready to face what he finds then. 'I gotta go, Jack.' We're at the hospital.

'Right, then. You take care.' He says the last three words slowly, like he really means them.

'You too.' I switch off the phone.

Charlie is still asleep. There's no one with him. Siobhan, playing with Sean, at the next bed, excuses herself and comes over.

'I stayed with him until he fell asleep. Then decided to make myself useful while still keeping an eye on him.'

'Thanks Siobhan. How was he?'

'Grand. He played on the iPad for a while then wanted to lie down.'

'He wasn't sore or anything?'

'No, just tired.'

And I hate to sound anal but: 'He got all his treatments?'

'Yes. They were IV and he slept through them.'

I bend over him and kiss his pale forehead. No tan, now, just a few stubborn freckles.

'Simon was around...'

I look up. 'Did he say anything?'

'He'll be in his office for a while if you want to talk.'

'I'll stay with Charlie if you like,' Mary offers.

'I'll head off, then,' Siobhan says. 'I'll just say goodbye to Sean. I'll see you tomorrow.'

'Thanks Siobhan,' I say. 'Mary, you go. You've probably loads to do.'

'It can wait. Go.'

'Are you sure? What about dinner?'

'Phil can explore his creative side.'

'I'll be quick.'

'Take your time.'

I knock on his door and wait. Nothing. I'm about to leave when it opens. He looks tired. Too much time in here.

'Jenny, hello. Come in, come in. Sit down. I wanted to talk to you.' Not words I want to hear.

He waits till I've settled.

'That was a bit of a knock this morning.'

'Yeah.'

'It's not the kind of news I like giving.'

'No.'

'And you seemed to be coping so well.'

'Yeah, well, there you go. Not your fault.' *What is he doing – trying to start me off again?*

'How are you now?'

'Fine.'

'How did this afternoon go?'

111

'What, going home?'

'Yes.'

'Good.'

'Did you get some rest?'

I nod.

'Good, good. You need to keep your strength up.' He seems to realise that I've no intention of discussing how I am and changes tack. 'We have some results back.'

My stomach lurches.

'They're good, Jenny. Charlie is responding to treatment.'

'But I thought you said he wouldn't.'

'I'm sorry. I mustn't have explained myself properly. In the long term, the original treatment course will not be adequate. Charlie will need a bone marrow transplant. But the current treatment is to induce remission. And so far, that is going according to plan.'

I nod, afraid to say anything that will change our luck.

'Is there anything you'd like to ask about the bone marrow transplant? We haven't discussed it.'

My mind is bursting with questions and I'm sorry I haven't written them down. I know I'll forget something.

'How soon can we start looking for a donor?'

'Straightaway. But it might take a while to find one.'

'How long?'

'It varies. It could be months.'

'Does that give us enough time?'

'Yes, it should.'

Should? 'Do you think we *will* find a match?'

'I would be very hopeful. We have two ways of searching. Immediate family and through a register of donors.'

'Which is the most successful?'

'It depends, Jenny. The best matches are usually found among siblings. Charlie has no brothers or sisters?'

'No. Only me.'

'And his father?'

'Yes,' I say, looking down. Everything has speeded up, taken off without me, again.

Silence.

'I'm sorry. It was insensitive to ask.'

'What about grandparents?' I ask, looking up.

'In fairness, it would be unlikely for them to be a good match. But of course, we can try, if they're willing.'

Suddenly, I wish I had a great big brood of children. A family of Waltons lining up with their sleeves rolled back. *God. What will I do?*

'I'll get to work on the register, then?'

'Yes. Of course. And you can do whatever test you need to do to me – right now, if you like.'

'It's a simple blood test for tissue typing. We can set it up for the morning if that suits you.'

'I'm going nowhere. How long do the results take?'

'Two to three weeks.'

'And you'll let me know as soon as you get them?'

'Of course. I know how anxious you must be. But please, try not to get your hopes up too much. We rarely have success with the first person we try. This may take a while, Jenny. Maybe you would like to talk to Pat.' The psychologist.

'Do you mind if I think about that?'

'Not at all. We're all here if you need us.'

I've taken in enough. I'm conscious of Mary waiting outside and start to make moves to go.

'Jenny?'

'Yes?' I say, looking up from bending to get my bag.

'Would you mind if I told Debra? She thinks she's baby-sitting Thursday night.'

'Oh God. I'd forgotten, Debbie. The yoga. I'm sorry. Of course. Tell her, please. Or maybe I should.'

'I'll talk to her tonight. She'll probably be a bit sensitive. Her mother...'

'Yes. Yes, of course. Poor Deb...'

'One more thing, Jenny? I don't think we need tell Charlie

about the bone marrow transplant until closer to the time. Better to concentrate on getting thorough the initial chemotherapy and home. There are a lot of ups and downs associated with looking for a match. I think we can protect him from that.'

'Thank you.'

'He is doing remarkably well. If he keeps responding like he is, I would hope to have him home in less than two weeks.'

'That's great.' But terrifying. *Home. Alone. No support. No advice. No Simon. What if Charlie gets an infection? What if he bleeds and bleeds and I can't stop it? What if? Stop! They won't let us home till we're ready. But what if we're ready and then Charlie gets sick again?*

I look at Simon now and wonder what he's been saying. He smiles and stands.

I do the same.

He walks from the other side of the desk and puts a hand on my shoulder. 'Things will get easier. This is the worst time.'

Charlie and I stay up late, sitting side by side on the bed, eating popcorn, watching *Toy Story* and pretending that everything is normal.

I watch him examine Charlie. *Is it unfair to keep him from knowing that he might be touching his own son, feeling his breath, listening to his bright chatter? No, because Charlie might not be his son. And even if he is, Simon mightn't want to know it.* I watch him now and remember what Mary said about him being the first doctor she's seen who 'doesn't just dive in and poke around.' She's right. He doesn't rush. Instead, he chats with Charlie, asking about his iPad, genuinely interested. He's not just pretending to care. When he does get down to business, he's sensitive to the fact that Charlie knows the routine now, and wants to lead the way, pulling up his top without being asked, coughing when the stethoscope rests on his chest, volunteering to stick out his tongue and say, 'aaah'. And because he's allowed the freedom to do this, it's a game not a chore. They're like a two-man company, putting on a performance. And I know that Charlie trusts Simon. Who approaches everything with a quiet confidence that makes you feel as if all's being taken care of, nothing forgotten, overlooked.

He washes his hands now, using his elbow to dispense the pink medicated liquid soap from its container. Round and round his hands move over each other – good hands with thin, straight fingers and short, clean nails. He gives them three quick shakes, holds the paper roll with a wrist and yanks off a section the other hand. You'd know he was a doctor just by the way he washes his hands. He does it unconsciously, without taking his eyes off Charlie, who continues to fill him in on his favourite Internet games.

'They had nothing like this when I was a boy,' Simon says.

'When were you a boy?'

He smiles. 'A long time ago.'

'When the dinosaurs were?'

He laughs and looks at me, still smiling. 'Not quite that far back, Charlie.'

'When Jesus was born?'

'A bit later than that.'

'Same time as Mum?'

'Well, I don't know if it was *that* far back,' he jokes, looking at me.

'Yeah. She's ancient.'

Simon laughs.

'Thanks, Charlie,' I say, smiling.

'So,' says Simon. 'Do you still want to be a doctor, Charlie?'

'No.'

'Why not? I could do with a good helper around here.'

'I don't like hospitals, Simon. I'm going to be a hairdresser.'

'Now, there's an idea,' he says.

Simon pulls back the curtain from around the bed. I catch sight of a man leaning awkwardly against the entrance to the ward, arms folded, looking down at his shoes. A little pile of bags circles his feet. He stands like Jack. He is Jack. He waits for Simon to pass, nods to him, then slowly collects up the bags and walks our way, smiling self-consciously. I know I wasn't enthusiastic about him coming in, but now that he's here, I want to throw my arms around him. A familiar face!

'I'm not staying,' he excuses himself.

'You'd better.'

He seems to relax a little. 'Just brought you in a few bits and pieces,' he says, shoving them under the bed with a foot.

'Sit down. It's great to see you. I know how you feel about hospitals.'

'Ah, they're all right. How's he doing?' he asks quietly, looking at Charlie, who has managed to switch on the Pink Panther with the remote.

'So far, so good, Jack.'

'Good.'

'How're you doing, Charlie?' asks Jack.

'I can't hear,' he whines.

'Oh, sorry,' says Jack.

'Charlie, don't be rude. You know there are no words in the Pink Panther. Jack asked you a question.'

'It doesn't matter, Jenny. Let the kid watch the telly.'

'Jack asked how you are.'

'Fine.'

'Fine, thanks, Charlie,' I remind him.

He ignores me. I roll my eyes.

Jack lowers his voice. 'So, what's the story?'

'Well, he seems to be responding to treatment, for the moment. It's one step at a time.'

'I know.'

'Thanks for coming in, Jack. How are things?'

'Sure, grand. The page isn't the same, of course.'

'I hope you're not trying to persuade me to start writing...'

He looks horrified. 'Can't a man give a compliment without being taken up wrong?'

'Sorry.'

'I got you that stuff you wanted on the Philadelphia

Chromosome.' He fishes an expandable A4 envelope out of one of the bags and lands it on the bed. 'I couldn't make head nor tail of it.'

'Thanks, Jack. It's all right. I'm used to reading medical jargon.' I pick it up. 'God, there's a lot.'

'I got as much as I could, just in case.'

'Thanks. I'll go over it later.' I put it in the locker so no one sees it. Don't want them thinking I'm checking up on them.

'Got you a few magazines and things,' he says, nodding at the bags.

'Aw, thanks, Jack.'

'And a few bits and pieces for the lad. Does he like snakes?'

'He loves snakes. How did you know?'

'He's a boy, isn't he? I got a book on them. It's pretty good. How about spiders?'

'I thought you didn't know a thing about kids?'

He looks chuffed.

'You'll have to read them to him though,' I say. 'I've arachnophobia.'

He chuckles. 'God, he really loves the old Pink Panther, doesn't he?'

'Takes after his mum.'

'Sure, isn't he lucky then?'

He stays for a half an hour, then starts to get edgy. 'So how long will you be in?'

'Not sure – two weeks maybe, if all goes well.'

'Sure, I might call in again, so.'

'That'd be great, Jack. You know, it's great to see a friendly face.'

'Especially an old codger like me?'

'Especially an old codger like you,' I say, smiling.

I walk him to the door of the ward. I'd go out with him only Charlie won't leave the Pink Panther and I won't leave him. As we are saying goodbye, he surprises me with a hug.

'Good luck, now,' he says and hurries off.

sixteen

I sit beside a sleeping boy. The light is dim, the ward quiet. I squint my way through every page of Jack's printout. Leukaemia. The Philadelphia Chromosome. Bone marrow transplant. I take in factual medical details, trying to stay equally factual myself. No cause, it says. *That they know of*, I think, then tell myself to stop. There are case histories from websites, mostly American, set up by parents whose children had leukaemia. Their diaries, open for all to see, chronicle their hopes, battles and ultimate heartbreak as their journeys end in tragedy. Tears blur my vision. I'm crying, not for my boy, but for Ben and Shaun and Nadim, who didn't make it, despite their fierce will, despite their undying hope. I do not sleep. I do not try, just sit in the chair beside the bed, knowing now that finding a donor doesn't always translate into finding a cure.

Next morning, I'm walking back from the bathroom, half-asleep, when I see Simon walking onto the ward. He looks so full of energy, so full of life. He stops when he reaches me.

'Are you all right?' he asks.

'Just a bit tired.'

'You didn't sleep?'

'Off and on.'

'Maybe you might doze later, when Charlie has a rest.'

'Maybe.' I'm about to walk off when he hands me a small parcel wrapped in *Monsters, Inc* paper.

'From Debra,' he explains.

'Aw, that's so sweet. She needn't have.'

'Try stopping Debra when she wants to do something.' He smiles.

'How did she take the news?'

'Badly, I'm afraid. But, in fairness, I'd anticipated that.'

'Poor thing.'

'She really wants to see Charlie but the thought of going back into a hospital, especially under the circumstances... It's too much for her.'

'Of course. Tell her we absolutely understand and we'll see her when Charlie gets out.'

'Apparently, there's a note in there for you. She said to make sure you got it. There's something she wants to ask. And I need an answer before leaving this evening or my life won't be worth living.' He smiles again.

'Sounds mysterious.'

'Not really. But I'm sure she'd like to ask you herself. Anyway, I'll leave you to it. I'll be around later.'

'OK, thanks.'

He strides off down the corridor, like he strides everywhere – always something to do. He is relaxed and unhurried when talking with you, making you feel that Charlie is his only patient. Then he shoots off. Reminding you that he's not.

I walk back to the bed smiling at Mark as I pass, and saying hello to a woman who, I guess, must be his mother, perched on the edge of her chair, looking weary and falsely optimistic. Like the rest of us. Her shy hello has a Donegal lilt.

Charlie is watching his *Monsters, Inc* DVD. It's almost at his favourite bit. He doesn't notice when I sit back in the armchair and open my note from Debbie.

Dear Jenny

I am so, so sorry about Charlie. I can't believe it. I just can't believe this could happen. It's so not fair. But he'll be OK, I know he will. He just has to be. I want to mind Sausage, Jenny. I know you'll be polite and say no, but I really, really want to. I have to do something. I've thought about it and I've asked Dad. We both think it would be good. You've enough to worry about besides a dog. I would love so much to come in and hug Charlie but I just can't. So I'll hug Sausage instead. And he can cuddle up to me, because I know how much he must be missing his family.

I really hope you say yes.

Lots of love.

Debbie.

PS Will you read Charlie's card out to him please?

I feel so bad for her. Without a mum at fifteen. Her dad spending so much time in here. Now this.

I open Charlie's card. And smile when I see that her message is more like a letter.

Dear Charlie,

I hope you're feeling OK. It's not easy being in hospital but I know you are being very brave. I can feel it in my bones. You're lucky to have your mum in there with you. Don't forget to give her plenty of hugs, especially when you're fed up or sore.

I would love to come and see you and it's hard to explain why I can't but I want you to know that I'm thinking about you all the time – when I get up in the morning, when I'm eating my Coco Pops, when I'm going to school. I'm thinking about you all the time.

Would you like me to mind Sausage for you while you're in hospital so he won't be lonely? If you'd like me to, nag your mum a bit, OK? Here's a baby Sausage to keep you company until you come home. You decide what to call him. He's really cuddly, isn't he? That's the little beans inside him. I love his eyes. I think he looks like Sausage. Don't you? If you can't think of a name, how about Cocktail because he's like a cocktail sausage and his tail cocks up in the air. See what you think.

Lots and lots of love, and millions of hugs, but no kisses, 'cos I know you don't like them.

Debbie

PS I'll come and see you the minute you come home.

How can I read this out to Charlie without crying?

'What's that, Mum? Is it a present for me?'

I look up.

'Yes, sweetie. It's from Deb. Let's turn off the telly.'

'OK. Can I have the present now?'

I hand it to him and he rips at the wrapping. I switch off the television, glad of the silence.

'He's just like Sausage!'

'There's a card. Want me to read it?'

'Yeah!' He says, very excited.

I've almost made it to the end when he asks, 'Are you crying, Mum?'

'No, sweetie.'

'You look like you're crying. Are you sad?'

'No, Charlie. I'm fine.'

'Do you've a pain in your leg?'

'No, I'm fine. Really. I think I might have a sneeze coming on or something. Anyway, what do you think of Cocktail?'

'He's good,' he says matter-of-factly. 'Can Debbie mind Sausage? He's lonely, on his own without us, Mum. And Debbie loves him. And he loves Debbie.'

'We'll see.'

'Aww. Mu-um.' He bangs his heel onto the bed.

'I'd need to talk to Simon. It would be his decision not mine. He owns Debbie's house. And he mightn't like a dog in it. Especially if he isn't used to dogs. And he isn't.'

'Can you ask him now?'

'He's a busy guy, Charlie. I'll ask him when we see him.'

'Aww.'

'If you keep that up, I won't ask him at all.'

Instant silence.

Charlie calls out a message to Deb. I scribble it down in my jotter.

Hi Deb,

I hate hospital. The food's soggy. I want to come home. It's a good idea about Sausage. I think Mum will say yes. I've a friend. His name's Mark. He's big. Love, Charlie. Thanks for the present. I think Cocktail is a good name. Bye.

I tear the paper out, slip it into the envelope Charlie's card came in, write 'Debbie' and draw a smiley face. When Simon drops by just before lunch, I hand it to him.

'I'm under instruction to ask about the dog,' he says with a smile.

'Simon, it's really kind to offer but the last thing you need is a dog.' I see Charlie glaring at me. 'Mary's husband, Phil, is walking and feeding Sausage. He'll be grand, honestly.'

'In fairness, it wouldn't interfere with me at all. Debra has it all planned. The walking, the feeding, brushing, whatever needs to be done. Actually, she really wants to do this. I think it would be good for her, Jenny, you know, to feel she's helping in some way. I'd encourage it.'

He really does sound genuine. 'In that case, that would be amazing, thank you. But, please, if it isn't working out, just tell me, OK?'

'I will.'

'Yes!' says Charlie victoriously.

I smile. 'This must be a first.'

'What?'

'Your doctor minding your dog.'

He smiles. 'Don't tell anyone in case it catches on.'

'You sure you don't mind?'

'Honestly, it'll be an adventure.'

'Thank you.'

'Yeah, thanks a million, Simon,' Charlie says.

Later that afternoon, I'm in the kitchen zapping vegetable soup for Charlie, one of the few things he'll eat. Mary brings in cartons that we label and store in the fridge, along with other favourites – cranberry juice, salami, olives, pickles, Cheesestrings and salty crackers. I spend a lot of time in here. For practical reasons, yes, but also to escape. There is nobody sick in here. And nobody trying to heal the sick. Just kitchen staff that arrive for their shift, listen to the radio, and serve up 'food' – simple uncomplicated people with simple, uncomplicated lives, or at least that's how it seems to me.

I'm alone now, my only company the sun, filtering in through opaque windows, filling the room with ethereal energy. On the radio, Coldplay sing, 'Let's go Back to the Start.' I loved that song. Until it took on new meaning. I can't listen to it like I used to anymore, unaffected. I imagine people all over the country – teenagers, businessmen, mums, busy doing whatever it is they're doing, half-listening, oblivious to the words. It's about death. Separation. And rewinding the clock. I think of Charlie, of life without Charlie. I let my guard down, just for a second, and cry.

Someone kicks the bottom of the door, then starts to push it in. It's either a staff member or a parent who knows their way round because that's the quickest way to get in. I turn my back to the door and run the flat of my hands over my face to clear the tears. Normally, I'd turn and smile because, in here, you need smiles like air. But now, I just can't. I hear the person open and close a cupboard, then the fridge. They arrive quietly beside me, waiting to use the microwave. Charlie's soup was ready ages ago. I take it out. Then turn to offer that smile.

Wait. I know that face. Elaine. Elaine…something.

'Jennifer? Jennifer Grey. How are you? What are you doing here? Another interview?'

As soon as she says it, she seems to realise her mistake. If I were interviewing someone, what would I be doing in the kitchen using the microwave?

'My son is a patient.'

'Oh. I'm sorry.'

'Yeah, well, there you go. Life, right? How is your daughter?' I try to remember her name. It was one of the most moving interviews I ever did. *Jessica? Was it Jessica?* 'Jessica,' I say, just in time.

Elaine's head falls forward as though she no longer has the energy to hold it up. For a moment, she says nothing, then takes a deep breath and sighs. 'She's not well, Jennifer.' She looks at me. 'She's had a relapse.'

'Oh, Elaine, I am so sorry.' Automatically, I touch her arm.

'I really thought we'd make it.' Her voice is beginning to rise. 'We did everything, fought all the way. Took every dose, did every test, went to alternative healers, set up the support group, prayed. God, how we prayed. But you know all that. You did the interview.'

Yes, I did the interview and I so admired this woman. So much fight in her, so much hope, so positive, facing the worst possibility in the world. How could she think of others in the same situation, setting up the support group, when she could have been so selfish about her energy? And then I went on to the next interview and forgot about her. How could I do that, just move on, when she was stuck, in trouble?

I look at her now, head down again, a tear hanging precariously from her chin. It falls into the dry Ready Brek she's holding, displacing tiny flakes. I take the cereal bowl from her and set it down on the counter. I put my arms around her. She sobs and shudders and I hold her.

'I never gave up hope,' she says, pulling back. 'And where did it get me? I was so naïve. I even had Jessica believing she'd make it. Mind over matter, I thought. And now, now, the prognosis is...well, there is no prognosis, and she still thinks she's going to make it. Dr Grace says we have to talk to her...'

'But surely there's hope. It's just a relapse...'

She shakes her head. 'It's the end, Jennifer, the end.'

I hold her to me. She gives in, lets her body go limp. There is nothing I can say. I should have known that. There is nothing anybody can say – and nothing worse that some eejit with false hopes. We stay drowning each other until we both feel the pressure of our sick children waiting for us, expecting us to return. Somehow, we emerge from the kitchen, with perfectly heated vegetable soup and Ready Brek, each of us with the right bowl and the right stiff upper lip. How is she going to tell her daughter?

seventeen

The following day, I'm waiting outside the bathroom for Charlie when Simon comes out of Jessica's room looking distracted, bothered. Then he sees me and stops dead. He stares at me as though seeing a ghost. Colour drains, not just from his face, but every visible patch of skin.

I know, instinctively, what's happened. To Elaine, I'm Jennifer Grey. Somehow, I must have come up for discussion. He knows who I am.

I don't know what to say. Neither, clearly, does he because he turns in the opposite direction and strides from the ward as though his life depends on instant disappearance.

So that's it. He knows. I feel suddenly sick, suddenly guilty, strangely relieved.

We don't see him for three days. He sends his registrar, Dr

Howard, instead. I catch sight of him, flying past the room, head down or dead ahead, always in the distance, talking with Anne or Siobhan in the nurses' station or showing other parents into his office.

I don't like Dr Howard, instantly suspicious of a woman who is on her feet all day but wears sling backs. My real problem is with her ratio of efficiency to caring. If I had to choose one over the other, I'd pick efficiency – obviously. But I don't see why I have to. I didn't before. And Charlie needs both.

He doesn't like her either.

'Where's Simon?' he asks. Repeatedly.

By day three, I'm ready to crack. This is ridiculous. He can't let what happened five years ago interfere with his job. Fine if he was a biscuit tester. It's Charlie's life we're talking about.

As soon as Charlie's asleep, I go to Simon's office, knock and walk in.

He stands up from his desk, looking like a fourteen-year-old caught with *Playboy*. 'Oh. Jenny. Hello.'

'This can't go on.'

'Sorry?'

'You're avoiding us. And, you know, that would be fine if Charlie wasn't sick and you weren't his doctor. But he is sick, very sick, and you have a responsibility. I'm not going to let him be seen repeatedly by your registrar. I'm sorry. I won't have him fobbed off. He's entitled to see a consultant. And if you're not prepared to see him, I'd like to know now, so I can take him elsewhere.' I try not to cry.

'Jenny.' He holds up both hands. 'Slow down.'

'I will *not* slow down. Charlie has leukaemia, not the common cold. I won't have his health put at risk because you're guilty about your past. The past is the past. I've put it behind me a long time ago...'

We stand facing each other across his desk.

'I'm sorry. It does seem bad from where you're standing. But, in fairness, I wasn't deliberately avoiding you. I was... I was just trying to sort this out in my head. I hadn't come up with a solution. And, though it might not look like it, I've been working as hard as ever on Charlie's health – just not visibly perhaps.'

'But we need visible. Charlie needs visible. I need visible.'

'Yes. I know. I'm sorry.'

'You're looking for a solution how to handle this? Here's a solution. Forget about what happened. It was five years ago. It happened. It's over. Both of us have got on with our lives. Charlie is sick now. He needs you. And, to tell you the truth, he misses you, Simon.'

'I'm sorry. It's not like me. At all. It's just that, well, in fairness, it was a bit of a shock. But you're right, it was unprofessional.'

'Look. I understand that what happened must have been very hard to live with considering... your situation...and everything...' *Oh Christ. Where am I going with this?*

'Yes, well...' He starts to fidget. 'Maybe we should go in to Charlie now.'

'He's asleep.'

We stand looking at each other. Stuck.

'Can we sit down?' he asks.

I sit.

He picks up a folder.

'I was going through Charlie's chart when you came in.'

I'm ever so slightly guilty.

'He's doing very well, Jenny. Better than expected. If he keeps responding like he is, I think he might be home in another week, maybe less.'

'Oh.'

'Have you spoken to Mairead about how you might handle things at home?'

'I don't need a social worker. I'm fine financially. I'll be able to look after Charlie full-time so he doesn't have to go back to school.'

'You don't want him to go to school?'

'It's not worth the risk.'

'Of infection?'

'Mainly. But I also don't think it would be good for him to be seen as different either.'

'I can see your point, though in fairness, I would like you to consider that there might be positive aspects to Charlie's returning to school. We won't discuss them now, but it is important to try to keep things as normal as possible for Charlie, psychologically – for him to have his friends, lead a normal life. We'll talk about it again. How is his form?'

'Good, apart from worrying about where you are.'

He looks apologetic.

'Other than that, he's fine. He has made friends, especially with Mark, whom he adores.'

He smiles. I notice he doesn't talk about other patients. Which I appreciate. If I want to tell other parents what's wrong with Charlie, I will. In fact, I have. And they have told me about their children, making me realise that it could be worse. Charlie could have leukaemia and kidney failure or leukaemia and Down's Syndrome.

'I'll call in to Charlie, first thing,' Simon says.

'Thank you.' I know I need to say more. 'Look, I'm sorry about earlier. It's just that I was, well, kind of frustrated, you know?'

'You were right to clear the air. I'm glad we spoke.' He stands. That's it then.

We walk up the corridor together. He continues home. I go in to Charlie.

Simon has become more attentive, appearing at Charlie's bedside two, sometimes, three times a day. I can't tell whether it's because of what happened or because Charlie's health is slipping. My little boy is paler, weaker, quieter. Dark circles, the colour of storm clouds, gather and build in intensity, not just under his eyes, but all round them. Even his lids appear grey. Blond hairs attach themselves to clothes, pillowcases, lips. Mine and his. Sometimes, I look at him and see a frail old man rather than a four-year-old boy.

I itch to get him home, feed him up and surround him with fresh air, fun and laughter, Debbie, Sausage, Dara. Operation Rosy Cheeks.

In here, I do what I can. I keep the window open until people complain of the cold. I teach him yoga, and laugh when he creates his own positions – gorilla, standing pencil and crocodile. I make up crazy games that get him off the bed – enemy capture and gung-ho ghouls. I ask Mary to bring in little messages from Dara, even if they are two lines. When Debbie sends in notes, presents or pictures of Sausage, we reply instantly to keep them coming.

'I'd give you the world if I could,' I tell him, one night I'm feeling mellow. We're lying side by side, doing nothing, just resting.

'Would this hospital be in it?' he asks without looking at me.

'I think maybe they could keep the hospital.'

I've become a big promiser. Already, I've agreed to a party, a coat for Sausage that says, 'I love bitches,' and a midnight feast. I've also become a deliverer – four large cuddly toys, every suitable game or book in the hospital shop – and a lot of unsuitable ones. All it takes is some kind of uncomfortable test, X-ray or scan, particularly when landed on us at the end of a long day. Simon was right – Charlie does know my buttons, which to push, when, and in what order to get what he wants. I let him. Hospital is an alien, scary place. He can behave out of character while he's here. I'll sort it out when we get home.

Despite being bombarded with chemicals, Charlie has had a growth spurt. From the waist down, he could be a clown. The gap between his wide-legged pyjama bottoms and giant cartoon slippers reveals an inch of pale, skinny ankle. The slippers are new, bought by Mary after his original ones had to be decontaminated and 'removed' when he sprayed them with radioactive pee. Special people in special uniforms with special equipment seemed to materialise, to take the slippers away and treat the floor. It was like a scene from *Monsters, Inc.* All I could think was, if a tiny bit of urine is such a danger to mankind, what about the amount of radioactive dye that must have been pumped into Charlie for the test. I joked about it, though. What else can you do?

In here, alone with Charlie, seeing other grandparents coming and going, I find myself thinking about my mother. The sensible part of me feels I should tell her – she is family; she should at least know. But the stubborn part won't have it. She has never shown any interest in seeing him, meeting him. I know I told her I couldn't take her anymore. That was five years ago. She needn't have taken me so literally. She could have made some kind of effort. She could have at least tried to find out about Charlie, how he's doing, how we're getting along. She never did. Well, apart from that one time at Great's funeral, but I wasn't myself then, wasn't ready. And she never tried after that. So, fine, let's leave it.

It's only eight but Charlie's already asleep and I'm tired. I drag my wafer into position and cover it with a sheet. I pull the curtain around the bed, take off my shoes and start to do a few gentle yoga stretches. On hands and knees, on my wafer, I'm in a position called 'cat'. I've arched my back upward into a feline stretch. Now, I let my lower back dip, sticking my bum in the air. *Loosening up nicely.*

A throat clears. 'Hello,' says a voice I recognise as Simon's.

Jesus! I drop my bum to my heels, kneel up. My hair covers my face. I flick it back, throw him a smile and an awkward, 'Hi,' then clamber to my feet. All this in three seconds. 'Yoga,' I explain.

'Is that what it was?' he asks with a crooked smile. 'I'm on call this weekend, so I thought I'd come by to see how everything is.'

'Fine...thanks.' I tuck my hair behind my ears.

Dressed casually in shirt and chinos, he looks more relaxed. Younger. *Friday night. He's probably going out. With a few friends. A woman? The gorgeous Dr Howard? Not his type – if he has any sense. I wonder, though... Stop. Obsessing. About. The. Hospital. Staff. God, I need to get out of here.*

'Well, enjoy yourself,' I say.

'I'll try. Debra's treating me to a movie.'

'Really?' *Oops. I sounded too surprised.* 'That's nice.'

'I don't know. She seems to have developed some sort of notion that I'm a case for self-improvement.' He grimaces.

I smile.

'She's getting me books from the library.'

'Anything good?'

'You don't think I read them.'

'She might ask you questions – make sure you have.'

'Shit. I hadn't thought of that.'

I laugh. 'What are you going to see?'

'Some documentary. It's "educational".' He puts his fingers in quote marks and pulls a doubtful face. 'I'll probably sleep through it.'

There's something lost about him that reminds me of another time. It catches me off guard. And I tell myself that I need to get out of here before the furniture starts to look attractive.

eighteen

Mary's trying to get me to take time out. She's thinking, bath.

'Come on, I want you to try out these aromatherapy oils Phil gave me for my birthday.'

'When was your birthday?' I ask, sorry I missed it.

'Last May.'

I smile. 'And you haven't touched them?'

'Nope.'

'Poor Phil.'

'He's used to me,' she says, rummaging in her bag. She produces what looks like a pencil case, zips it open and pulls out a tiny brown bottle. 'Lavender,' she reads, 'for relaxation, healing and harmony.'

'Why haven't you used them?' I ask suspiciously.

'Too busy.'

'Isn't that the point? Rest, relaxation, harmony?'

She waves her hand dismissively. 'I've no time to be lolling around in baths.'

Suddenly, it hits me. 'You're spending way too much time here, Mary. You really are. You've a million things to do.'

'OK, so I'm lying. I just hate baths.'

I raise an eyebrow.

'Look, since Dara's started school, I'm practically a lady of leisure. Phil's even nagging me to take up golf so we can play together when the kids are gone.' She rolls her eyes. 'Already thinking of retirement.'

I imagine how great it must be to have that kind of easy, comfortable relationship, the security of having someone who loves you, thinks of you and plans your future together. Behind the tut-tutting, Mary loves it.

'I want to be here, Jen. What better excuse to sit on my bum, where I'm happiest? I've spent the last ten years running round in circles. Now that I've my mornings back, I'm going to take advantage of them. This break is long overdue. So, stop with the guilt and go have a bath. Go on – you're coming between me and Hello magazine.' It's one Jack brought in.

'In fairness, I could do with a soak,' I say. 'I can't believe I just said that.'

'What?'

'In fairness.'

'What's wrong with that?'

'Nothing,' I say, starting to get embarrassed.

'What? ...What?'

'It's just something Simon says. All the time.'

'Does he now?' she asks, looking at me, a glint in her eye. 'Can't say I noticed.'

'Oh for God's sake, Mary. Don't be ridiculous.'

'What did I say?' she asks innocently, palms up.

'Nothing. Forget it. I need to get out of here, that's all. I'm so bored I'm beginning to notice the habits of the medical staff.'

'I wouldn't say all the medical staff.'

'Mary, it's you who needs to get out.'

She just laughs. 'I can't say I blame you, though.'

'I'm going for my bath. I hope you'll have matured by the time I get back.'

She throws over the aromatherapy kit. 'Better take your time, then.'

'Will you take that stupid look off your face?'

'Make me.'

'Don't think I'm not tempted.'

She laughs.

And Charlie's rolls his eyes like he's thinking, *Women!*

Steaming water roars into the bath. I squint at the labels on the bite-sized bottles of essential oils. *Hmm, Clary Sage, for euphoria. Could do with a bit of that.* I tip the bottle upside down. *Oh my God!* I gag, hold my nose and breathe through my mouth. I quickly screw the lid back on. Risking second-degree burns, I yank at the stopper. Out swirls the water. Unfortunately, not the smell. I throw open the window and start to fan the air. An icy current rushes in and pokes at the steam. I search for the lavender oil. *Safe with that.*

Finally, the bath is full. I lie back, hold my nose and slide under the water, drowning out all noise. I try to empty my mind but keep thinking about what Mary said. *So what if I notice something Simon keeps saying? I'd be stupid not to. It's practically in every sentence. Sometimes, I want to laugh because it's not even in context. But so what? It means nothing – apart from the fact that I'm becoming institutionalised. Like a prisoner longing for mealtime to brighten her day, I look forward to seeing Simon. There's a good reason for that. Reassurance. A reminder that we're in good hands. I breathe easier when he's around. It has nothing to do with Simon the individual and everything to do with Simon the doctor. I do feel deflated when he goes. But that's just part of being cooped up in here, nothing to do, horizons contracted to a decimal point. I bet every mother in the place feels the same. He's probably got a whole fan club going on without knowing it.*

I surface for breath, go under a few more times, then, conscious that it's a communal bathroom, carry on with the job of cleaning. My head is covered in shampoo when I realise there's no shower attachment. I fiddle with the mixer, trying to find a balance between ice-cold and scalding. Crouching forward on my knees, head under the nozzle, I rub my hair rapidly until it squeaks. *Forget conditioner.*

I feel relaxed, clean, fresh. Even positive. *Could it be the Clary Sage after all?* For the first time since we came in, I put on make-up. And dry my hair properly. I slip on a pretty pink top that Mary insists she's finished with. Then my jeans. You can make out the shape of my hipbones through them. I need to get home. And eat.

Instead of, 'you look great', I'm greeted with, 'Urgh, what's the smell?' from Charlie.

Mary's look says, 'the boy's got a point.'

'It's Clary Sage. It's supposed to make you happy. I thought it was gone. Don't you smell lavender?' I sit beside Charlie and pluck a hair off his shoulder.

'Frankly, no,' says Mary at the same time Charlie offers, 'Pe-ew.'

He holds his nose and shifts up the bed.

'If you're not careful, I'll try some on you.'

'Urgh, no way.' He scrambles further up the bed, forgetting he's attached to a drip.

'Charlie, stop,' I shout, visualising his Freddie being ripped from his chest. He stops but not before the drip starts to bleep.

Oh God, something's wrong! I rush to get a nurse.

She turns of the drip. Checks the Freddie.

'It's fine,' she says.

I breathe again.

'Sorry,' I say to everyone, feeling like a fool.

A week goes by. Mary keeps us nourished. Jack keeps us in clothes, arriving with two pairs of olive-green *Action Man* pyjamas. They bring out the colour in Charlie's eyes. That is an accident –

Jack doesn't notice things like eye colour. The matching baseball cap, though, does strike me as impressive forward planning – getting Charlie interested in caps before he has to use them as camouflage. Charlie decides to sport the back-to-front look, the way SuperMark does. It suits him.

The following day, Anne takes me aside and suggests we shave off Charlie's hair, get it over with, end the torture of finding it everywhere. She can organise a hairdresser to come to the ward.

Can I do it, though, go from child with hair to child with no hair, just like that?

Could it be any worse than what I'm looking at now? His scraggy hair makes him look sicker. In any case, I could do with controlling something.

The appointment is made. Before the hairdresser arrives, Mark comes over and sits beside Charlie.

'I shaved my hair off, too,' he says.

'Did you really? Cool,' says Charlie. 'Did you shave it all by yourself?'

'Yeah. But I'm big. If I was four, I'd let the barber do it.'

'What's a barber?'

'Oh, like a hairdresser.'

'OK.'

'Do you like Winders?'

'Yeah.'

Mark reaches into the pocket of his tracksuit top, pulls out a Winder and hands it to Charlie.

'Thanks. D'you want half?'

''s OK. Just had one. Want me to stay while the hairdresser cuts your hair?'

'Yeah.'

'OK.'

Here is a boy at an age when his only worries should be girls, whether or not to shave, the odd spot, and his voice breaking, landed here with a terminal illness, a broken family, an absent father. Instead of feeling sorry for himself, he's focusing his energy on someone else. I look to my far left, then right, then up, to spread the tears that are flooding my eyes. I wipe my nose with the back of my hand and try to collect myself. I smile at them, the two buddies, chatting away, oblivious to their age difference, surroundings or fate. United by illness.

The hairdresser, a pleasant cuddly woman in her fifties, arrives. I try to hide how I feel as I watch clumps of blond hair, like sheep's wool, drift onto his shoulders, lap, and floor. It breaks my heart. But I continue to smile. I sneak a lock for myself, wrap it in tissue, hide it away. Without his hair, Samson lost his strength. It makes sense, suddenly. I look at my new boy and try to adjust. His face seems so small now compared to the size of his head. It doesn't dominate any more. His eyes are the same though. *Focus on his eyes, Jenny, his soul. Not his body. Which keeps changing. And will keep on changing. His eyebrows will go. His lashes. His face might swell. But he will still be Charlie, my Charlie, my boy. Smile Jenny. And keep on smiling.*

'Cool, Charlie,' I lie.

'Want to look in the mirror?' suggests Mark

I look in panic at Anne. She nods to go ahead.

'Yeah, OK,' says Charlie, happily, game for anything as long as he's with Mark.

The hairdresser hands him a mirror.

He just sits and stares.

'Well?' asks Mark.

Charlie looks up at him. 'I'm like you now, amn't I?'

'Yeah.'

'That's OK then,' he nods.

'Would you like one of my Nike caps? I've two.'

'Cool. We'll be like twins.'

Mark smiles at him, lands his hand gently on Charlie's head and rubs it back and forward, making me feel like it's OK; it can be touched, it won't break. And I think how Mark must be a great brother. And how much he must miss his own.

nineteen

Every day, Charlie has his blood tested. I wake, worrying what the results will be. I think of little else. Until I find out. I try not to let it affect my mood. It did in the beginning, until I learnt a trick. I write the results in a record book that they've given me and try to detach. The plan is, once I record them I can forget about them. Sometimes it works. Sometimes it doesn't. Sometimes there are bad days, when everything seems to be going against us.

I've become a bit of an expert. I know the levels of each blood cell, what's normal, how far from normal Charlie's have been and how he has progressed. Not steadily but in waves and troughs. It's hard not to become obsessed. When your child has leukaemia, your constant fixation is how close to remission he is. Remission is your dream, your Utopia, your escape. You just have to believe that when there's a dip, it will turn again.

At the end of our second week here, Simon arrives at Charlie's bedside, looking happy. There is no intro, no preamble. He just says it straight out. The cancer cells have disappeared from Charlie's blood! Before I know it, I've thrown my arms around him and actually lifted him off the ground.

Totally embarrassed, I drop him. 'Sorry.'

He laughs. 'It's fine.'

'What are you doing, Mum?'

'Acting like a complete idiot.'

'Why?'

'It's good news, Charlie, really good news.'

'Am I better?'

'Yes, sweetheart, much better.'

'Can we go home, now?'

I look at Simon. Who sits down beside Charlie.

'Charlie,' he says. 'We are winning the fight against the bad cells. They have all gone from your blood now.'

'Good.'

'We just have to do a test to see if they have gone from your bones too.'

'Oh.'

'Do you remember when we put you to sleep the last time for the bone test, the bone marrow biopsy?'

He nods.

'Well, we're going to do that again.'

Charlie looks at me, eyes wide. 'The space ships, Mama.'

'Sweetheart, that was just a dream,' I say, lifting him up and settling him on my lap. 'Like the nightmares you had before.' I rub his cheek with my finger. 'If we do this test, and if the bad cells are gone, that means we can go home. Doesn't it, Simon?'

'Yes. It does.' He smiles at Charlie. 'You will be in remission.'

'Remission,' I say. I hold my breath and pray.

This time, it works. Charlie. Is. In. Remission. He has made the first step to freedom. It's what we've hoped for, prayed for, dreamt of. But now that we're here, I'm thinking of the next step, the bone marrow transplant. *When will we find a match? Am I one? When will I get the results of my blood test?* I stop myself. Because, today, I'm allowing myself a sliver of happiness, a slice of relief, a segment of victory. For the rest of the day, I'm going to stop thinking ahead.

Mary smuggles in a baby bottle of champagne. The night nurses pretend not to notice.

Simon, Anne, Siobhan, Mairead and the rest of the team prepare us for discharge, what to expect, how to look after Freddie and how to take the medication. They write everything down. They give me booklets. Website details. Phone numbers. A medi-alert bracelet for Charlie. I know what to look out for – temperatures, bleeding, bruising, rashes. Anything unusual. I have the direct line to the ward and Simon's mobile. We will be in once a week for chemotherapy but I am to call or come in at any time, if I'm worried. If Charlie gets a temperature, we have to make it back in an hour. These are the things that worry me.

I'm afraid of having to cope alone but know that when I get home I *will* cope. Because that's what we do, in life, cope. We're thrown into situations and we get on with it. Because we have to. I just need to get home, walk through the door and start again. Back to a normal atmosphere where Charlie can have a healthier life – fresh air, organic food, exercise. He won't be the sick boy anymore; he'll be the boy who is getting better. And we will cope.

I feel guilty looking around the ward at the other children and their parents, still waiting for that news. But they are delighted for us; as I would be for them. We're all fighting the same thing. And if one of us has a victory, it makes us all more hopeful. Mark gives Charlie his favourite cap and his mobile number. He tells him to text. Charlie's mouth falls open. Texting a teenager; he's made it.

We've said goodbye to everyone except Elaine and Jessica. They are in a room on their own. The door is closed. Part of me wants to steal away. But I can't. I leave Charlie with Anne and force myself into that sweet-smelling room, that room that smells like death.

Their energy is flagging. But they're so happy for us, it makes me want to cry. They offer hugs and hope and tell me to keep fighting. I manage to hold off the tears until I walk out of the room. I hide in the bathroom until I'm ready to go back to Charlie.

I want to get moving now, get out, away. Mary has taken home most of our things. I have the remainder packed, ready to go. We have to be officially discharged by Simon. He comes, at last, all smiles and chat with Charlie. He writes a prescription that seems to go on forever. I watch his thin, confident, black scrawl and wonder how I'm going to get all that medicine into such a small person, every day. He signs his name with a whoosh. He writes with his left hand, I notice, like Charlie. This catches me by surprise. Everything becomes embarrassingly personal. Though of course it isn't. He is a doctor writing a prescription. That's all. He hands me his card, forgetting that he's already done this. Our hands touch and I blush. *What is wrong with me?*

He smiles professionally. 'How are you getting home?'

'We've a car.'

'Are you OK to drive?'

'Fine.'

'I'll walk you out,' he says.

'It's OK. You're busy.'

'I insist.'

On the way out, he checks that we have everything, know everything, are ready for this. Leaving feels like walking a tightrope, with nothing below me, anymore, to break my fall.

We're all set. In the car. Charlie strapped in. Stuff in the boot. Simon standing at the hospital entrance, waiting for us to take off. I turn the key. Nothing happens. There isn't even a sound. I try again. I close my eyes. *Come on!*

Nothing. It's flat. Totally flat. I can't believe I didn't think to come out and warm up the engine. It's not exactly a Merc.

Charlie starts to whine. After the stifling heat of the hospital, the car is cold and damp.

'It's OK, sweetie.' I take off my coat, reach back and cover him with it.

There's a tap at the fogged up window. I jump.

'Everything OK?' It's Simon.

'It won't start,' I say, feeling useless.

'There's been a lot of rain. You're not the first person it's happened to. Can I give you a lift home?'

'God. No. Thanks. You're busy.'

'Muum,' Charlie calls from behind.

I turn around. 'It's OK, Charlie, everything's fine.' I turn back to Simon. 'Maybe I could bring Charlie back to the ward while I look for someone with jump leads. It's the battery. It has to be.'

'I've jump leads.' He disappears. And returns, minutes later, in a Merc. His jump leads are almost as big as the Mini. Charlie is jigging up and down in his car seat at the excitement of it all. Simon pulls up, his engine purring like a tiger.

In seconds, he's hooked up the wires.

And I breathe out in relief as the mini starts, first try.

When he disconnects us, I rev the engine continuously not risking the embarrassment of cutting out again. He comes to the window and smiles.

'Bingo.'

'Thank you so much, Simon. Sorry for taking up your time.'

'No problem. Safe home.'

'Thanks, Simon,' shouts Charlie from the back.

Simon winks at him. 'Mind your Mum, OK?'

'OK!'

'We'd better go,' I say. 'Thanks again.'

He puts his hand on the car. 'Call if you've any worries.'

He waits until we reverse out and drive off.

We stop at a pharmacy close to home. The hospital has given us a supply of medicine to get us over the first day or two but I want to get on top of things. We have to wait for ages, though, while they fill three paper bags full of medicine containers. Mairead, the social worker, has signed Charlie up for a long-term illness scheme where he gets free medication. I just have to fill out a form. When I see how much we would have had to pay, I nearly drop. The pharmacist looks sympathetically at Charlie. She offers him a lollipop from a glass jar. He takes ages to choose one and I wonder if she is as tolerant with children who have hair. She doesn't charge for the lollipop.

One more stop for milk and bread, then we're home.

The flat is warm and tidy. A big Welcome Home banner is stuck to the wall. Brightly coloured balloons are everywhere. An unfamiliar vase stands on the coffee table, holding an enormous bunch of white, unopened lilies. In the kitchen, there is a Bart Simpson cake with four candles on it. Charlie is running around, laughing, asking if it's his birthday.

The fridge has been emptied and completely restocked with a mixture of essentials (milk, butter, fresh bread), healthy food options (soup, salad, probiotic yoghurt) and all of Charlie's favourites. Mary has left a note:

Jenny,
We thought of jumping out from behind couches and shouting 'surprise' but felt you might be tired. I'll call tomorrow. But if there's anything you need, just pick up the phone.

She is an angel sent by God. Or maybe Great.

'Where's Sausage?' Charlie asks.

'Remember? I told you, Debbie will drop him back after dinner. We're going to have a little rest first. OK?'

'But I want him now. I need to give him a hug.'

'I know, sweetie. But he'll be here, later. When we wake up.' I told myself that as soon as we got home, I'd be firm. No, nonsense. It's not as easy as I thought.

I put the medicines up on top of the fridge-freezer, to 'keep them out of reach of children'. Ironic, given the effort it takes to get them into him. There are about twelve containers of various shapes and sizes, standing together, like the Manhattan skyline. I wonder will we ever get through them. I give Charlie his first dose and take his temperature, just to be sure. Then, we head to bed. We climb in together. The warm glow of the lamp fills the room on this grey November day. We're home.

twenty

Simon has arrived with Debbie and Sausage. I'd forgotten that he would have to come. But I'm glad he has. Sausage is slobbering all over Charlie and I'm silently freaking about germs. I look at Simon.

He mouths, 'It's OK.'

I relax again and start to enjoy the reunion – Charlie reunited with Sausage and Debbie at the same time.

Debbie bends down. They both rush to her. She grabs them, one in each arm. Sausage barks and licks her face.

'OK, you're going down, buddy.' She puts him down then stands, lifting Charlie's face up to hers. She smiles. 'How are you?'

'Good.'

'I'm so glad you're home. I missed you. I've loads of news...' She carries him to the couch.

Simon is hovering. I guess we both are.

'Would you like a coffee?' I ask.

'Only if you're having one.' He looks at Debbie and Charlie on the couch and smiles. 'Doesn't look like I'll be going anywhere for a while.'

'Do you want to sit down?' I nod to the counter that separates the kitchen from the sitting room.

He pulls up a stool and I head for the kettle.

'She's a great kid,' I say, catching him looking at the two of them.

He looks surprised.

'She's so good with Charlie,' I add.

'He seems to bring out the best in her, all right.'

'She's a good kid anyway. You can always tell.'

'She has her moments. But you're right, she is. Since she started to mind the dog – well, no, it was before that – since she heard about Charlie...she's changed.'

'How?'

He shrugs. 'Easier to live with. Calmer. More co-operative. Less...explosive,' he says like he's articulating it for the first time himself. 'It's been difficult since her mum died. In fairness, I don't think I've been handling it very well. Anyway...' He smiles. 'We're talking again. Properly. She even asks my opinion sometimes.' He looks so surprised, I want to laugh. 'No, I have to say, we're getting on very well.' He looks equal parts relieved and bemused.

'Even though it means you get dragged along to the movies?' I smile

'Actually, it wasn't that bad. A bit of escapism.'

'You're lucky?'

'Why?'

'Deb could be like I was when I was her age.'

He looks surprised. Then amused. Then interested. 'Oh, really?' he asks, eyebrows up.

I grimace. 'I was a bit of a handful.'

'Is that right?'

'You don't want to know.'

'Oh but I do.'

'I shaved off my hair.'

'All of it?'

'All of it.'

'Fashion statement?'

'More of a rebellion. It was the only thing my mother ever complimented me on.'

'Ouch,' the parent in him says.

'Yeah, she blew up. Which only encouraged me. I started wearing Docs, ripped black woolly tights, short skirts. And black. Lots of black. Buckets of eyeliner. And white make up.'

'You sound scary.'

'I was. To some people.' I'm serious now. 'Especially teachers. They came down hard. So I started mitching. My mother lost it completely.'

'Why were you so keen to upset her?'

I shrug. 'Maybe I just wanted her to love me.' I laugh at how ridiculous and psychobabbly that sounds.

'She didn't love you?'

'Let's just say, she put politics first. I pretty much grew up with my gran, Great. I mentioned her.'

'Yes, yes you did.' He thinks for a second. 'Is your mother Kathleen Dempsey?'

I nod. 'Belongs to her constituents. Always chasing the vote. Some eejit rings in the middle of the night with a blocked toilet she'd practically go over there herself, roll up her sleeves and shove her own hand down the loo.'

He looks shocked.

'OK, I'm exaggerating. A bit.'

'What about your dad?'

'She's his world. They should never have had kids. Well, kid.'

'Where are they now, your parents?'

He must mean, where are they in relation to the hospital, in relation to Charlie being sick, because it's obvious from the media where they are – larger than life and living in Dublin. Coming to a television near you. Mother at least.

'We don't keep in touch.'

He picks up on my end-of discussion tone. 'Sorry. Didn't mean to pry.'

'You weren't.' I realise that the kettle boiled ages ago. I go to make the coffee. As I do, I start to hope that I haven't freaked him out, talking about rebellious teenagers.

I return to the counter with two mugs of coffee. Then get milk and sugar. I sit on the stool beside him while he helps himself to milk.

'Anyway, Debbie is wonderful. And don't worry, she won't start any of that attention-seeking behaviour I just frightened you with. Because she has your attention. And that's the main thing. Take it from one who knows.'

'I'm just relieved. I had just gone out and bought a load of books on teenage behaviour. They were terrifying.'

I smile. *Ah, God.* 'So have you worked out why you are being taken in hand, artistically?'

'No. But I'll suffer a little sophistication.'

After a while, Simon notices that Charlie is tiring. He tells everyone it's time to go. Sausage looks from Debbie to Charlie and back again. He doesn't know who to go with. In the end, he decides he's home – luckily, or there would have been one deeply wounded boy.

Charlie feeds him, while I rustle up supper.

I pump my son with the vitamins I am allowed give him (everything except folic acid, which counteracts one of his drugs), then go through the stressful procedure of giving him his medication. His temperature is fine.

He wants me to lie down with him until he sleeps. I stay longer, gazing at his little face – so pale, so still. Too still. I rest the back of my hand on the pillow, near his mouth, to feel his breath. I rub his cheek with a finger to see if I can bring some colour back. It's no use. He is disappearing – first his complexion, then his hair, eyebrows, lashes. He is being rubbed out. And there is nothing I can do to stop it. Even his face is beginning to lose its familiar, sweet shape. *The steroids, like they said.*

I take his limp hand in my two, close my eyes and try to

remember the way he was. Picture him, before. But his present image keeps intruding and I get frustrated, upset. I get up and leave the room. In the kitchen, I go to the windowsill and pick up a picture of him. I stare at it for ages. I'm going to get him back. If it kills me.

I make another coffee and sit down. The empty mugs remind me of my conversation with Simon and how little you really know about a person. You can have sex with them. See them every day for two weeks. And still know nothing about them. In my mind, Simon's gone from unhappy widower and doctor to struggling father, lone parent, like myself. Confident doctor, hesitant father. Trying to do his best like the rest of us.

I like him.

And I'm curious: Why he chose to be a doctor and why a children's oncologist...how he got the thin, white scar just below his right cheekbone...what makes him laugh...what makes him angry. I know what makes him sad. Why did he never remarry? Did nobody live up to Alison? How often does he think of her? Is he still guilty about what happened? Do I ever pop into his mind? If so, in what context? Sometimes I think he likes me. But then, I figure, no more than any other parent. And sometimes – obviously when I'm really tired – I feel that if things were different, I mean completely different, like we were stranded on a desert island, with no history, there might be something between us. Which is ridiculous, childish, desperate. Charlie is sick. But what if all this *is* because Charlie is sick. Maybe it's some primal instinct driving me to find a mate to get us through this. Clearly, I'm losing my mind.

Mary gives Dara the day off school and we take the boys and Sausage to Brittas Bay, an endless white sandy beach in Wicklow, to let them gulp great breaths of fresh air. The sky is clear and blue but, after a windy night, the water's wild. It's beautiful. Waves pound, smash and roar to the shore, the smell of salt, invigorating. Cappuccino froth foams at the edge, as the angry sea sweeps forward onto the flat, wet, caramel sand. The boys, in their Wellies, run ahead with sticks to join up prints left by horses' hooves.

I treasure every inch of sky, sand, sea, every pebble – smooth and round, in varying shades of wine, slate grey, luminous white. My favourites are grey with white stripes. Looking up, I follow the trail of a plane slicing through the sky. *I will appreciate everything from now on*, I tell someone – God, maybe. *So please give me back my life, my boy.* I watch Charlie draw in the sand. It's a Christmas tree made of three triangles. *Will we have found a donor by then?*

Walking back to the car, I look at the shadow of the two of us walking, hand in hand. We look normal. In shadows you don't notice pale faces or missing hair.

Dara finds a bright green Frisbee. We don't know where it's been, who's had it. But what the hell? We let him keep it.

twenty-one

To get Charlie to exercise, I employ a variety of sneaky techniques. Firstly, timing – as soon as he gets up and after he rests. Secondly, I trick him into it. One of my favourites is to stick my bum out and get him to slap it. I start out walking, a bit like a gorilla, then speed up, forcing him to run. We both end up laughing and out of breath. We dance to the *Lilo and Stitch* CD the hospital let us borrow. It consists mostly of Elvis tracks and Charlie loves it. He moves like a little Elvis, though he's never seen the king.

'I'm a huk, a huk, a burning luv,' he sings, all husky, into a toy microphone Louis bought him, which unfortunately gives great 'amplification'.

We walk to the shop to buy treats.

'Let's get you a treat,' he says, meaning, 'let's get me a treat'. But if it gets him moving and out in the air, that's fine with me.

Then there's the 'we-better-bring-the-dog-for-a-walk' excuse.

When Dara calls over, I organise games that require energy but not too much – treasure hunts, musical chairs, hide and seek. And maybe I'm a little too organised, too controlling but there's too much at stake not to be.

Getting Charlie to eat used to be a problem. Now it's the opposite. Steroids have given him the appetite of a rugby team. I have to watch his weight. They've warned me about that. Just like they've warned me his face might get puffy (it has). And that his moods might become erratic, making him giddy, hyper. Most of the time, he's too wiped out to be either.

I'm anal about his drugs, making sure he gets every dose on time, the syrups syringed in, millilitre-by-millilitre, the tablets crushed and disguised in food. I have to be equally fussy about preparing his food and keeping him away from anyone sick. Hand washing has been drummed into us and Charlie is really careful. I've given him responsibility for the oral hygiene routine they want us to follow – washing his teeth four times a day, swishing round an antibacterial mouthwash and then swallowing an anti-fungal liquid. It's strange watching a child so small take an almost obsessive interest in caring for himself. But it's better than having to argue with him to do it four times a day, every day.

A liaison nurse from the hospital calls to see how we are managing. She checks the way I clean and disinfect Freddie and arranges for a public health nurse to call. I continue my Zero Spoiling campaign.

'Thank you, Mum,' I remind him whenever silence replaces manners.

'Thank you, Mum,' he repeats.

I try not to give him everything he wants or jump to attention for minor requests. But the hardest thing is reminding other people, especially poor Deb who tries too hard, maybe to make up for not coming to the hospital.

'Is that OK?' she asks him in a gentle voice, covering him with his baby quilt.

He is crashed on the couch, like a child with ME.

She has already supplied a pillow.

'I want a drink,' he says.

In the kitchen, I take her aside.

'Deb, you're so great with Charlie. But we have to be careful not to spoil him. When he gets through this, we want to be able to live with him.'

She looks horrified.

'I know it's hard but please, if you can, just try to treat him as normal.'

'But he's sick.' She looks at me like I'm Cruella Deville.

'Even if you just try to get him to say please. That would be great.'

They spend a lot of time drawing and painting. It's something they both like and it's calm, restful work that doesn't take much energy. The only problem is, when Deb's not there, he expects me to be as good as she is.

'Can you draw a crystal for me?' he asks.

'OK.' I've no idea how to draw a crystal but I make a stab at it.

'It usually has lines coming out of it.'

'Oh, like light?'

'Yeah.'

'OK.' I produce some rays and he seems happy enough.

He notices a mark on the back of my wrist.

'What's that?' he says holding it.

'I burned myself.'

'How?'

'With the iron.'

He frowns. 'Did you cry?'

'No. It was OK.'

'You're so brave,' he says, lifting my hand and kissing it better.

'Thanks, sweetie.' I hug him because he's the brave one.

It's not my first accident. I've become scatty, constantly dropping, spilling and losing things, bumping into corners, forgetting plans, I've even locked us out. I infuriate myself.

They advise us not to get too involved with the other parents. All children are different, they say, with different conditions, tests, treatments and 'outcomes'. Another person's bad experience might not be yours and will only drag you down. It makes sense. Still, I ring Elaine every day. I can't help it. I feel a duty to her. We talk or, at least, I listen. And try to hide my shock. Everything is being handled with such practicality, such efficiency. Jessica has picked out a headstone, the songs she wants at her funeral. *How can she do that? Face death, straight on, eyes open. Could I, could Charlie, be that brave?* I'm in awe – when I allow myself to believe it.

If there's one good thing about what we're going through, it is this: I've learnt who my friends are. Real friends. Not the ones who call to say how sorry they are, then never show up. No, not them. I'm talking about the ones who keep coming, helping, even when you think you don't need it, but you do. The ones who knuckle down, get their hands dirty. Like Elaine's sister. Always there. Always helping. Or Mark's granny. Same thing. For me, it's Mary who knows what we need before we do ourselves. But also Jack. We always got on, Jack and I, but he wouldn't have been the first person I'd have called in an emergency. He has been a surprise.

After his first visit he became a regular. Arriving with newspaper cuttings and printouts from websites. Then, new pyjamas for Charlie. He bought me a pillow when he discovered I didn't have one. Oh, and a life supply of Lucozade which he reminded me, 'replaces lost energy quickly'. He has read Charlie his snake and spider books while I've left the room 'for some fresh air'. Since we've got home, he has been equally, if not more, attentive. He calls with takeaways from the best restaurants so I needn't worry about how the food is prepared. He baby-sits while I nip out for a walk or catch up on jobs. He e-mails constantly. And now, after arriving with and helping us polish off a lasagne, he has just presented me with a voucher for a local beauty salon. I laugh.

'How did you know about Jackie's?'

He smiles.

'And how did you know I love Indian Head Massages?'

'That article you did about beauty salons?' He's fidgeting with the lapel of his jacket.

'But that was ages ago.'

'Yeah, well, I looked it up. Do you want it or not?'

'I want it. I want it.' I give him a hug. He really is such a gruff little cutie.

'Jesus. Get off. If you do it some evening, I'll mind Charlie.'

'You sure? You'll be alright on your own?'

'I won't be on my own. Aren't we two men? We can watch the snooker. I'll bring popcorn.'

'Or you could make some. I've got the stuff in the cupboards...'

'Don't push it.'

'How did you know he likes snooker?' Charlie loves snooker, stands two inches from the telly, fists clenched. When a ball is pocketed, he hops up and down.

'All men like snooker.'

'Right.' Everything is so simple with Jack. But he always seems to get it right.

'Jen?'

'Hmm?'

'I wanted to talk to you about something.'

'Sounds serious.'

'I hope you don't mind. And it's none of my business, I know, but have you thought of telling Dave?'

I look at him, my stomach flipping.

'I mean, as Charlie's father, don't you think he should know?'

My shoulders stiffen. 'Jack, if I'm a match, I won't need to tell Dave.' My tone says don't-go-there.

But he does. 'I'm not talking about that, Jenny. I'm talking about just letting him know what's happening.'

'I don't want to disturb him.' Or the status quo. Everything has settled. I don't want to stir it all up again.

'Jen, I think he'd want to know.'

'How do you know what he'd want?' I snap.

'I don't want to argue, I'm just making a point. I think he should know. That's all.'

'I should have known you'd take his side. Is that why you've been so good to us? You were just waiting for the right moment to put Dave's side forward. Your old pal.'

He looks hurt. 'I'm disappointed you'd think that.' He starts to get up.

'Sorry. Jack. I'm sorry. I shouldn't have said that. Sit down. Please. I didn't mean it. I don't know, I just get upset when people talk about my life as if they know best.'

'I'm not taking anyone's side, Jenny,' he says, sitting at the edge of the chair, ready to bolt.

'I know. I'm sorry. It's just that, well, sometimes, everything looks so easy from outside. And it's not, believe me, Jack, it's just not. OK?' I hear tiredness in my voice, the emotion.

'OK. Look, I'm sorry, Jenny. I just wanted to say it and I've said it, now. You're right, it is none of my business.'

'I know you were only trying to help. But you don't know the full story, Jack, that's all I'm saying.'

He looks at me. Expecting it.

'Thanks for the voucher, Jack. And thanks for calling.'

'OK.' He says, getting the message.

He pats my arm on the way out so I know we're still OK.

People nag me to look after myself. But I am. By default. Making sure Charlie eats well, means I do too. The same with fresh air, exercise, sleep. There is another reason to stay healthy. If I catch something I could pass it on to Charlie. With his immune system down, a simple sore throat could quickly whip up into something more sinister.

I decide to use Jack's voucher and take him up on his offer to mind Charlie. I'm thinking about my health; it's also a no-hard-feelings gesture.

I take up the yoga classes again. The first one is like a tonic. Physically, mentally. I lie on my back, focusing only on my breathing and the gentle stretches I am doing. Yawn after yawn, my eyes water. I relax deeper and deeper, the smell of incense calming me, easing the tension in my body. I feel guilty, though. Charlie could really do with this. He *is* the sick one.

After class, I tell the instructor about what he's been through. She suggests I bring him to see her privately. She has an available slot, next day.

We go to her home, a small three-bed semi, in a pretty estate in Dalkey. There is a very good feeling about the place. She shows us to a room where she does her treatments. Charlie is a little giddy, probably nerves, but she calms him down by asking him to sit on a peculiar chair made of two flat planks, one to sit on, the other for his knees. She asks me what treatments he has had, takes out a tuning fork, hits it off a block and then slowly runs it around Charlie's body, clearing his aura, which she says has been damaged by radiation from tests and X-rays. Charlie doesn't like the sound and she stops.

She lays him on a plinth and chats to him while holding her hand over different areas of his body, a few minutes at a time. She is re-energising his chakras, she explains. They play together with large squares of silk. Red and orange, the colours of energy and happiness. This is the bit Charlie likes best. He sits on her lap, mesmerised.

'Do you know what a guardian angel is?' she asks him.

'Yeah, an angel in the garden.'

I can't believe I haven't told him about his guardian angel. What kind of mother am I?

'You have a guardian angel, Charlie.'

'Have I?'

She nods. 'Do you want to know what she does?'

'Is she a girl?' he asks, disgusted.

'Guardian angels usually are. But if you'd prefer a boy you can ask for one.'

'Who?'

'God.'

'Can I ask him now?'

159

'You can. Do you want to know what they do first?'

'Yeah.'

'They mind you. They look after you.'

'Like Great.'

She looks at me. I explain in two words. His great-grandmother.

'Guardian angels give you whatever you want,' she says.

'No, they don't. Great doesn't.'

'Well, whatever's good for you. And they love you; I forgot the most important bit. They love you.'

'I'd like one, please.'

'Well, you have one now. And you can talk to him whenever you want. If you're sad or sore or need help, your guardian angel will be there for you. Isn't it nice to know you have someone there helping you out all the time?'

'Like my Mum.'

I smile at him. My angel.

There was a time I might have been cynical. And maybe I'm desperate, trying anything. But I do believe in it. At the end of this half-hour session, Charlie has a pale pink glow in his cheeks and an energy. And he's leaving with something new, his guardian angel. I'm taking all the help we can get.

I buy Charlie a wardrobe of red and orange clothes, including pyjamas and undies. I go a bit mad with towels, cushions and flowers. My mood is on the up. Maybe it's the colours. Maybe it's the fact that I'm doing something positive, taking action. In the pharmacy, we find a tiny guardian angel brooch. It's silver with a little droplet of glass. Not bad value: a guardian angel for five euro. We take it. I clip it to the corner of Charlie's pillow.

twenty-two

We have to go back for chemotherapy. The sight of the uniformed woman buffing the floor and the mingled smell of floor polish and disinfectant remind me, like a slap in the face, that we are back. The sick, nervous feeling at the pit of my stomach returns. My shoulders tense up. My heart pounds. My breathing falters. Charlie grabs my leg and I almost fall over. I bend down to him. His little worried face! I hug him, lift him, then carry him off, our cheeks together. He looks over my shoulder at the disappearing hospital entrance.

His hospital voice is back. It's weak and filled with fear. I remind him (and myself) that we're only here for the day. It helps that Anne and Siobhan are on duty. Charlie looks for Mark and is told he has gone home. I explain why that's a good thing and that we should be happy for him.

'We'll send him a text when we get home,' I say.

'Can't we do it now?'

I smile. 'We can do it now.'

There are no surprises with the treatment. Nothing we haven't seen before. After a while, Charlie nods off. I ask Siobhan to stay with him while I go see Elaine and Jessica.

It is a matter of days. The shock of that silences me. Stunned, I return to Charlie. Siobhan touches me on the shoulder and leaves. I sit looking at my little boy, praying like I've never prayed before.

Simon appears. He tells me he wants to talk. He's not smiling. To his office, then.

The latest news: I am not a match.

'Now, don't be disappointed.'

Don't be disappointed?

'It would have been unusual for the first person we tried to be a match. The chances were very slight.'

'But there.'

'We still have the register...'

I squeeze my lips between my teeth, pinch the inside of my hand, look up and to the right.

'I know it's a disappointment... '

I shrug, look out the window and sneak my finger up to plug the beginnings of a tear.

'Is there another family member we could try? Charlie's father?'

'We're going to have to, aren't we?' I snap. I close my eyes, then take a deep breath. 'Sorry. It's been a long day.'

He nods. 'There's no rush, Jenny. You don't have to decide now. Take your time.'

'I can't! We have to find a donor. Charlie won't get better without one...'

'Take a day or two to think through your options. A day or two won't make a difference.'

I look down at my clenched fists. And open them. I think of Dave, the man I haven't seen in five years, the man I sent away. He owes us nothing.

'Can I ask you something?'

I look up.

'Technically, this is none of my business but does Charlie's father know that he's sick?'

Assuming that Charlie's father is Dave, and not you. 'No.'

'It might be a place to start.'

I just look at him, not believing that we're having this conversation.

'He might surprise you. And, technically, he has a right to know...'

'You're right, Simon. This is none of your business.'

'Of course.'

My hands go to my temples. 'I'm sorry. I know I have to contact Charlie's father. I know. It's just that he has his own life. Everything has moved on. He won't want to go back. And I don't want to bring him there. I have to, I know...' I think for a second about the logistics of it. I take down my hands. 'Would a person living in another country have to come home to do the test?'

'No. They'd just need a simple blood test. We could link up with a hospital in that country.'

'So it could be done without him coming back to Dublin?' Just to confirm.

'Yes.'

I nod. 'OK.'

We're home by teatime. I try to get some soup into Charlie but he just wants to sleep and for me to lay down with him. Into bed we climb. Charlie wants to talk to his guardian angel and Great. I'd like a word too, only not as polite. We do it his way. And there is some comfort in it, I suppose.

'Tell me a story of when you were a kid,' he says, sleepily.

'OK. Let me think.' I smile, then. 'OK. I've got one.'

He props his head up on his elbow.

'Great took me on a boat once.' He's never fussy; he'll take any old story from my childhood, which is just as well, because there isn't much to tell. 'She was wearing a bright yellow jacket and it got covered in greenfly.'

'What's greenfly?'

'Little tiny flies that are green.'

'Oh. Do they sting?'

'No.'

'Why did they go after her?'

'She said it was her perfume. But I said it was because she looked like a daffodil.'

'Did she?' he asks, smiling, imagining.

'No. She looked like a buttercup.'

He looks at me sideways to see if I'm serious. Then laughs. He's quiet for a second, then frowns. 'I don't like the smell in the hospital.' He flops down on the pillow.

I rub his cheek. 'Neither do I.'

'It makes me sick in my tummy. My tummy was sick today. I'm not going back again. 'K?'

'We'll see. Now close your eyes,' I say gently.

He gives in to the pull of sleep, going so deep it's scary. I worry about how to get him to hospital again. I worry about how to ask Dave. I worry about not finding a match. Then I force myself to stop. I try to concentrate on remembering those positive affirmation things Pat keeps talking about – 'whatever happens I can cope'. *Hmm.* I try some 'positive visualisation', imagining Charlie's body recovering from today's onslaught. *His latest blood tests are good,* I remind myself, which eases the worry. For about eight seconds.

I get up. Drag on a warm jumper. Tidy up. Put on a wash. Iron things I don't usually iron. Pick up a heap of neglected post, and sit up at the counter with it. I decide to be methodical and get out the chequebook, envelopes, stamps. I take the letters as they appear. Bill, bill, a CD I've won in some competition I don't remember entering, an Air Mail envelope. I pick it up, look closer. Dave's handwriting. Dave's address in the corner. *It's not Christmas. It's not my birthday. Not that we mark those anymore.* I run my thumb under the thick fold of expensive paper. I pull out a card. It's an invitation. To a wedding. Dave and Fiona. So few words, say so much. They're just details: a church, the time of the wedding, the venue afterwards. But they say:

'I've found another woman. A woman who will marry me. A woman who loves me. A woman I love. So, bye, Jen. I'm getting on with my life. Oh and I don't expect you to actually come.'

The biggest shock is my reaction. I am winded. Floored.

I tell myself I don't care. *I didn't want him. I don't want him now. So what if he's gone? So what if I'm alone? So what if no one loves me? Who'd want me anyway, sitting here in a crappy jumper with shag-all make up and a fuzzy head of hair? Bet she's beautiful. Fiona. Funny. He went all the way to America to find a Fiona. There are loads of them here. Loads of Fionas.* We had our invitations made. Jenny and Dave cordially invite you... I lower my forehead onto the cool oak table and cry.

It is Charlie, calling out in his sleep, who finally focuses me. And though he doesn't wake, it is Charlie who gets me up, gets me moving, and ultimately gets me looking for stationery. Nothing else matters only getting him better. At least now I have an address.

Dear Dave

I'm sorry that it's taken five years to send you a proper letter. And I'm sorry that in this letter I have to ask for your help. But I do. Charlie was diagnosed with leukaemia, three weeks ago. And it's not just any old leukaemia, it's a special kind that requires a bone marrow transplant. If he doesn't get it, he will die.

I thought I could handle this by myself but I've had a blood test and I'm not a match. I need your help, Dave. You don't have to do much, just a simple blood test that you can do, there in the States, through your own doctor. No need to come home. Charlie's doctor can co-ordinate with yours. It's unlikely that you'll be a match. But you understand, I have to ask, I have to check. I know you've a new life now and I'm so glad you've found someone else. Congratulations! I'm sorry to butt in like this but Charlie is my life. I can't lose him.

If you say yes, and I so hope you do, I'll find out exactly what you need to do.

I'm so glad you're happy. You mightn't think it, but that's what I've always wanted.
Jenny

I don't say I'm sorry I let him go, though that's how I feel. I don't say I miss him, but I do. I don't say I've made the biggest mistake of my life but I have.

My head is full of decisions queuing up to be made. *Do I contact my parents to see if they are a match or do I wait to hear from Dave? Do I send Charlie back to school for a 'normal' life and risk infection or keep him home and risk smothering him? Do I tell Simon that he may be able to help, how and why?* In my mind, I switch from problem to problem without working out any solutions. At last, on the verge of driving myself crazy, I decide to tackle the easiest first. Parents.
Or is it the easiest?
The chances of them having the right tissue type are negligible, but there. I take a breath, try to detach from my feelings towards my mother, try to be logical and think. This takes two mugs of coffee. But the decision does come. And it's this: Because the chances of them being any help are tiny, I'm going to wait to hear from Dave. I'll give him a week. If I hear nothing, I'll rethink.
They tell me at the hospital that it would be 'healthy' for Charlie to go back to school. But they've also given me a booklet that warns against him catching chicken pox or measles, which could kill him because his immune system is down. He is going to miss nine months of school after the bone marrow transplant and will have to repeat the year anyway. He is only four. Many kids start at five. So, I'm not sending him. I want to build him up for the transplant, have him ready. Ensure nothing can go wrong. If I smother him, I smother him. I'll get on to the Department of Education and Skills to see if I qualify for Home Tuition. If I don't, I'll teach him myself, or ask Mary or Debbie. As for other faces, Dara can come over. And Jack. As long as their vaccinations are up to date.

As for Simon? That's the one decision that doesn't get made. *Two out of three is progress. 75% progress. Almost an A.* Or so I tell myself, before crawling in beside Charlie for the last few hours of darkness.

twenty-three

Charlie likes to swim but can't with a Freddie. So he's in the bath wearing his togs and swimming hat. And he's happy enough to pretend.

'Do seals eat penguins?' he asks.

'Fish, I think.'

'Fish eat penguins?'

'No.' I smile. 'Penguins eat fish, and seals eat fish.'

'And what do fish eat?'

'Fish. And other stuff.'

'Oh.'

'D'you know what Great used to sing to me when I was a kid and she was giving me a bath?'

'Row, row, row your boat?'

'How did you know?'

'That's what she used to sing to me.'

'Of course she did. Silly me.'

'Why did she sing that?'

'Because she was a bit mad.'

'Yeah. I know.' He smiles.

'I like people who are a bit mad,' I say.

'You're a bit mad.'

'Thanks. So are you.'

'Ow.'

'What?'

'You hurt me.'

'What did I do?' I'm only washing his face with the softest of cloths.

'You hurt me on the forehead.'

'Where? Show me.'

'Don't touch it.'

'I won't. Let me see.'

'Ooow. I said don't touch.'

'There's nothing there, Charlie.'

'But it's sore.'

'OK, let's get you out of the bath, dry you off and have another look.'

I can't find anything.

Should I call the hospital?

And tell them what: Charlie has a sore forehead but there's nothing there?

Two days later, I notice a small red patch with tiny blisters.

'Is your forehead sore, Charlie?'

'Nope,' he says, reaching for his iPad.

'Is it itchy?'

'No.'

'Were you scratching it or anything?'

'No.' As in, leave-me-alone.

'Weird.'

'What?'

'Nothing. It's probably nothing.'

I feel like an idiot ringing Simon for a few blisters. But they did say to ring if I was worried and I am, maybe, not *worried* but suspicious.

He doesn't dismiss it.

'And it's nowhere else on the body?'

'No.'

'When did it appear?'

'This morning.'

'Is it sore?'

'No.'

'Was there any soreness before the rash appeared?'

'No. Actually, wait, yes, it was sore the other day but not in the exact spot, it was closer to his ear.'

'Jenny, I think you should bring him in.'

'When?'

'Well, now, if it suits. It might be nothing but it's best to check.'

We're driving into dark, grey clouds. The sun in the rear view mirror is blinding. It's like we're leaving it behind. Stopped at lights, I stare blankly into the back of the space wagon in front. Two boys are fighting. Their heads have been closely shaved but strong stubble juts out of their healthy scalps. I can feel the energy coming from them. Wish there was such a thing as an energy transplant. I'd hook up jump leads to their car and steal some energy for Charlie. They've too much anyway.

We arrive at the hospital in a downpour. The red neon 'full' sign in the car park glows. Where can I park? I drive down a nearby street, which is jammed with parked cars. I can't walk this far in the rain. I'd have to carry Charlie and he's getting so heavy from retained fluid. To hell with it. I drive up to A&E, park on double yellow lines and run in, carrying him.

Simon shines his surgery lamp onto Charlie's forehead and moves in for a closer look.

'It's getting worse Simon, even since this morning.'

'It's all on one side,' he says like he's thinking aloud.

'Yes.'

'And he's had chicken pox.' He lightly fingers a pockmark just over the place Charlie's eyebrow used to be.

'Yes.'

'It's not sore,' says Charlie, who has developed an expertise of knowing what doctors are going to ask before they do.

Simon smiles at him. Then looks at me seriously.

'It looks like shingles, Jenny.'

'But children don't get shingles.'

'It's not very common, but they can, especially if their immune systems are down.'

'Shingles is very painful, though.' I wrote an article on it.

'Shingles in children usually isn't.'

'Oh.' Then I think of something. 'But he hasn't been in contact with anyone with chicken pox.'

'Not that you noticed. It's highly infectious. He could have picked it up anywhere.'

'But I didn't send him back to school.'

'I know. Sometimes no matter how careful we are, we can't prevent these things. It's shingles. It's in the very early stages. We'll have to admit him, Jenny. He'll need intravenous anti-viral drugs.'

'Oh, no,' says Charlie, mirroring my thoughts.

'I'm sorry, Charlie. But it's the best thing for you. This time you'll have your very own room.' Simon takes me aside and explains that Charlie will need to be kept in isolation to stop the shingles spreading to other children.

'Maybe we could treat him at home? I could give the drugs into his Freddie. I already flush it twice a week with heparin and saline.'

'Jenny, Charlie is immuno-compromised. Any infection like shingles in the immuno-compromised is very serious. We need to admit him and start treatment straight away. And, in fairness, I need to tell you that there is a risk of damage to his eye. Now,' he says, in a try-to-be-calm-now-that-I've-frightened-the-shit-out-of-you voice, 'we've caught it early, and if we start treatment immediately, there's a good chance that disease progression can be halted before it gets to his eye.'

'What's wrong with my eyes, Mama?' Charlie asks.

'Nothing, Charlie. We just have to give you some medicine to stop the rash, that all.'

'I don't want to stay here. I want to go home.'

'It's just for a little while. And I'll be with you. And Simon and Anne and Siobhan. And Mary will call in.'

'Will Debbie mind Sausage?'

Here we go, again.

An unfamiliar nurse brings us to the ward. She hands us over to another nurse we don't know.

'Where's Anne?' Charlie asks.

'Day off,' she says, barely looking at him.

Charlie calls out a few more names.

This time she ignores him.

'What about Siobhan?' I ask.

She looks at me blankly.

'Are you new?' I ask.

'No. Just here on loan from another ward. There's a shortage of oncology nurses today.'

'Great,' Charlie says.

I look at him in shock. Sarcasm at four?

She shows us to a single room and tells us that Charlie is only allowed leave to go to the toilet. I ask her which would he pass on – chicken pox or shingles. She doesn't know.

I look around the room. A bed, locker, window with a brick view, and a TV, mounted high on the wall. No cartoon pictures, just 'no smoking' and 'no mobile phone' signs. The old-fashioned radiator is the kind you see in convents. At least we have a sink. There's a bin beside it with a sticker on the top: CLINICAL WASTE that I've a sudden urge to vandalise.

The nurse leaves, closing the door behind her. I read through a paper sign that has been stuck up on the other side of the glass panel, ISOLATION (backwards).

I settle Charlie. Switch on the TV. We watch it together. I keep waiting for someone to come with his anti-viral drugs, but no one appears. After almost an hour, I'm panicking. If it's so dangerous where are the bloody drugs? I switch on my mobile and call Simon's.

Minutes later he strides past our room. Another few minutes and the Nurse From Somewhere Else wheels in an electronic drip. She tells me it's the medicine Charlie needs and it will take about thirty minutes to go in.

I relax a little.

Not so Charlie.

'Where are your sterile gloves?' he asks her. 'You should have sterile gloves for this.'

She looks at him, her colour rising. *Is it anger, humiliation or both?*

'Have you done this before?' he asks.

'Yeah, I have, actually.'

He is watching, examining, her every movement. He's right. The last thing we need is for his Freddie to get infected. I've seen it happen with other kids and it's serious.

I watch the drops fall rapidly inside their little capsule, imagining the drug whizzing through his veins, zapping the virus. At last.

She leaves.

'She didn't wash her hands,' he snorts.

Ten minutes later, Simon appears.

'How's everything?' he asks.

'That nurse didn't do it right. She didn't have the sterile gloves. Mum has to wear sterile gloves at home when she does my Freddie. She's very careful about it. That nurse isn't careful. That nurse should be careful.'

'You're right Charlie. I'll have a chat with her. She's not used to this ward.'

'She's not as good as Anne.'

'Anne will be back tomorrow.'

'Good,' says Charlie.

Good, I think.

'And she didn't wash her hands.'

'Oh, dear,' says Simon. He smiles at me and is gone again.

We've probably made an enemy. But at least now, hopefully, she'll do it right, not just for Charlie but for everyone else. It's lives we're talking about here.

I smile at my son. 'You're a great little fellow, d'you know that?'

Ah, God. His smile.

We go back to watching the TV but my mind starts to fill with questions I should have asked Simon: Can Charlie continue his chemotherapy while on the Acyclovir? Will it delay the transplant? And what has happened to my head?

When Anne calls to the room, first thing next morning, I know immediately something is wrong. She brings me outside and across the corridor to the little room for parents, though Charlie is still asleep. And then she tells me. Last night, while we slept, Elaine was losing her daughter. Jessica died.

I sink into a chair. I don't mean my thoughts to come out but somehow they do. 'Poor Elaine. Her baby is gone. Yesterday, she was there. She was dying but she was there. Elaine could talk to her. Jessica could feel her touch. Now she's gone. Gone.' I look at Anne, horrified.

She smiles. 'Elaine doesn't feel like that. It's a relief, Jenny.'

'A relief?'

'She's at peace now. No more pain, no more suffering. That's the way Elaine sees it.'

'Should I go to her? I don't know, what should I do?'

'Elaine and Jim sat with Jessica all night. They held her for a long time after she'd gone.'

I start to cry, imagining the horror of it.

'They're going to take her home now. For one last day together.'

I stare at her.

'It helps.'

'I'd like Elaine to know I'm thinking about her.'

'She knows.'

'So there's nothing I can do?'

'There will be, but not yet.'

What will I tell Charlie? is my next thought but I can't ask; how selfish would that be?

It's like she reads my mind. 'About Charlie.'

'Yes.'

'Are you OK about telling him?'

'I don't know, Anne. Do you think I should tell him?'

'It's better that you do, Jenny. He'll ask about Jessica when you stop mentioning her and going to see her. Or he'll overhear you talking about her to someone else. He'll find out somehow. And he needs to trust you Jenny. So, yes, I would tell him.'

'How?'

'I'd keep it very simple. I'd just say that Jessica got very, very ill...'

'He knew that she was very sick.'

'And that will help prepare him. I'd just say something like, "you know the way Jessica was very, very sick, well, she didn't get better, Charlie." Then I'd tell him that she died last night and is in heaven now.'

'He never got to know her, really. I was afraid, Anne. I used to go to see Jessica and Elaine on my own. To protect him.'

She smiles sympathetically. 'I know. And that will make it easier for him. But he's still likely to be upset and worried. I wouldn't talk about it too much with him but I'd encourage him to express how he feels. Maybe later, just ask him how he is. And take it from there. Pat might come round to have a chat.'

It's like the cancer has won a major battle in a war that is fought in here every day. A brave soldier has fallen. For once, I'm glad Charlie is in isolation because I don't want to face any of the other parents. I don't want to see fear in their eyes. I just want to stay in there, tucked away staring at a TV screen and pretending to notice what the Pink Panther is doing.

twenty-four

Jessica's funeral. I race along the corridor, late. Charlie wanted to come at the last minute and had to be talked out of the idea. Poor little fellow. He wanted to say goodbye. I rush on, trying to remember where I parked. The double yellow lines! *Damn, damn, damn.* I stride outside and find the car, a white square on the window, a yellow triangle on the wheel. *Shit.* I check my watch. Twenty minutes to make it to the church. I look around in panic. *Where are the taxis when you need them? Nowhere.* I'm taking out my mobile to phone for one when I see Simon and Anne coming through the exit, coats on. I hurry over, ask if they're going to the funeral and tell them about the car. All in one breath.

'You're welcome to come with us,' Simon says. 'As long as you mind fast driving. We've cut it a bit fine.'

Simon and Anne chat to each other, up front, while I look out the window in the back. The day is grey and bleak, standard issue for Irish funerals, like it's been prearranged.

The church is heaving with people. I follow Anne up the centre aisle. We're walking towards a little white coffin and I can't breathe. Head down, I follow her sturdy ankles. Finally she stops. We excuse ourselves as we squeeze in front of three pairs of knees and find a tight spot in the pew. I'm sure we've lost Simon, but no, he crams in beside me.

All is quiet apart from throat clearing and coughing. Someone is tuning a guitar. I check my bag for handkerchiefs. They're there, a thick bundle of real, fabric handkerchiefs, strong enough to withstand a tidal wave. Because, I know what's going to happen. The coffin has already shot the first arrow at my heart. The coffin that holds little Jessica, who only a year ago, sat at her kitchen table with her twin sister, making their father a surprise birthday card while Elaine brought me into another room to talk about living with cancer. I have to stop myself thinking about the child lying up there so still, surrounded by dark, and wood, and air because if I don't, I just won't get through this.

It starts. And for a while I hold it together but then my ability to block things out starts to fail me. Suddenly I notice it, the utter, devastating tragedy: the paintings of horses on the altar, done by Jessica, her black velvet riding hat and recently polished boots, the heart-shaped display of rosettes, little conquests that don't matter anymore, the songs she picked for the ceremony, especially, *No Tears In Heaven*. And then there's the message Elaine reads from her daughter to the congregation, saying goodbye and thanking the nurses and doctors each by name, the people who donated blood, but most of all her mum, family and friends. She has a special goodbye for her twin, Laura. Her parting words to us all are, 'Treasure each day. And give blood.'

Then the most disconcerting thing happens. Laura comes to the microphone. She is identical, or at least was, until cancer and chemo got involved. *How surreal; how unfair on Elaine.*

'Jessica was my sister and my best friend. I don't know why she got sick but I wanted to get sick too. I tried so hard but I couldn't. I thought she'd get better. But she didn't. Even though I prayed and promised to be good. Mum says it was meant to be and that she's in heaven now and she's happy and not a bit lonely. But I'm lonely. I miss her so much. I don't want to go to school without her...' Her voice breaks and she stops, her head drops and she shakes. A delicate little fist goes up to her eye. Elaine steps back beside her daughter, puts her arm round her and leads her back to their seats. I hold my breath so I make no noise, but sobs shake my body. Hands are going up to faces all round. Noses are being blown. Only the statues remain unmoved. Everyone united in grief. I fumble in my satchel for another handkerchief. They are used and wet. Soaked. But I've nothing else. I'm about to use a wet one when a clean, folded, white one appears in front of me. I take it from Simon without looking at him. Ann puts an arm round me.

When the time comes, Simon and Anne go to the top of the church to pay their respects. I can't. I try to collect myself but as soon as Jessica's father puts his arms around his daughter's coffin and carries her out of the church as though there is no barrier between them, as though the coffin is not there, I feel actual pain in my heart. It is the last time he will ever carry his little girl.

Leaving, I see Elaine standing in the churchyard surrounded by people yet temporarily alone. People are hugging her children, her husband, but for a brief moment there is no one with her. She's standing, staring straight ahead, in shock. I forget everything and go to her. We just look at each other, say nothing and hug. Finally, she pulls back. She looks like she's going to say something, but nothing comes. I try to smile but my lip wobbles and I'm off again.

'Sorry. I'm hopeless. I wanted to say something, do something...'

'You came.'

I feel someone beside us now, someone who wants to say how sorry they are. I smile one last smile, squeeze her arm and turn. I hurry away, head down, embarrassed by my inability to provide some comfort, however small. I feel a hand on my shoulder and look up.

'Oh. Simon,' is all I manage.

'Are you alright?' he asks, softly.

'Yeah.'

'Ready to go?'

'Mm hmm.' I sniffle.

We walk towards the car park.

'Anne,' I say, turning round. 'We forgot Anne.'

'No, she's off duty. Gone shopping, then home.'

'I sometimes forget that you have lives outside the hospital.'

He smiles. 'Sometimes we forget ourselves.'

Silence.

'That was tough,' he says.

I sigh. 'Yeah.'

'You OK?'

I nod.

'Ready to go back to the hospital?'

'No.' I laugh.

'Would you like a coffee first?'

'Don't you have to get back?'

'I could do with something myself. We're not immune, you know, doctors.' We're almost at his car. 'It's not easy,' he says, 'when we lose.'

I want to hug him. 'You did your best, Simon.'

He doesn't answer.

We get to the car. He bleeps it open.

How silently such heavy doors close.

'So, coffee?' he asks.

'That'd be nice.'

'Where?'

I shrug. 'Somewhere quiet.'

'I have to call home. I can make us one? Or would you prefer to go somewhere?'

'No, actually, that'd be better. I'm a mess.'

'You're fine.'

'If you like red, puffy eyes and swollen faces, then I'm fine.' I smile.

He leaves me in the sitting room while he makes the coffee. A mistake. By the time he gets back, I'm at it again. I hear him come in and look up. He puts down the two yellow mugs with smiley faces.

'I'm sorry,' I say, wiping my nose with the palm of my hand.

'For goodness sake,' he says gently, 'don't worry about it.' He sits on the arm of the couch, then is up again. 'Hold on a minute.' He's back with a sheet of kitchen paper.

I take it from him and blow. 'I'm sorry,' is all I seem to be able to say. That, and, 'I don't know...'

He sits beside me now, and puts an arm around me. 'Shhh. It's OK,' he says and takes my wet sticky hands in his. 'Shhhh.'

I start to hiccup. Feel such a fool.

He draws me into a hug. And, God, I needed that. He smoothens back my hair. 'Shh,' he says. I sob involuntarily. He pulls back, lifts my chin with a finger, looks into my eyes. 'It's OK, it will be OK.'

I lean forward, my mouth seeking his. Our lips touch. It's like flicking a switch. And we're back, kissing passionately, frantically, my face in his hands, his in mine, so much hunger for each other. I tug at his shirt, too impatient for buttons, tiny, annoying, stupid bloody buttons. He yanks at mine causing one to pop out and hit me in the eye. It makes me laugh and stops us.

'I'm sorry,' he says, mortified. He runs a thumb over my lid, kisses it, then the side of my nose, then full on my mouth. He takes my upper lip between his, then my lower. Then lips, mouths separate us no longer, the boundary melts. We lie back together. He cups the back of my head in his hand and I'm shocked and thrilled by the feeling of his tongue running, flat, from the base of my neck to my chin, like a predator staking a claim. Our eyes hold each other now and it's like this was meant to be. He kisses my mouth, neck, then buries his face in the swell of my breasts. He groans. His hand slides up my leg and caresses me through my, thankfully, silk underwear, the only reason I'm wearing is they're black and I wanted everything to be black today. But I need to forget that now. And he makes me. *Oh God.* I arch my back, aching for him. Our eyes are locked when he enters me, locked when we move together like we were destined to, locked when I explode in waves and bite his fingers. And they are locked when he calls my name and tightens his grip on my hair. He shudders and I hold him tight. He lies very still now and I don't want to let go. Just stay like this forever. Not move. Not get up. Not carry on. He lifts his head now and we face each other, eyes only far enough apart to keep each other in focus. Pupils dilated. Staring. Bonded. When he takes his away, the spell will be broken. We will remember who we are and the reasons we can't be together. I have a sick child. He is that child's doctor. I am his guilty past. And it will be over. So I hold his stare, until he looks away and takes himself away, the warmth of his body replaced by unheated November air. I pull my skirt back down over my knees, reach for my shirt.

'I'm sorry,' he says, sitting on the edge of the couch, head in his hands.

I want to run my hand along his back, kneel behind him and cling to him. But I don't.

'I shouldn't have let that happen,' he says.

I look away. Don't want to hear. Almost block my ears.

'Charlie is my patient. You're his mother. This isn't right.'

'It is,' I say quietly but defiantly.

'No, Jennifer, it isn't.'

I shake my head.

'How would an outsider see it?' he asks.

I don't answer.

'They'd say I took advantage of a young mother trying to cope alone with the recent diagnosis of her son.'

'They'd be wrong.'

'It won't happen again.'

I say nothing. Give up. What's the point?

'I'm sorry,' he says again.

Me too.

'If things were different...'

'But they aren't. So let's forget it, OK?' I say, coldly. 'I need to go to Charlie now.' I get up, start to button my shirt, crucial button missing. I try to flatten out the creases in my skirt. Pointless.

'I'm sorry,' he says.

'Could you just drop me home, Simon?' I close my coat and try to hold myself together. 'I'll get a taxi to the hospital. Thanks.' I clutch my satchel to my chest, the way I used to carry my school bag on the short walk home. I'm ready. But I'm shaking, my whole body reacting, screaming, 'this happened...you didn't dream it...it happened, Jenny.'

'You don't need to take a taxi. I'll wait while you get whatever you need.'

'It's OK.' *I'm alone. And I'm good alone. How could have I forgotten that?* 'Let's just go, OK?'

'Of course. I'm sorry.'

'Yeah. I know.'

I shower and change, chin high. I turf out the soggy handkerchiefs. I pack clothes for the hospital. I get a new tube of toothpaste from the bathroom cabinet, catch my reflection in the mirror.

Weakling!

I get scissors. Cut off great chunks of hair.

And no, I don't need a drink.

Charlie and Mary are sitting on my bed, looking at the iPad together. They look up, stop what they're doing and stare.

'What?' I ask, crossly, impatiently.

'Your hair,' says Charlie.

'Are you alright?' asks Mary, standing slowly, coming towards me. She looks worried.

'I'm fine.' I turn my back on her, using the excuse to put my coat away.

'Jenny? Did something happen?' she asks quietly.

'No.'

'It's just that, I don't know, it's not just your hair...'

'I was upset. I went home. I cut my hair – so what? It's just hair.' Coat sorted, I turn to face them again.

Mary looks at me a questioningly, but saying nothing. She sits back down.

'Did they grave Jessica?' asks Charlie, kneeling up on the bed.

'Yes, sweetheart,' I run my hand along the side of his cheek, 'they buried Jessica.' I sigh, take off my shoes, sit up on the bed beside him. 'Can I rest on your pillows for a sec, Charlie?'

'OK.'

I lie back on the wall of pillows and close my eyes.

We're quiet for a second. I feel him on the bed, moving up towards me. His hand rests on my leg. 'Do souls have mouths, Mum?'

I hope Mary will answer.

She doesn't.

I open my eyes, look at him, then at Mary. She's rummaging in her bag.

'Do souls have mouths?' he repeats.

'I don't know, Charlie. I don't think so.' I close my eyes again.

'Why don't they?'

'I don't think they eat in heaven,' I continue, eyes closed.

'What's heaven like?'

I force my weary eyes open. 'I don't know. Nice.'

Go on, says his face.

Oh, what the hell. 'I think it might be like a big garden where everyone's happy and the sun is shining.' The Irish approach to heaven – the weather's got to be good.

'Are the angels and the souls having a picnic?'

'That's a nice idea, Charlie. Yes, I think, they probably are.'

'Well, they'll need mouths then.'

Mary smiles over at me.

'Do they have McDonald's in heaven?'

'No.'

'Why not?'

'Because it's run by humans not souls.'

'I bet souls could make chicken nuggets and chips just as good as human beans.'

'Maybe you're right.'

'Where is it, Mum?'

'What?'

'Heaven,' he says impatiently. 'Is it on the top of the world?'

'It's in the sky somewhere, I think.'

'Is it in space?'

'Probably.'

'Is it beyond space?'

'You're right. That's where it is. Beyond space. Probably.'

'I think I might go someday.'

And that's what wakes me up. 'Not yet, Charlie. Not yet, love. Come here, sit on my lap, I need a cuddle.'

'OK, Mum.' He sits up on me. 'But can I go tomorrow?'

'Wait a few years Charlie, OK?'

'OK, Mum.'

Later, Pat, the psychologist 'happens' by.

'How are things?' she asks too innocently. Mary has said something, I know she has.

'Fine,' I say, not in the mood to be analysed. Charlie is asleep. It's time for peace now, quiet. No more questions.

'It was a tough day,' she continues.

'Yes.'

'Terrible thing to bury a child.'

'Yes.'

'How are you feeling?'

'Fine.'

'I see you've cut your hair.'

'It's just hair – you don't have to analyse it.'

I expect her to react but she doesn't.

'Is there anything you'd like to talk about?'

Well, yes, actually, now that you ask, I fucked Dr Grace today, how's that? 'No.'

'Well, you know where I am if you need me,' she smiles. 'Try and get some sleep.'

I feel like laughing.

I find myself in the chapel, looking for the answer to one question. Why? That's all. Why? Why do children get sick? Why do they die? Why bring them into the world in the first place if You're going to kill them off before they experience anything? What's the point? To make us stronger? I can be strong. You don't have to take my child. I can be good, be a better person. Don't take my boy. But there's nothing here, only echoes. And a register of deaths. A great tome, recording all the children who have died in this hospital. What is that supposed to do? Remind us they are mortal? Or remind us that they lived?

twenty-five

I can't forget. It's not that simple. I watch him wash his hands and remember how they felt on my skin. I look at the back of his neck where his hair twists into a V and want to run my finger over it. I look at his gentle face and want to take it in my hands and kiss his mouth. Start it off again, the spark. Sometimes I see it in his eyes too. Or think I do. We might be discussing Charlie's blood count or shingles or how much he's been peeing during the day – business – when I catch him looking at me with such softness that it throws me and I can't remember what I was thinking or what he was saying. But then I look again, and it's gone, leaving me wonder if I dreamt it to distract myself from the reality of blood counts, angry rashes and 'blasts' that might come back if we don't find a donor. We are doctor and parent again, make no mistake. Professional, civil, even friendly, at times. It's just the eyes, every so often, the eyes. And if I'm dreaming, then I'm dreaming and I'll keep on dreaming until I get out of here, get home, away from him and his eyes, get on with my life. Forget.

The slow, steady creep of shingles seems to stop. Or is it just fooling us, ready to strike blindness as soon as we dare to relax? Maybe I should hope for that though, because, what God would blind your son and then take him? But days pass and the rash starts to recede. And I thank that God and tell Him I'm sorry for doubting Him.

But another worry lunges in to take its place. I haven't heard from Dave. It's been ten days. It can't take more than five for a letter to reach the US. I had the right address. I remembered to include our phone number. Which means: he doesn't want to do it. Why should he? I told him to go and he did. And still, I ask Mary to pick up my post and answering machine messages.

I don't know what to do. Wait another day? Or approach my mother, ignore how I feel, just get down and dirty, seek her blood like a politician seeking a vote? Or should I approach Simon, tell him the truth, admit what I've been hiding from him all this time? After what we've just been through, that seems impossible. Only one thing's certain – I need to do something.

I'm walking Charlie back from the bathroom, pushing along his drip for him, looking down to make sure I don't knock its sprawling legs into his feet or move them in front of his slippers causing him to trip. Something, I don't know what, makes me look up. Two people, one uniformed, are standing at the door to Charlie's room, talking but watching us. One of them, I see now, is Anne. The other looks like...Dave. But it couldn't be. Dave's in New York. I keep my eyes on him till I get close enough to see that...it is Dave. It really is. An Americanised, denim-ised, loafer-ised, grey T-shirted version of Dave. His hair is longer, his body fitter. He smiles. And suddenly it's the Dave I know, the face I know.

'Here they are,' announces Anne.

I've stopped. What is it about men? I cope perfectly well without them but as soon as they turn up, I'm jelly.

'What is it, Mum?' asks Charlie, looking up at me.

I shake my head. 'Nothing sweetheart.' It comes out as a whisper.

'Who is it?'

'A friend. It's just a friend.'

They walk to us, Dave leading the way. Still smiling.

Anne says something cheery to Charlie, lifts him up and carries him to the room, pushing the drip with her other hand. Chat, chat, chat, she goes. He looks back. Suspicious.

I'm stuck.

He comes to me.

'I can't believe you came,' I say, whipping away escapee tears.

'Of course I came.'

'I hadn't heard from you. I was about to give up.'

'Oh ye of little faith.' One of his sayings, which makes me laugh and cry at the same time.

He puts his arms round me and I feel tiny. He smells familiar, comforting. 'We should have stayed in touch. Properly.'

'I know.'

He pulls back. 'It's good to see you, Jenny.'

'You too.' I smile, half-afraid to look at him.

'You've changed so much. Your hair. It's beautiful.'

I touch it, embarrassed by the recent hacking episode, still obvious, despite Mary's best efforts with a scissors. 'It needs a cut.'

'But it's so long.'

'It was a lot longer.'

'And the colour. I never liked those highlight things. You look really great.'

'Hardly,' I say, thinking of how exhausted I do look, how drained, how thin.

We stand awkwardly. I fold my arms. He stuffs his hands in his pockets.

He looks towards the room. 'How is he?'

'He's OK, Dave.' We start to walk, very slowly, back, heads

down. The movement gives us purpose. 'He's in remission but we had to come back in because he has shingles.'

'The rash on his face?'

'Yeah.'

'Poor kid.'

We start to walk again.

'It's not sore. And it seems to be clearing. We got it early.'

He stops again. Making me stop. 'You should have told me, Jenny.' It's a statement of fact. And, now that it's out, I know he's right.

'I know. I'm sorry.'

'Why didn't you?'

I shrug. 'Didn't want to bother you.'

'Bother me? He could be my son, Jenny,' he whispers, 'He has a terminal illness. This is something I should know.'

'I know. I know. I'm sorry. I wasn't thinking.'

'*I* wasn't thinking. Going off to the States, leaving you here, alone, pregnant with a baby that could be mine.'

'I told you to go.'

'I shouldn't have listened. It's taken this to make me realise it. I shouldn't have left you.' His thumb is at this temple and two of his fingers are rubbing back and forth over his forehead, like he always does when he's upset.

'You didn't just go off and leave, Dave. It was the right thing.'

'I had responsibilities. That little boy in there could be my son.' He sweeps out his arm dramatically. 'In there, dying, without a father.'

'Dave, Charlie is not dying.'

'If he doesn't get a transplant he will.'

'He'll get the transplant. He has to. We can't think of any other option.' I'm not going to cry. I'm *not* going to cry.

'I'm sorry.' He takes my hands in his. 'Of course he'll get the transplant. I didn't mean to upset you. I was just disappointed you hadn't told me. That's all. OK? Let's forget it now, let's just get him better. OK?'

I nod.

He hugs me and we stand together quietly for a moment. I close my eyes and rest my head against the side of his neck. Then I feel the pull to get back to Charlie and to let Anne back to work. I lift my head, open my eyes. And look right into Simon's. He's standing outside the nurse's station, holding a chart, not looking at it, but at us. Instantly, he drops his gaze as though mine has burnt him. He slots the chart into a filing trolley and disappears into the nurse's station.

'We better go in to Charlie,' I say to Dave.

'Who are you?' Charlie demands of Dave. What would normally be an impressive frown just manages to wrinkle the bottom of his now enormous forehead.

'Charlie,' I say, 'be nice.'

'I'll leave you too it,' Anne says, getting up. 'See you later, Charlie.' She taps him on the shoulder.

'See ya, Anne. You might win me the next time. If you're lucky.'

She laughs. And is gone.

Charlie squints at Dave. 'Did you make my Mama cry?'

'No, Charlie,' I rush, 'Dave didn't make me cry.'

He looks at me. They both do.

'I just got a shock. I wasn't expecting to see Dave. Some people cry when they get a shock. But see, I'm not crying now.' I produce a grin. 'I'm glad Dave's here, very glad. He's my friend. And he's very nice.'

Charlie gives him a not-so-sure look.

'He's come all the way from America to see you. Remember the big yellow country on the globe?'

'The United States of America where Disneyland is?'

'Yes,' says Dave, smiling.

'Cool. Are you a yank?'

Dave laughs. 'Nah, but I know lots of them.'

'D'you know the Hulk?'

Real, genuine laughter now. 'No, but I'll keep an eye out for him for you, when I get back, OK?'

'Cool. Want to see my iPad? I've lots of games. I'm really good at them. Especially when I'm playing with Anne. She's useless.'

Dave looks at me as if to say, 'what a character', then sits on the bed beside Charlie. They get into the game.

'Ah, get me out of here. Yikes. Oh my God. Got him. Phew. It's OK, I've got another life.' When Dave glances at me proudly, five minutes later, he looks like a Dad. This is the way it could have been. I turn, go to the sink and splash my face with cold water. 'The boys,' I might have called them or 'my boys'.

Dave stays for the rest of the day and I get a sense of how it must feel to have someone to share this with, not just the laughter, but the worry, the responsibility. They walk to the bathroom together, Little Man and Big Man, allowing me a tiny break from the routine. Big Man reads to Little Man, plays Ludo with him, listens intently to him, allowing my head time to clear. Amazingly, Big Man becomes the only person Little Man will take medicine from outside of me. To be able to avoid that battle, just for once, is such an incredible relief. I feel my mood lift. Everything seems easier all of a sudden. Manageable. But, I remind myself, it's just for a day or two. *Don't get cosy, don't get used to it.*

Dave's an instant hit with Mary, who calls as usual but doesn't stay long, afraid of interrupting the happy family unit I can see she is imagining (judging by her furtive eyebrow raising). I walk her to the hospital entrance, prepared to set her straight.

As soon as we're safely off the ward she turns to me, her hand grabbing my arm.

'He's goooorgeous, Jen. How did you ever let him get away?'

'Mary.'

'But he is. And he just dropped everything and hopped on the first plane?'

'He came because of Charlie.'

'Who seems to really like him,' she says, in a problem-solved manner.

'Now all we've got to do is walk into the sunset.'

'Don't see why not.'

'Mary. What's wrong with you? First Simon, now Dave. Why are you in such a hurry to pair me off?'

'I'm just saying he's cute. Nothing wrong with that.'

'He's engaged.'

'Maybe you better remind him. I saw the way he looked at you.'

'Mary, please don't,' I say, seriously. 'Dave and I have been through so much. It's over. He's with someone else. Please, don't talk about happy endings. Not for us.'

'Sorry.'

'There is only one happy ending and that's a bone marrow transplant. Nothing else matters.'

Finally, Little Man sleeps. I make coffee, then sit with Dave in the relative's room across from Charlie's. We keep the doors open, so we can hear if he wakes. There's so much to talk about, so much to ask. I start with the practicalities.

'How did you find us?' I ask, then answer it myself. 'Jack.'

He smiles.

'Where you staying?'

'Somewhere near the hospital, probably.'

'Probably? You mean you haven't organised it?'

'It's not a priority.'

'Stay at the apartment.'

'Nah.'

'Why not?'

'I don't know, you mightn't want me there.'

'Of course I do. I wouldn't want you anywhere else. You've come all this way for us. Stay.'

'Really? You sure you don't mind?'

'Dave, of course I don't mind.'

'Alright then, if you're sure.'

'How long are you over for?'

'As long as it takes.'

'It only takes a few minutes. You could have done it in the States.'

'I'm not talking about the blood test. I came over to be with you for this and I'm staying as long as you need me to. Until everything's sorted.'

'What do you mean? Until we find a donor?'

'If that's what it takes, yes.'

'But that could take ages. What about Fiona?'

'She understands.'

Does she? What has he told her?

'What about your job?'

'I'm owed some leave.'

'How much leave? It's the States.'

He just smiles.

'Dave, you don't have to stay. I mean, it's great to see you, really great, but if you do the test tomorrow, you can go. You can always come back if you turn out to be a match. Everything's working out for you in the States. You have a life. You're getting married.' I smile. 'Still can't believe it.'

'Let me do the test, wait for the result and take it from there, OK?'

'It'll take at least two weeks.'

'Fine. Two weeks. That's fine. I'd factored in two weeks.'

'You sure?'

'Sure.'

'Thanks so much, Dave.'

'You're welcome.'

'So tell me about Fiona.'

'Fiona?'

'Fiona.'

'She's nice.'

I laugh. 'Nice? The woman you're going to marry is nice.'

'Yes.' He smiles.

'Is she American?'

'Yep.'

'Must be Irish-American with a name like Fiona?'

'She is.'

'Aa-nd?'

'And what, she's a nice Irish-American girl, called Fiona, and I'm going to marry her. OK?'

'OK.' No point asking how they met, what age she is, what she looks like, then. 'How's the job?'

'Grand. So what happens next with Charlie?'

'Well, once he gets over the shingles, I presume it's back home. And we keep looking for a donor.'

'Who else have you tried?'

'No one.'

'What about him?'

'No.'

'Does he know?'

'No.'

'Jenny.'

'I'll tell him...if I have to.'

'You mean if I'm not a match?'

It sounds so calculated – if Dave doesn't work out, I'll try the next guy. But it's not like that. I'm just trying to keep everything the way it is, simple, uncomplicated, under control. Is that so bad?

The door opens. Simon pops his head in. 'Just saying goodnight. Oh, sorry, I didn't realise you still had company.'

'No, no, it's fine.'

Suddenly we're all standing.

'Eh, Dave, this is Charlie's doctor...'

'Simon Grace,' Simon says, confidently, offering his hand.

'Sorry?' Dave's head juts forward.

'Simon Grace?' says Simon, taking back his untouched hand.

Dave shoots me a look. 'Is this some sort of joke?'

'Dave, it's OK,' I say. 'We need to talk.'

He turns to Simon. '*The* Simon Grace?' So much anger.

Simon checks the corridor, steps into the room, closes the door. He squints, shakes his head and says, quietly, 'I'm sorry, do I know you?'

I can't believe this is happening.

'No, you don't know me. Why would you know me? I'm only the person whose life you wrecked.'

Simon looks at me as if to say what is going on? Who is this person?

'Dave, please,' I say. 'Leave it.'

'No. I won't leave it. Why should I leave it? I left it before and lost everything. I'm a fucking walkover, that's what's wrong with me. I'll tell you who I am, Simon Grace,' he almost spits. 'I'm Dave O'Neill, Jenny's ex-fiancé. Our engagement ended five years ago. Not long after an incident in Brussels.'

'Dave, please,' I say. *Oh God.*

'Someone should get things out in the open, Jenny.'

'I understand,' Simon says.

'Well, that's big of you,' says Dave.

'Look, I'm very sorry about what happened. I had no idea. But I don't think this is the time or place.'

Dave is quiet.

'I'm sorry to have disturbed you,' says Simon. 'I'll see you in the morning, Jenny.'

'Goodnight, Simon,' I say quietly.

And then he's gone.

I glare at Dave.

'Why didn't you tell me?' he demands before I can say anything.

'Dave, keep your voice down. I was about to tell you when he walked in.'

'I'd have been prepared, handled it better.'

'Is that an apology?'

'I don't know. But what d'you expect? That guy pissed on my life.'

'He didn't know that, though, did he?'

'The end result is the same.'

'Dave, he knew nothing about me. I don't think he even saw me properly.'

'He didn't give a shit, though, did he?'

'You know the story.' I sigh. 'At least you didn't tell him about Charlie.'

'He doesn't know?'

'That's what I was telling you.'

'I thought you were saying he didn't know that Charlie had leukaemia.'

'Well, he obviously knows that, he's his doctor.'

'Yeah, but I didn't know that.'

'Simon knows Charlie has leukaemia. But that's all he knows.'

'When I left, why didn't you tell him?'

'Dave, I didn't even know him. Why would I want him involved? I can't believe you thought I would.'

He looks down now. 'When you didn't want me, I thought it was because you wanted him.'

Oh my God. 'Dave. I told you. I explained.'

He looks guilty.

'You didn't believe me, did you?'

He says nothing. Won't look at me.

'Are you telling me, you were over in the States thinking I was with him?'

'No. Jack told me you were on your own.'

'You asked Jack?'

He looks at me now. 'No. I didn't want to talk about it. Jack was playing Cupid.'

'Poor Jack. But didn't that tell you, the fact that I was alone?'

'I thought you might have wanted him but he, well, he didn't...'

'Jesus, you've a busy mind.'

'You'll have to tell him now, though.'

'Not if you're a match, I won't.'

'I'm sorry. I shouldn't have gone off like that.'

'S'OK. But try to be civil to him, Dave, please. I'm going to be here long after you go back to the States. And he's Charlie's doctor.'

'I'll stay out of his way.'

'And if you happen to bump in to him?'

'I'll be civil.'

'Thanks.'

'You OK?'

'Yeah.'

'I'll go.'

'OK.'

We walk back to the room. He collects up his things. He's about to walk out without saying goodbye.

'Dave?'

'Yeah.'

'Thanks for coming.'

'Yeah.'

I know he's killing himself. He's like that.

'You'll need the key.'

twenty-six

It's time for Dave's blood sample. Charlie talks him through it like a pro. Reassuring stuff like, 'Yeah, that's the magic cream. It kind of works. Take a deep breath, now, yep, in it goes. Are you OK, Dave?' And finally, 'That's it, all over now, good man.'

Once he gets into the swing of educating Dave, he can't stop. He gives him the lowdown on leukaemia, what's happening at bone level, how it affects the body, the drugs he has to take, in what order, how to turn off a drip, which nurses are the best. And which are 'hopeless'. Dave keeps throwing me, 'can-you-believe-this-guy' looks. It's hard not to smile. He's like a bite-sized lecturer. All he needs is a pointer and a little less attitude.

'Oh, and it's nobody's fault,' he finally ends.

Once he's sure that Charlie has definitely finished, Dave produces presents he's brought from the States. Charlie perks up. There's a tiny book of edible paper, so you can write secret notes and swallow the evidence. Charlie draws the sun and eats it. Then he shouts to everyone who passes the room:

'I ate the sun.'

Dave's also brought two sticks of candy with *Muppet Show* characters attached. Charlie doesn't really know the *Muppet Show*. He's a *Sesame Street* man. Fossie Bear and Beaker are lost on him.

I pick up Beaker. 'Brilliant,' I say, straightening his orange mop of hair. 'Did they have Dr Bunsen Honeydew as well?'

'No, they'd only six. Kermit, Miss Piggy, Animal, Fossie, Beaker and...I can't remember the last one, but it definitely wasn't Dr Bunsen Honeydew.'

'Good to know Beaker's appreciated.' I do the little Beaker noises and make the scared Beaker face and mouth movements. 'Ah, God, look at his little lab coat.'

Charlie has moved onto his iPad.

Dave watches him with a smile. 'I didn't know what he'd like. So I went for the kind things you used to.'

'You remembered my love for Fossie and Beaker?' Even I'd forgotten.

'It's not the kind of thing you'd forget, Jen.'

So there, I mustn't have been all hot ambition back then. Must have had *some* good points. And here's the man who knew them.

'Thanks, Dave.'

'They're for me, Mum,' Charlie says, suddenly looking up.

'Oh, yeah. Sorry.'

'I can get you more,' Dave says to me.

'It's OK, I can play with these when Charlie's asleep. Can't I guys?' I say to F and B. 'You know, I never noticed that Fossie had lavender eyelids. So cute. So fetching,' I say, cuddling the stick of candy to my cheek.

'You're mad,' they both say, then look at each other and laugh. They're good together.

I was a fool.

When Charlie falls asleep, Dave bombards me with questions. Prognosis. Success rates for bone marrow transplants. The likelihood of finding a donor. These are the questions that allow you plot your chances on an imaginary graph. Been there, Dave. Know what you're up to.

Simon keeps his distance. Official. Very official. Hard to believe that he is the same man who is looking after our dog. Or that his daughter is our babysitter. Or that we ever lost ourselves in each other. I know that it's partly to do with Dave's outburst, but how much, and whether or not he's just using it as an excuse to withdraw, I can't figure out. He stops calling to say goodnight. I don't care. He channels as much as he can through Dr Howard. I don't care. He never says my name. I. Don't. Care.

Our days fall into a routine, Dave calling early, leaving late; Mary popping in to let us out for a blast of late November air, or even, one night, a drink. Charlie inches towards recovery from shingles. Anne and Siobhan are as warm and caring as ever but I appreciate them more now that Simon has distanced himself. It is a shock to be reminded once again how much love you need, when you're isolated in a children's hospital.

And then it comes. News that Charlie can be discharged. He is out of danger and can continue his antiviral medication at home in the form of creams, eye ointment and oral suspension. We're packed and ready to go in minutes. Dave rushes ahead with our things to collect his rent-a-car from the car park and be out front when we get to the hospital entrance. No trying to remember where I parked, no lugging things for miles, no getting soaked, and no worries about the car starting. Just arrive like landed gentry at the pickup point where our chauffeur takes care of the details, opening the doors for us with a flourish. The car is clean, tidy, fresh. It smells new. I should upgrade the mini to something safe, practical and without temperament. Sitting up front, I feel like a locum princess, waiting to be whisked off, not quite into the sunset, but at least away from the clouds for a while.

But a cloud does follow us, hovering overhead. Dave's test results. They won't be back for another week.

'I'll get a room,' he says, pulling up at traffic lights.

'No you won't. There's plenty of space. Charlie sleeps with me now. You can have his bed, can't he Charlie?'

'Eh, yeah, OK, if you want.'

'Thanks, Charlie.' To me, he says, 'It's OK. I'll get somewhere.'

'But I want you to have a sleepover,' whines Charlie. 'You're my friend.'

'Can't argue with that,' I smile.

'I don't want to get in the way, Jenny.'

'Dave, if you were getting in the way, I'd tell you. Seriously, I could do with the company. It's been great having you here. And you'll be gone soon enough. Please stay. We'd like it wouldn't we, Charlie?'

'Yeah. And you can play *Scooby Doo* and the *Phantom Knight* with me. But if you don't practise, Dave, I'll keep winning, I'm warning ya.'

'With an offer like that...' He smiles and pulls away from the lights. 'You sure?'

'Yes.'

'Alright, then,' he smiles. And I know he's happy.

We settle in. Aim for cosy. I turn on the heat and every lamp in the place, then settle Charlie on the couch with his pillow and quilt.

'Put on, "Mama, I feel my temperature rising,"' he says. I find his favourite song and hand him my iPhone. He lies back and crosses his legs, like a woman on a beach in Juan Les Pins. He holds on to the headphones and nods enthusiastically, singing loudly and off key. I look at him and am reminded of what a softie he still is. He might watch all the latest cool movies, but his favourites are still *101 Dalmatians, Lady and the Tramp and the Lion King*. It's so easy, when he's whiny and bossy, to forget how hard this all is, the tiredness, the endless hospital visits, the tests. I kiss him on the forehead and go to start dinner.

Dave puts on some music and gets a fire going.

After a while, the doorbell rings.

'I'll get it,' Dave offers.

'No, sure, your hands are black.' I move the pasta to a cold ring and head for the door.

In bursts Sausage, skidding on the wooden floor. Like a missile, he homes in on Charlie.

'Debbie,' I say. 'Hi, come in. How are you?' I check the hallway behind her. Empty.

'Dad told me Charlie was home. I thought he'd want to see Sausage.'

Dave, squatting at the fire, turns to say hi.

'Debbie, this is Dave...a friend.'

She flushes.

Dave produces a dazzler. 'Can't shake,' he says, holding up his hands.

'That's OK,' she says, shyly.

'Hiya, Deb,' shouts Charlie. 'Thanks for bringing Sausage. D'you want to stay for a sleepover? Dave's having a sleepover.'

She looks at me, shocked.

'Charlie,' I say to avoid confusion, 'Where would Debbie sleep? Dave will be in your bed.'

'She could squeeze in.'

The poor girl is deep shade of tomato.

'Not tonight, Charlie,' I say to him.

'Aw.'

I ask Deb to dinner. She says she can't stay. First time I've seen her in a hurry to leave.

It's weird. Though Charlie and I are like an elderly couple, set in our ways, with our own little routines, idiosyncrasies, Dave slots in like an egg in a cup – helping just enough, stepping back just enough, knowing when to make himself scarce. And knowing when to take over – bringing Charlie to the park so I can catch up on everyday stuff like bills and rent and shopping. He makes the odd meal when I'm too tired. He answers the phone when I'm in the middle of something. We settle into a routine of cosy domesticity. Of sorts. Fiona keeps ringing. I hear snippets of hushed conversation.

'I miss you too...There's no need, really, I'm grand... How are you?... Yeah?...That's great... He's an amazing kid... I offered to find a room but Jenny won't have it... Any day now... Yeah, OK, better go. You too. Bye.'

He takes us out every day. The zoo, Sealife, the movies, the Natural History Museum, art galleries. The Phoenix Park:

'Do you see the squirrel?' he asks Charlie, pointing.

'Where?'

'Up there, on that branch.'

'Oh, yeah. I see it. It's laying an egg.'

Dave laughs but doesn't correct him. Neither do I. I like the idea of squirrels laying eggs.

I look around. Suck fresh air into my lungs. It's so peaceful here, surrounded by nature. Deer, metres away, lock antlers and push forward, backs arched. The females are disinterested, sitting, looking away, chewing. I like animals. They don't stare. They don't ask. Just mind their business. Pushing each other around.

'There's the ranger,' says Dave.

'Where? Where's the reindeer?' Charlie asks enthusiastically.

Dave and I smile at each other.

'I need a wee,' says Charlie.

'Can you hold on?' I ask.

'No.'

'OK, well, just go in these bushes.'

'People will see my bum.'

'No they won't. I'll stand in front of you. Anyway, there's no one around.'

'OK. But don't look.'

'OK.'

Ah, God his little bum!

'Why is there steam on the leaves?'

'You're pee is hot.'

'Oh, yeah. Cool.'

'Is it supposed to be red?' asks Dave, trying not sound panicked.

'It's OK. One of the drugs turns it red.'

'Christmas pee,' Charlie says. Then he turns around. 'Can Santa fly on his own, Mum?'

It's so good to have someone to share this with, the thinking, the worrying, and the practical stuff. Dave is going back, I know. I try not to dread the day. I try to prepare Charlie for it. Try to prepare myself. Enjoy him while he's here. Don't think ahead.

Dave wants to know everything about Charlie. What he was like as a baby, his first steps, first words, first laugh, favourite toys, favourite food, little accidents. Whenever they have something in common, Dave notices. We go through photos. All the birthdays. Great keeps popping up. And it's so wonderful to see her again, remember her, touch her face. Then she isn't in the photos any more. He asks what happened. Leukaemia, I explain. He can't believe it.

'I didn't know,' he says.

'How could you have?'

'I'm sorry I wasn't there.'

I shake my head.

We talk about Great and laugh at funny stories, like the first time they met and she asked if he was a virgin, and what his 'intentions' were regarding me. She was very liberal, Great, until it came to protecting her granddaughter. It's the first time since she died that I've spoken about her to anyone who knew her. It feels good to admit how much I miss her, how much I loved her.

Then, one afternoon, when Charlie's asleep, the call comes.

Dave answers.

'It's him. Looking for you,' he says, his hand over the mouthpiece.

I take it. Dave stays put, eyes scanning my face.

Doesn't take Simon long to get to the point. 'I'm sorry, Jenny, but Dave O'Neill is not a match.'

I have to sit, catch my breath.

'I thought you'd want to know as soon as we found out.'

'Yes, thank you, Simon. That's fine, thank you for calling.' I hang up.

He knows. Just by looking at me. He knows. 'It's a no, right?' he confirms.

I nod.

He slams his fist down on the arm of the couch. His jaw tightens. He grabs his coat and storms from the apartment. I stay where I am, holding my head in my hands. Another hurdle. Another fall. When is our luck going to change? Is it?

'Where's Dave?' asks Charlie when he gets up.

'Gone for a walk.'

'He didn't bring Sausage.'

'Oh, he must have forgotten. Why don't you give him his dinner to cheer him up?'

'OK,' he puts his hand into the sack of dog food and pulls out about ten fistfuls.

'Wash your hands, pet.'

'You don't need to tell me, Mum.'

I feed Charlie. We watch a video and later I put him to bed. I stay up, lights out, curtains open, staring at stars, waiting for him to come home.

He doesn't.

Finally, I go to bed.

The red figures on the clock say 01:32. The date is the 23rd of the eleventh month. Our anniversary. If we'd married. We should be celebrating. Instead, I'm lying beside my son, time ticking, options narrowing. I so wanted Dave to be a match. To save Charlie and also, I know now, to have him stay. He has no reason to, now. He will go, leaving us alone, again, back where we started.

Dave turns up next morning, pale and unshaven. 'Hi,' he says, awkwardly.

'Hi. You OK?'

'Yeah.' He takes off his coat. 'Sorry about that.'

I wave my hand dismissively. 'I'm making coffee. Want some?'

'Coffee would be good.' He sounds rough.

I smile. 'Sit down.'

He yawns, sits at the counter, propping up his chin with his hands. He looks younger and older at the same time.

I make the coffee and give him a mug. 'If it's any help, I know how you feel.'

'I thought it would work. I thought I could just come home and fix everything. Make it right again.'

I smile. 'The knight in shining armour.' I pull out a stool and sit beside him.

'Something like that.'

'The chances of you having the right tissue type were slim, Dave.'

'But there.'

'Funny.'

'What?'

'That's what I said when they told me I wasn't a match.'

He stares into his coffee.

'It's like you're useless, isn't it?' I say.

He turns to me. 'It doesn't mean I'm not the father, though, does it?'

I've thought about this. 'No, Dave. I'm his mother and I'm not a match.'

'Right.' He takes a sip. Then looks around. 'Where is he, anyway?'

'Over at Dara's. Thought it'd be good for him to have a change of scene. Get away from his mother for a while.' I smile.

'I don't know how you keep going.'

'Don't have a choice.'

'So many ups and downs, though.'

'Yup.' I look out the window.

'What do we do now?' he asks.

'Keep searching.'

'I rang Fiona last night. She thinks I should come home.'

'There's nothing to keep you here.' Though it kills me to say it.

'Do you really think that?'

'Dave, we'd love you to stay. But Fiona is your fiancée. And she obviously misses you.'

'What about you and Charlie? I have a responsibility...'

'Dave, you've taken care of your responsibility. You did the test. There isn't anything else you can do.' *Outside of being here for us, like you have been, which has been so amazing.*

'He could be my son, Jenny.' His voice cracks. 'I can't just leave him. I'm not going to. Not yet. Not until we find a donor.'

'Dave, that could take weeks, months. You can't expect Fiona to wait that long. And they won't hold your job.'

'I'm not walking out on you just because my blood isn't good enough.'

'But Fiona...'

'Can come over.'

'Dave, you should go home.'

'I'm going to book Fiona and myself into a hotel for a week. It'll be a holiday.'

'Not much of a holiday.'

'I'm not changing my mind.'

Thank You, God.

He goes into Charlie's room to call Fiona.

He comes back smiling.

She's going to organise it with her boss and come over as soon as she can.

Jack rings. 'You're coming to lunch. Today.'

I smile. 'Who's coming to lunch?'

'You, Charlie, Dave.'

'Charlie's not here.'

'Right, then you and Dave.'

It'd be so good to get out of the apartment. 'Let me just check with Dave.'

For somewhere Jack booked, the place is a surprise – modern and bright with a Scandinavian feel to it, pale wood and stainless steel. Simple lines. Orange flowers add a splash of colour on each table. The staff is young and attractive, dressed in trendy black. I feel light years away from my life and wonder if maybe Charlie is right – maybe heaven and food are related.

Wine? Sure, why not?

Before I know, it we're on coffee, that part of a meal when business people get down to business. But we're not business people and there's no business.

'I'd a call from someone you know,' Jack says to me.

Was I wrong? Is there business? 'Who?'

'Your mother.'

I sit straighter, suddenly alert. 'What did she want?'

'To know why your columns have stopped.'

'What did you tell her?'

'Nothing.'

'You must have told her something.'

'I told her you were taking a break.'

'That's all?'

'I said I'd pass on her message to you.'

'Which is what, exactly?'

'That she's asking after you and hopes everything's alright.'

I raise a cynical eyebrow.

'She seemed worried about you, Jen.'

'So she called you?'

'She reads your column every week.'

'She's a politician. She has to read the papers.'

'She's very proud of you, Jen.'

I laugh. 'Don't you get it, Jack? She's putting on a show for you. You're a newspaper editor. VIP to her.'

'I think you're being a bit hard on her,' he says.

'You should tell her about Charlie,' says Dave as if none of this is news to him.

'Hang on. You knew about this?' I say, turning on him.

'Yes, I did.'

I look from one to the other. 'Are you telling me you planned this lunch to tell me about my mother?'

'You're looking for a donor, aren't you?' It's Dave.

'You don't waste time,' I snap.

'How much time do we have?' he asks, eyeballing me.

'Thanks, Dave.'

'Look, Jenny,' he says. 'You don't get on with your mother. It happens. But Charlie needs a donor and your parents might be able to help. That's two possible donors.'

'You've it all sorted.'

'At least I'm trying.'

'Now, now, children,' says Jack. *Quite bitchily,* I think.

'You plotted this, the two of you.'

'Three of us,' says Dave. 'The lunch was Mary's idea.'

'Mary?' I'm stunned.

'Yes, Mary, your friend, your very good friend, who cares about you, about Charlie. And who knows how to pick a good restaurant,' says Dave.

Jack nods enthusiastically, until he gets to the bit about the restaurant.

And finally it becomes clear. The people I love are just trying to help.

'Sorry,' I say.

'So are you going to ring your poor mother?' asks Jack.

'No. She rang you, not me. If she wants to talk to me, she can call. I'm not going to beg. If you want to tell her what's happened, that's OK. But it's up to her to call me.'

'What if she doesn't?'

'Then I'd have wasted my time asking, wouldn't I?'

'She'll call,' says the ever-hopeful Dave. For some bizarre

reason, he has always had time for my mother.

'Let's just see what happens.' Inside, of course, I hope she'll ring.

twenty-seven

Fiona. Childfree singleton with time for self. Body familiar with the inside of a gym. Hair short, blonde, layer-free, cut in at the neck. I imagine some leading New York stylist who also does celebrities. Hands slender and manicured. Designer clothes. And boots. But forget all that, let's see some ID, this woman can't be more than twenty-two. And maybe that explains the You're The Woman Who Wants My Man vibe. I don't want her man. But am I going to tell her?

NO.

I tell myself to stop. It can't be easy, coming to his country, the hub of all his connections, memories, ties, the home of the woman he'd planned to spend his life with, the boy who might be his son. If I was her, I'd want him safely back in the States too. So I try.

Dave moves out. The apartment is quieter. No one now to dilute the intensity of what we're going through, distract us from ourselves, each other and 'it'. I take up the job of story time again.

Dave bought Charlie *The Gruffalo*. It has become his favourite.

'You're not reading it properly,' he whines, taking his disappointment out on me.

I'm not doing the voices right. Or the faces. Worst of all, my pace is off.

I try to improve.

He turns on his side, away from me, to sleep.

'Pat my head like Dave.'

'What do you mean?'

'When I go to sleep, Dave pats my head.'

'What, like this?'

'No. Like this.' He holds my hand and moves it over his head, stroking.

I give it a go.

'You're not doing it right.'

'Sorry,' I say, realising how close to tears he is.

'Your hands are too small.'

I keep trying, slowly, carefully, until I fall into a pattern. His breathing becomes regular, calm. He sleeps, his little chest rising and falling. I get such a strong protective urge; I would kill for him.

Dave calls to see us every day, sometimes with Fiona, most times not. It doesn't work when she's here. Everyone's on edge. Even when he's alone, the magic's gone; it's just not the same anymore. He seems stressed, under pressure. She wants him to go back. I know it.

Five nights after she has arrived, Charlie is in bed. I'm on the Internet looking up bone marrow transplants. The doorbell rings. I get up, annoyed at being interrupted when I'm working. Because this *is* work. Getting Charlie better is my career now.

I open up.

Fiona stands there. Alone.

'Can I come in?'

'Sure,' I say, standing back.

In she comes. A woman on a mission.

'Would you like a coffee?' I ask.

'No thanks. I've come to talk with you.'

'Do you want to sit down, take off your coat?'

She slips out of her elegant navy overcoat, folds it, then positions herself at the edge of the couch, back straight. This works wonders for my posture. I'm strangely prepared for attack.

'This has gone on too long,' she says. 'He has to come home now. You have to make him.'

I don't have to do anything.

'There's no reason for him to stay. He can't help anymore than he already has. He should leave now, with me.'

'Shouldn't you be having this conversation with Dave?'

'I have but you've such a hold on him.'

'I'm sorry, Fiona, but that's simply not true. He's here for Charlie.'

She starts to wrap the strap of her bag round and round a finger. If it's possible to garrotte a finger, she's doing it.

'Yeah but he can't stay here forever.'

'I think he knows that.' She sees me examine her garrotting technique and quickly unwinds the strap. Her finger is white, bloodless, squished. She doesn't see it.

'He's guilty about the past, about leaving you before. He won't come home unless you tell him to. And you have to. He'll lose his job. He's getting too involved here.' She's wrapping her finger again. And unwrapping when she becomes conscious of what she's doing. 'It's not fair. He thinks he's Charlie's father.'

'He might be.'

'Might isn't enough to hold him here. Can't you do a paternity test? It's only fair. Dave should know whether he's Charlie's father or not. We all should. It's gone on too long. What are you trying to achieve?'

'I'm not trying to achieve anything. Apart from saving my son.'

'Do the paternity test. Then let him go.'

'What if he is Charlie's father?'

217

'Then we'll deal with it. But at least we'll know.'

After she's gone, I stride, wall to wall, wanting to pound my fist through one. She comes into my home and tells me what to do. She doesn't care about Charlie. She has zero compassion. And how dare she ask me what I'm trying to achieve? I asked Dave for blood. I never asked him to come. And I haven't asked him to stay.

I walk and rant and rant and walk. I call her a bitch. I call her worse. And yet, in the end, I know she's right. I hate it. But she is. I haven't given Dave the information he needs to make the right decision for him. He's here because he might be Charlie's father. If he isn't, then it's unfair to let him hope. If he is, then let him have that fatherhood, the certainty of it. He wants to do the right thing. I owe him the freedom to do it.

I'll arrange a test. Once I know how. Once Dave agrees to it, which I expect he will. He has nothing to lose.

But, actually, he has. Everything to lose. Charlie. I know how close they've become, though it's only weeks. I know how much in awe of each other they are, how much time they've spent together, how happy they've made each other. And I know he wants to help. If he's not Charlie's father, what excuse does he have to stay? But maybe what Dave wants isn't what he needs. Maybe he should go back to the States, pick back up his life and…marry…Fiona.

twenty-eight

Dave says we don't need to do the test. But doesn't put up much of a fight. I suspect someone has been working behind the scenes. I ring my GP. She can't do paternity tests but directs me to a private hospital nearby. I make an appointment for the three of us. Charlie wants to know where we're going, what we're doing and why. And I hate lying to him.

They take swabs of saliva from the inside of our cheeks, to check for DNA. Normally, they'd take blood but Charlie has had a transfusion in the last three months and has other people's cells in his blood. I can't think about that.

I feel a surge of anger with myself when she takes the sample from Charlie. We shouldn't be doing this now. Not with him sick. But then, Dave has given enough, been patient enough. So I say nothing, just open my mouth when it's my turn.

The swabs have to go to a lab in the UK for genetic testing.

The results will take six weeks. I can't wait that long. I have to approach Simon to see whether or not he's a match. If it was one week, even two, I could have waited. Then either go to him with the certainty that he is the father, or not go to him at all. Now, I'll have to tell him he might be Charlie's father and hope that he'll do the test. Will might be enough?

'You've a mother!' says Charlie. 'I didn't *know* that.'

    'Yes, Charlie, I have.'

    'Where is she?'

    'In Dublin.'

    'Dublin? But we live in Dublin. Why don't we see her?'

    'She's been kind of busy.'

    'Like my Dad,' he says moodily. 'Everyone's busy.'

    'Well, she's not busy today. She wants to meet us.'

    'Great. D'you think she'll bring treats?'

    'I don't know, Charlie. Don't always think about what you can get.'

    I should offer myself the same advice.

    When we arranged to meet, I chose the venue and time. Half nine, at a playground that's not local, but not too far away. Reasons for choice: 1. It'll be deserted. 2. It's designed for small children, so Charlie won't need much supervision. 3. It's not in the neighbourhood, so we shouldn't meet anyone we know.

    I wrap him in his quilted coat, cap, scarf and mittens. Colour scheme orange and red, like a confused traffic light. She's already there, sitting on a light blue bench with chipped paint, huddled against the cold. Not marching around in her usual business-like way. No entourage. Posture gone to hell. She hears Charlie's chatter and lifts her head. She smiles and stands. Charlie runs to her.

    'Hi,' he says loudly. 'Are you my mum's mother?'

    She bends down to him, takes his hands. 'Yes, Charlie, I am.' She smiles. 'And I'm your grandmother.'

He pulls his hands away. 'No, You're not. My granny's in heaven.'

She looks at me, horrified, as if I've told him she's dead.

'No, Charlie,' I say. 'You're thinking of Great.'

'Yeah.'

I try to explain. 'Great was my granny, your great-granny. That's why her name was Great. But this is my mother, your granny.'

He looks confused. 'I thought she was called Great because she was great.'

'That too, Charlie,' I say, smiling and giving him a hug.

He stands, hands in pockets, eyeing up his new grandmother.

'Hello, Jenny,' she says.

'Hello, Mother,' I say, coldly.

'What's wrong? Aren't ye friends?'

'Charlie, look,' I say enthusiastically, 'no one's on the slide. Quick, come on, you can have a go.'

'I want to talk to my granny.'

'I know. You can in a minute. But if you don't hurry up, other kids will come and you'll have to queue for everything.' He hates queuing.

'OK,' he says, 'but I'll be back in a minute.'

I rub the dew off the slide with a hand towel.

'Why don't you like her?' he whispers.

'I do.'

'No you don't.'

'Well, Smarty Pants, you play away here for five minutes and let me see if I can make friends with her, OK?'

'OK.'

'Call me if you need me.' I hold his chin between my thumb and finger and give it a little shake. He turns and climbs the toddler's slide, both hands gripping the ladder, the way I taught him.

I go back to her. Unfortunately, I need her blood.

She's on the bench again. I sit beside her, say nothing.

'He's a lovely child, Jenny. Is he...alright?'

'He has leukaemia, Mother.'

'Yes, but how is he doing?'

'He's in remission. For the moment.'

'Thank God.' She lets out a breath. Seconds pass, then: 'Why didn't you tell us?'

I just look at her.

'We've had our differences. But we're still your parents. We still expect you to call if you're in trouble.'

'And you'll come rushing to the rescue? All Charlie ever was to you was an unwanted pregnancy.'

She closes her eyes. Finally she opens them. 'Jenny, I'm sorry about that. I reacted badly. I was just worried about you...'

'About yourself. And your image.'

'That's not true. That's not true at all.'

'It's all you're interested in. It's all you were ever interested in.'

'That's not fair. I tried to get on with you but you always pushed me away.'

'Wrong.' I fold my arms. I'm not budging on this.

'Look, Jenny, I know I never understood you the way your grandmother did but I did try. And just because I never knew how to talk to you doesn't mean I didn't love you.'

'So where were you, then?'

'Jenny, a politician's life is a busy one. There are so many demands...'

'Here we go.'

'Whatever free time I had, I wanted to spend with you but you weren't interested. You were always with your grandmother. You preferred her, got on better with her.'

'And why do you think that was?'

'I don't know, Jenny. I did try.'

'Did you? Because it certainly didn't feel that way. I'll tell you why I got on with Great. Because she was there. She cared. I didn't have to wait around until she had five minutes, squeezed in between clinics and the funeral of someone she'd never met. She was always there when I needed her. When I had a problem. She didn't just rush in and try to catch up by asking me deep and meaningful questions that just stressed me out. She was just there.'

'And I wasn't,' she says, lowering her head.

'You treated me like a toy you could pick up whenever it suited you. I wasn't a toy. I was a child who needed her mother. Anyway, forget it. I'm a big girl now.' But I can't forget it. 'It just makes me so mad when you say I got on better with Great. Of course, I got on better with Great.'

'Mu-um.'

Charlie's coming over. 'Will you push me on the swing?' he asks, watching us carefully from under the peak of his cap.

'OK,' I say. Anything to get away. This isn't going to work. I knew it was a mistake.

I push the swing and pretend not to notice that she has got up and is walking slowly away from the bench, head down. She starts to rummage in her bag. She pulls out a hankie, dabs her eyes and blows her nose. *Oh, great. Another of her stunts.* I pretend to be busy with Charlie. Maybe she'll go.

'Is Granny crying?'

'No.'

'She is.'

'No, Charlie, she's fine.'

She returns to the bench and puts the hankie back in her bag. She tilts her head back as though taking a deep breath.

'I want to get off,' says Charlie.

I stop the swing and hold it while he jumps off. He runs over to her. I follow, slowly.

'Granny, are you OK?'

'Yes, sweetheart, I'm fine, thank you,' she says, rubbing his cheek. 'How are you?'

'Fine. D'you want to see me go on the slide?'

'I'd love that.'

'OK.' He runs off. I'm about to follow, when she calls me. I walk over, avoid eye contact, sit down, fiddle with the car keys.

'Jenny,' she says, 'look at me.'

She has been crying.

'I love you,' she says.

First time she has said that.

'I loved you from the first moment I held you.'

She's not like that. Politician, first. Mother, last.

'Something went wrong between us and I thought it was a phase, that it would just get better, that you'd grow out of the resentment you had for me. But it never got better...Just worse and worse.' She's crying now, really crying, tears flooding her cheeks, dropping off her chin, splashing onto her coat. This is not an act. Unless she's a complete genius. I've never seen her cry. I'm mortified. I check to make sure no one's coming. She won't stop. *Jesus. Charlie's coming over now.*

'What's wrong, Granny?' he asks, rubbing her the back, the way I do with him when he's upset. 'Are you OK?'

'Yes, sweetheart, I've got something in my eye.'

'Let me have a look.' He puts his face right up to hers. 'Tears,' he says. 'Yeah, I see them.'

She laughs, rubs his cheek again. 'You're a lovely little fellow, aren't you?'

'Yup.'

She laughs. 'Would you like to sit on my lap?'

'What'll you give me?'

She's laughing again.

'A hug,' she says.

'Hugs are OK. But no kissing, right?'

'Right,' she says with a decisive nod. Up he goes.

Why can't I get on with her? Charlie doesn't seem to have a problem. Dave definitely doesn't. Is it me? It is weird, this sight, my mother and my son. Together. Happy. And the strangest thing happens. From nowhere, a memory flashes. We're at a park; she's young, pretty. Her dress is yellow. With flowers. I'm at the top of the slide and she's at the bottom, waiting for me, her arms out, smiling. And I trust her. I want to go to her. *Where did that come from? Did that really happen?*

'Are you any good on iPads?' he asks her.

'No, sweetheart. I don't think so, but maybe you could show me, someday?'

Don't push it.

'Yeah, that'd be cool. D'you want to come to my house now? We've no plans.'

She laughs. 'You're full of business, aren't you? Like your mum.' She looks at me, still smiling.

I blank her.

She sighs.

'So are you coming?'

'Not today, Charlie.'

'Don't tell me. You're busy,' he says, pulling a face.

She smiles at him, kisses his cheek and hugs him. Her face is so sad when she looks at me.

Stupidly, madly, crazily, I feel sorry for her.

'Will you come a different day?' he asks.

'I really hope so, Charlie,' she says, looking at me.

'Charlie, one last go on the slide and we have to go, OK?' I say.

'OK.'

Charlie climbs down and walks off. A little man's walk.

'I want to help, Jenny.'

'Why?'

'Please. I'm sorry about the past. I'm sorry I didn't have enough time for you. I'm sorry about how I reacted to the pregnancy. You don't know how much I regret that. We are two obstinate people...'

'You want to help?' I ask coldly.

She nods.

'Charlie needs a bone marrow transplant. We have to find a donor. I'm not a match, Dave isn't...'

'Dave? Is Dave home?' she asks, full of hope.

'For the moment,' I say flatly. 'He's engaged.'

'Oh.'

'And she wants him back home in the States where she can keep an eye on him.'

'Oh, dear.'

'Did you see that, Granny?' shouts Charlie, proudly, from the bottom of the slide.

'Yes, wonderful, Charlie,' she says, clapping.

'Will you do a blood test, see if you have the right tissue type?'

'Of course, I'll help in any way I can. And your father will too.'

'Do you want me to do it again?' shouts Charlie.

'Yes, love. I'd love to see it again,' she calls back.

'The chances of grandparents being a match are tiny.'

'When can we do it?'

'Whenever you want. Sooner rather than later would be good.'

'I'll talk to your father.' She seems happy now. A new campaign. 'How are you, Jenny?'

'Fine.'

'Are you looking after yourself?'

'Yes, Mother.'

'Your father is well.'

'Great.'

'He said to send his love. He would have liked to come but he thought... I'm sorry we haven't been in touch. But that's what you wanted isn't it?'

'Yep.' I look away, hoping she'll take the hint and go.

'But maybe it wasn't such a good idea. Because we've missed you. And we've missed seeing that very special little boy grow.' Her voice starts to break.

I stand up. 'I'd better be going. You have my number so you can ring to arrange the blood test.'

'Yes. Thanks, Jenny, for seeing me. And letting me meet Charlie. I hope you're very proud,' she says looking at him coming back over to us. 'He's a wonderful boy.'

'He's alright.'

'No, Jenny, he's much better than that.'

I need a distraction. It needs to be something out of the ordinary. Passing a car showroom, on impulse, I pull in.

'Let's have a look at these Golfs,' I say to him.

I'm in the driver's seat, eyes closed, savouring the smell of new car, the steering wheel, sturdy in my hand, imagining myself on a bumpy country lane, wind in my hair, long, silvery grass on either side, butterflies, wild flowers and swallows. Beside me is the happiest, most energetic little boy, his thick blonde hair flapping in the breeze and his cheeks the rosiest in the world.

Whoa! The radio blares suddenly, snapping me out of my dream.

'Charlie!' I flick off the radio and turn to him, laughing.

Oh God. There's blood everywhere. All over his top, face, left hand. It oozes from his nostrils. He rubs it with the back of his hand, too busy looking at the car to notice.

I don't want to panic him.

'Charlie, love. You're having a little nosebleed. It's OK, I had them all the time when I was a kid. I just have to pinch your nose, OK, sweetie? Breathe through your mouth, now.' I hold his nostrils together. The blood feels warm and sticky. With my free hand, I fumble in my bag for a hankie.

He looks down at the blood, so calm, it's scary.

'Now, lean forward a tiny bit. Good boy. Try not to swallow, OK?'

'DohK.'

We sit like this for about five minutes until the salesman pokes his bird head through the open window. Instantly, he loses his plastic smile.

'Can you get a cold, wet cloth, please?' I ask calmly. 'It'll help stop the bleeding.'

'Can you get out of the car?'

'Not without bleeding all over it. Now, can you get the cloth please? Thank you.'

I may look calm. I may sound calm. Inside I'm thinking: *His platelets must be low. That's why he's bleeding. If they're down, it's going to be hard to stop. And he can't afford to lose any blood or he'll become anaemic. Or more anaemic than he already is.* I need to get him to hospital.

The salesman returns. I press the cold, wet cloth to Charlie's forehead.

'I'm tired, Mama.'

'Can't you stop it?' asks the salesman.

I ignore him.

'It's OK, Charlie. It's OK, sweetie. It'll stop in a few minutes and then we'll go to the hospital.'

'The hawpital? Oh dno. Not again.'

twenty-nine

His platelets are down. He needs a transfusion. Anne is in the nurses' station setting it up.

I go find her.

'How did they drop so fast?' I ask. 'He's only had a test and his levels were fine.' All I can think is, *relapse*.

'Platelets can fall because of chemotherapy.'

I know this already. Doesn't help. 'Can you test his blood for cancer cells?'

She looks at me. 'We are, Jenny.'

I take a deep breath. There's nothing to do but go back to Charlie. We need this transplant. Fast.

Minutes later, Anne hooks Charlie up to the drip.

'I'm never going to get better,' he says, lying flaccid on the bed, watching a line of dark red run into his Freddie.

'Sweetheart, of course you're going to get better.'

'No, Mama, I'm not.'

'You will, Charlie and we'll have a party and...'

'I don't want a party. I just want to get better. I'm tired, Mama. I'm really tired.' He starts to cry.

I have to be strong. I can't give in. Not now. Not ever. 'I know, sweetie.' I stroke his head. 'I'm so proud of you, Charlie. D'you know that? You're such a brave boy.'

'I wish my dad was here.'

'I know.'

'Doesn't he know I'm sick?'

I don't answer, just continue to stroke. I kiss his temple.

'Where's Dave?'

'He's coming love.'

'But he won't stay. He never stays anymore. Just goes off with her.'

I kiss his forehead. 'I'm here.'

'Everyone goes away.'

'No, they don't.'

'Great did. My Dad did. Simon and Dave were my friends and now they hardly come at all.'

'Dara and Debbie are your friends and they haven't gone anywhere.'

'But they never come to see me in here.'

'You have Mary. What about Mary?'

'Mary's Dara's mum. I want someone for myself. I want my new granny. She'll come.'

'Your granny?'

'Yeah, she'll come. I know she will. Ring her, Mama, please.'

Damn.

'Please.'

'OK, Charlie, I'll ring her.'

I get up, knocking a bright red, toy Elmo off the bed.

'I feel great', it says.

She comes, of course, like the cavalry, only quicker. She fusses over him and asks to see his iPad. She pretends it's the most fascinating thing in the world, acts dumb and gets him to take her through it. Lots of ooohing and ahhing, lots of 'you're so clevers'. I have to give her credit. He's not as down as he was. He even sits up. I take her aside and ask if she could try getting a drink into him. He won't do anything for me. And she's on an obvious roll. She adopts the unoriginal, 'Bet you can't drink all this,' tack. He's so busy trying to impress her that it works. She stays for hours, a surprise, considering there's an election coming up. She hasn't really got time for this.

They ignore me. Which is fine. As long as he's happy.

When she finally goes, Charlie makes her promise to come again.

She looks at me.

I nod. As long as she continues to work her magic, she can stay.

There are no cancer cells in the sample. My body deflates in relief. The blood transfusion goes in.

We can go home.

Driving out of the car park, I remember. I never told Simon. I have to. Especially after today. No more frights.

Everyone's giving blood. My parents, Mary, Jack. Who knows, maybe my own little register of potential donors will be more successful than the official one. Wouldn't be hard. My biggest chance is Simon.

Where do you arrange to meet someone to announce that they may be the father of your child, that you need them to try to save his life – oh, and that, you're sorry for not mentioning it before now?

There *is* no suitable place.

I call him on his mobile.

'Hi, Simon, it's Jenny.'

'Is everything alright?'

'Yes, thanks. I need to talk to you.'

'You've caught me at a good time. I'm in my office. Do you want to call the landline?'

'No, Simon, I need to talk to you. In person.'

'Oh.' A pause. 'Do you want to come in to the hospital?'

'Could I meet you somewhere else? There's something I have to tell you.'

Silence now.

'When suits you?' I ask. Because I have to do this.

'Today?'

'Yes, today.'

'Eh, after work would be best...although I said to Debra I'd cook her...'

'Debbie's coming over here, Simon. I invited her for dinner. I hope that's OK with you. I thought she'd checked.'

'I'm sorry, she did. I'd forgotten. I'm a bit under pressure. Well, then, after work, if that suits you.'

'What time?'

'About seven?'

'Fine.'

'Where?'

'I don't know.' *Did I just say that?*

'Somewhere local?'

'Yes.'

'Like a bar?' he asks.

'No. Not a bar. Eh...' *Quick, quick.* 'The Four Seasons?'

'Fine.'

'See you there, then?'

'The lobby?' he asks.

'The lobby.'

Jesus. I've a cramp in my hand from holding the phone so tight.

'Where are you going, Mum?' Charlie asks.

Three faces look at me questioningly – my son, his babysitter and the dog.

'Just meeting a friend. Are you sure you don't mind babysitting for a while, Deb?'

'No problem. I was here anyway.'

'Thanks.'

'What friend? Mary?' You couldn't call him a quitter.

'Eh, no.'

'Jack?'

'No, Charlie. Someone else. OK, see you later, bye.'

'Who, Mum?'

I can't admit that it's Simon. But I can't say it's someone else in case Simon mentioned to Debbie that he was meeting me. 'It's just a meeting, Charlie.'

'For work?'

'Mm-hmm.'

'Are you going back to work?' he asks, surprised.

'No. But I'm meeting someone to say I'm not going back, OK? Look, I gotta go, bye.' I kiss his head, wave to Deb.

Well, it's official, I made a mess of that.

First to arrive, I find the quietest spot and hide by a large plant. I order a glass of freshly squeezed orange juice and wait, going over the conversation in my head.

Then he's there, stopping, looking around. He sees me. I nearly spill the juice.

I stand up when he gets to me.

'Sorry I'm late,' he says. 'I had to wait for some results.'

'It's fine.'

He takes the antique chair at right angles to, but beside, the dainty couch I'm on. He puts his satchel on the ground. It's practically the same as mine. How have I never noticed?

'How's Charlie?' he asks.

'OK. A bit tired.' My mouth is dry but I'm afraid to go near the juice.

'Due in for his chemo tomorrow?'

'Yes and you're probably wondering why this couldn't wait

till then but it has nothing to do with Charlie's illness. Well, it has, in a way. Look, I'm sorry, I need to tell you…' I squint. 'Do you want a drink or something?'

'I'll wait for someone to come round.'

'Oh. OK.'

He looks at me, expecting me to continue.

I shift in my seat, clear my throat. 'This thing I have to tell you? I should've told you before. And I don't exactly know how to, now, but I have to, you see, because of Charlie. I'm sorry.' I take a breath. 'It's about the bone marrow transplant.'

He looks relieved, as if happy to discuss something clinical, manageable, impersonal.

'Simon?'

'Yes.'

'You know the way, I wasn't a match, and Dave wasn't a match?'

'Yes but I wouldn't worry…'

'I was hoping one of us would be, so I wouldn't have to tell you what I have to tell you.'

There's no visible movement yet suddenly he seems to be sitting an inch off the chair, bracing himself.

'You may be Charlie's father.'

A lounge boy, dressed like a penguin, is standing beside the table.

'A Jack Daniels,' Simon chokes.

'Yes, sir,' he says, then looks at me.

I shake my head.

He scuttles off.

'Charlie was born on January 25th,' I say.

'I know.'

'You know?'

'I saw it on his chart, the first day he came to the hospital. Charlie was born the day my wife died.'

There are no words.

The whiskey arrives. The waiter leaves.

Simon takes a gulp. Then another.

'Charlie was born nine months after the conference in Brussels.'

Silence.

'Did it ever cross your mind that he might be yours?'

He shakes his head.

'Not once?'

He puts down the drink, looks at me intently. 'You need to understand... What happened in Brussels was out of character. Not me. At all. I couldn't let it interfere with my life. My wife,' he pauses, 'Alison, was everything to me. She was dying. What happened was... I erased it from my mind. It was the only way I could live with myself. Do you understand?'

I nod.

'It never occurred to me that it might have affected your life. I didn't think. Didn't realise. It broke up your relationship with Dave, didn't it?'

I nod again.

'I'm sorry.'

'Not your fault. Just one of those things.'

'Can I ask you something?'

I look at him.

'That time I thought I recognised you, why did you dismiss it, why didn't you tell me who you were? You knew who I was, didn't you?'

I nod. 'I didn't want to embarrass you – or myself – by bringing up the past. I thought about changing babysitter but Charlie loves Deb and I couldn't find a replacement and then they discovered they were each missing a parent and I couldn't separate them.'

We're quiet for a moment. Then he smiles.

'You know, I tried to stop Debra babysitting too.'

'I know. She told me. Were you worried I was a bad influence or something?'

'A bad influence?'

I shrug. 'Single mum.'

'No. God, no. It was school. She'd just started Junior Cert

Year. I didn't want her to take on too much. God. I'd never think that. *I'm* a single parent. I know how hard it is. I've great respect for people parenting alone, especially with sick children. Believe me.'

I smile. 'I do.' I've never heard him get so emotional about anything.

We're silent again.

'Jenny, you said I may be Charlie's father?'

'I was in a relationship with Dave.'

'Who then left you,' he says, guiltily.

'No. He didn't. I ended it.'

'Why?'

I shrug. 'What happened would have come between us in the end. At least I thought it would have. Maybe I was wrong.'

'And you never did a paternity test?'

'Actually, we just have. We'll have results in six weeks.'

'Six weeks.'

'Simon, I can't wait that long. I need you to check to see if you're a match for Charlie. I know it's awkward, you working at the hospital, but there must be some way of keeping it confidential. Could you do it yourself, put a false name on the test tube, I don't know, something? There must be a way. I know the chances are small, but you understand, I have to try.'

'Can you let me think about this?'

What's there to think about – a dying boy, a chance at life? But I've just landed this on him. I need to be fair. I sigh. 'OK.'

'I think I'll go now, if that's all right. There's nothing else you want to say?'

'Just sorry. For landing this on you.'

'No, *I'm* sorry. If I hadn't been such a dumb fuck... Sorry. But you know what I mean.'

'I told myself the same thing so many times – until Charlie.'

He smiles and nods. He picks the bill up from the table.

'I'll get this,' I say, reaching for it.

'Already done,' he says, slipping a twenty between the leather covers.

'Thank you.' I get my coat.

He walks me to my car.

'Goodnight, Jenny. I'll see you tomorrow.'

'Night, Simon,' I say and try not to hope. I've no doubt that Brutus is an honourable man. It's just that Brutus doesn't know if there is anything *to* honour. Maybe Brutus won't feel a responsibility to do anything unless it's proven genetically that he has one. Maybe Brutus will want to wait six weeks.

thirty

Charlie's tired, weary and in no mood to make the trek back to what has become our second home, only to be made worse by more chemo. I'm not exactly tripping over myself to get there either, having spent the night awake, worrying about Simon and what he'll say. Or won't say. Dave, who has promised to spend the day with us, is not in great form either, but won't talk about it. So here we are a bunch of miseries, driving together to the hospital.

And here we are now, same bunch of miseries arriving at the ward, so familiar with the place that there's no longer uncertainty, no longer confusion, just routine.

Charlie wants to watch a DVD. And I get that. Anything to take his mind off this.

Dave switches on the TV and flicks through the channels.

'Stop, stop. I saw Granny!' shouts Charlie.

'Where?' asks Dave.

'Go back one, I saw her, I saw her.'

He lands on breakfast television news.

I look up.

There she is, outside the Dáil, dyed auburn hair being whisked about by an unkind wind. So that's why I've always wanted mine to be any other colour.

'But coming up to an election, Minister?' says the interviewer. 'The timing couldn't be worse.'

'I agree that the timing could be better, Fergal, and I would like to take this opportunity to apologise to the party and to the electorate, but I have compelling family reasons for retiring from politics.'

'With all due respect, Minister, family reasons are often quoted when people retire from politics. Are you sure your retirement hasn't anything to do with the recent fall in popularity of the party, reflected in the latest MRBI opinion poll?'

'Fergal, I think you know me by now,' she says, as though they're best friends, which she has probably made sure they are, 'there's nothing that motivates me more than a challenge. That opinion poll almost made me stay.' She pauses for effect. Then says, 'I have devoted over thirty years of my life to politics. I have always put it first. Someone reminded me of that recently.' She stops again. 'Time with my family is long overdue. Who knows how much time any of us has left?' She beams at him as if to say: That, young man, is all you're getting.

He thanks her, tells her she will be sorely missed and wishes her all the best.

'What'd she say, Mum?' asks Charlie.

'She just said she's giving up work.'

'Is she?' as in wow. Then: 'I didn't know Grannies worked.'

'Some do.'

'Why's she giving up work?'

'She wants to spend more time with her family or something.'

'Who's her family?'

'Well, us, I suppose.'

'That's great. She's going to spend more time with us. Cool.'

'I don't know Charlie. Let's just see what happens, OK?'

Dave has become as animated as Charlie. 'What. About. That?'

'I don't know what she's up to,' I say.

'Can't you just accept that maybe she's sorry? Maybe she's trying to make it up to you.'

'What are ye talking about?' asks Charlie.

'Nothing, Charlie, nothing,' I say, glaring at Dave.

He goes quiet, giving me a moment to decide what I feel. It is this: I'll believe it when I see it. And this: Don't count your chickens. And this: It's not that easy.

Buzz Lightyear is falling with style, on screen. Charlie is engrossed, Granny and chemo temporarily forgotten. Dave goes to 'stretch his legs'. Almost immediately, Simon appears and I wonder if he's grabbing his moment. I think of what he's here to talk about and my stomach clenches.

'Hi, Jenny, Charlie.' *How do I interpret that smile?*

Charlie doesn't hear, fists clenched and twisting, chin sticking out in excitement as the rocket explodes.

'If only we could all be as easily distracted,' Simon says. Then he looks at me. 'I'll do the test,' he says quietly. 'Of course, I'll do it.'

Thank. You. God.

I get up and we walk together towards the door. 'It's not awkward for you?'

'No. I can do it discreetly.' He looks at me. 'And I have to be discreet for Debra's sake. I can't have her knowing. It would break her heart to think that I …' He stops. Looks back at Charlie.

I can't believe I never thought of Debbie in all of this. We really never fully realise the implications of our actions.

'Of course. Thank you, Simon.'

'I'm sorry,' he says. Though there's no need.

'Fiona's going back to the States,' says Dave when he returns, over an hour later.

The movie is over and Charlie has fallen asleep. I wasn't far off it myself. I look up now, from where I've been resting my head on my arms on Charlie's bed.

He pulls up a chair and sits beside me.

'We had a bit of a tiff,' he says quietly.

'I'm sorry.'

'She thinks I'm spending too much time with you and Charlie.'

'Do you?'

'No.' He's quiet. Then, 'She thinks you have some sort of...' he makes quote marks with his fingers, 'hold... over me.'

I try to look surprised.

'It's ridiculous,' he says.

'Don't be so enthusiastic.'

We laugh.

'Go, Dave. Go with her. We won't have the results for six weeks.'

'I know but don't you need me around?'

'Not if you're going to be moping over Fiona.'

'I'm not moping over Fiona.'

'You should see your face.' I smile. 'Go on. Six weeks is a long time.'

'Did you talk to him?'

I nod. 'He's going to do it.'

'Great.' He takes my hand. 'But don't get your hopes up, Jen.'

'I'm not. At least I'm trying not to.'

'I'm staying.'

'What do you mean, you're staying?'

'I'm not going to let her push me around. I want to be here. So I'm staying.'

'What about work?'

'I'm going to do some stuff for Jack. I was just talking to him, there, on the phone.'

'Nobody could accuse you of being a slow mover.'

'I can think of one.' He smiles.

I frown. 'Are you sure you're doing the right thing? She really wants you with her. If you stick your heels in, you might lose her, Dave. She's young, remember?'

'Jenny, marriage is for life. You've got to have a bit of give and take. She must understand that I need to do this. She's going to have to love me warts and all and if that means being patient, well, she's just going to have to be patient. Anyway, I think a break from each other might be good – let her know what she's missing.'

'I don't know...'

'I do.'

'Then I'm glad,' I say, smiling. 'But go at any time, if you need to, OK?'

'OK,' he smiles back.

The Manhattan skyline on top of the fridge slowly turns into the Dublin skyline as the medicine bottles steadily reduce in number with every passing week. It's the season to be jolly. We've got a taller tree than usual, spent a fortune on decorations, Santa's being particularly generous this year. My mother and father are introducing Charlie to Scalextric. Mary has presented me with an agenda of Christmas shopping, crib visiting and carol singing that would floor an athlete – we'll have to organise a pared down version. Jack is coming over, Christmas Day. He invited us to his, but it's better for us to stay here, so I switched the invitation round. It'll be good to have company.

Dave has left for New York. He got an ultimatum, which he wasn't going to give in to, until I convinced him that there was no point losing his future for a few days. When the bad news started to arrive, I kept it from him. My parents: not a match. Mary: not a match. Jack: not a match. Though the chances were minuscule, each was as devastated as the one before. Not true – my mother took it particularly badly. And for a brief second, I might have loved her for it but I controlled that. She has given up politics and has been to see Charlie every day. High achiever that she is, her gaming skills are now exceptional. She and her grandson send regular emails to Mark and Dave. She seems to have developed a sense of humour.

I'm getting quietly desperate now. Christmas week and no news from Simon. The results must be back. I debate repeatedly about whether or not to call. In the end, I do.

'Simon, hi, it's Jenny. Just calling to wish you Happy Christmas.'

'Happy Christmas, Jenny. How are you?'

'Fine.'

'How's Charlie?'

'Very excited. He needed something to look forward to, get excited about.'

'I can imagine.'

'Have you heard anything, Simon?'

Silence. Then: 'Jenny, I was going to wait until after Christmas to tell you.'

My heart sinks. 'Then it's bad news.'

'I'm afraid so, Jenny. I'm sorry.'

Slowly, quietly, I put the phone down, sink to the floor and ignore it when it rings. He was my last hope. The phone keeps ringing. I hardly hear it. Just sit here thinking, *why does it always have to be bad news, time after time after time?* I can't get up. I can't do anything.

This is it. I. Give. Up.

But you can't give up when you've a kid because they won't let you. There's a loud bang on the door. The kind of bang Charlie makes when he comes home after being out for the day. They're back. I jump up, run to the sink, splash cold water on my face.

The bell rings.

I dry my face and hurry to the door.

'Hello,' chirps Mary but stops when she sees my face. 'Come on, boys,' she says loudly. 'Let's see what's on the telly.'

She puts them sitting in front of it.

In the kitchen, she makes coffee, strong stuff.

'OK. Tell me what's going on.'

'Simon isn't a match.'

'When did you hear?'

'Just now.'

'OK.' She thinks for a moment. 'It's a knock back...But...let's think of our next step.'

'There is no next step. I've run out of people.'

'What about the register?'

'What about it?' I ask glumly. 'Does it even freaking exist?'

'All right. You've had enough. I know. And I don't blame you. But I've been thinking about this, right, about what we'd do if no one we knew turned out to be a match. And I've come up with an idea. You're a journalist, right? You can reach people. Thousands of people, through the paper. Start your own campaign.'

I look up.

'Ask people to help. Set up your own register.'

'Could I?'

'I don't see why not? Someone out there has to have the right tissue.'

I start to brighten. 'Jack! Jack would help, I know he would.'

'You see, there you go, that's the attitude.'

'I could write an article about what we've been through. People would want to help. I know they would.'

'Definitely, they just need to know.'

I jump up, already thinking ahead. I've a mission now, something I can actually do. Jack will help; I know he will.

The phone starts to ring.

'D'you want me to get it?' Mary asks.

'No. It's OK. Thanks.'

She smiles. 'Atta girl.'

'Jenny? It's Simon.'

'I'm not talking to you anymore.'

Silence.

'All you do is ruin my life.'

More silence.

'When are you going to give me some good news?'

'I'm sorry Jenny, I...'

'I'm joking, Simon.'

Another pause. 'You have a point, though.'

'No. It's OK. I've recovered.'

'You sure? I was worried. I was going to call over.'

'I'm fine. I'm usually better at handling the disappointments. It's just that you were the last in a long line of hopefuls.'

'I know. Which was why I was going to wait till after Christmas.'

'I always prefer to know where I stand, Simon. It helps me think of other options.'

'We have the register.'

'Excuse me, Simon, but shag the register. I'm going one better. I'm going to start a campaign.'

'A campaign?'

'Yes, to get people to donate samples.'

'I see.'

'Would that be OK? Could we do something like that? If people want to give blood to be tested, could the hospital deal with it?'

'I don't know. I'd have to check. But in fairness, it's extremely unlikely that any such recruits would prove to be a match for Charlie.'

'But could you check, Simon, please? Just check to see if we could do it.'

'I'll look into it.'

'Great, thanks.'

Pat calls to the house. 'Just passing,' she says.

I don't believe her. In any case, I don't need her. I'm a woman with a mission now. Try and stop me.

thirty-one

Christmas Day, I'm woken at four to find something hard being shoved under my nose. It's a remote control car. A tiny hand grabs mine and drags me into the sitting room. I switch on all the winky lights, turning the apartment into a fairyland. Santa got it right.

Later, we go to Mass, say hello to 'baby Jesus' who arrived in the crib overnight, then share the first half of the morning with Mary and family. The older boys get 'really cool stuff', which reminds Charlie of Mark. We text him Happy Christmas. He calls Charlie back. My son's face shines brighter than any decoration. All is well with his hero.

It's back home at noon, for my parents. It's a Christmas miracle. We actually get on. Without effort. And something in my heart melts to see the way they fuss over Charlie. My father jigs him up and down on his knee and I remember him doing that with me. He calls him Poppet and Sweet pea, like he used to do with his own daughter. I'd forgotten. He chases Charlie with his dentures, letting them clap loosely together. Clack, clack, clack. Charlie runs away screaming, like I used to do. It's weird. But good weird.

After three, Jack arrives. We open presents. Pull crackers. Slide on paper hats (Jack, silver; Charlie, yellow; me, purple). We gobble up turkey, Brussels sprouts, roast potatoes. Chat, laugh. Take photos. Sing *Jingle Bells*. And smile at Charlie's alternative version of the song. Before we make it to dessert, he falls asleep, sitting back in his chair. I carry him to bed, tuck him in and send silent thoughts to Great, Jessica and Dave.

'I haven't forgotten you. Happy Christmas.'

I switch on his globe and swirl it, watching the world go round. Making my way back to Jack, I think about the day we've just had and smile. For one whole day, I managed to forget.

Jack and I are mellow now, me stretched out on the couch, him sitting low in an armchair, legs sprawled comically, looking like he could slide off. I'm drinking Baileys. Guinness for him.

'I never gave you your present,' he says.

'Jack! You brought wine, pudding, that disgusting electric tarantula, the snake that glows in the dark, the Lego set...'

'OK, if you don't want it, I'll just put it back.'

I smile.

He hands me an envelope.

Vouchers, I think.

I open it up. Vouchers alright. Airline vouchers.

'Jack!'

'Jenny.'

'Jack.'

'Jenny.'

'What are you up to?'

'Nothing.'

'You can't go spending that kind of money.'

'I didn't. The airline keeps sending me freebies. We're always plugging them.'

'But I can't go. Not with Charlie. He's still on chemo.'

'It's open. Go when it's all sorted. You'll need it.'

I start to get a little teary. 'Why are you so good to us?'

'Why wouldn't I be?'

'I don't know, it's just that you've been so great since Charlie got sick. I mean, really great.'

'I got a bit of a shock. That's all. It made me think. And sure, I'm not doing much.'

'Well, I appreciate the "not much" you are doing. You've been amazing. And the way you go on.'

'What d'you mean?'

'About being useless with kids. Charlie's mad about you.'

'Is that right?' He smiles.

We sit quietly for a while. I scratch a stain on the couch.

'Jen?'

'Yeah?' I look up.

He's sitting up, slouch gone. He's looking at me intently.

'What is it?' I ask, concerned.

'I have a child.'

'What?'

'I have a son. His name is Alan. He's fifteen.'

I can't believe it. 'How come you haven't mentioned him before?'

'You're the first person I've told.'

I don't know what to say.

'I walked out on them. Alan, his mother. Left as soon as I heard she was pregnant. I wasn't ready. For any of it. To be a father. To be tied to one person forever, no matter how great she was. I did an awful thing. I asked her how she knew it was mine. The oldest trick in the book.'

'Could it have been anyone else's?'

'No. That's the awful thing.'

'Did you love her?'

'I don't know. I might have told her I did. But we hadn't made any big plans. We were just plodding along, enjoying the craic.'

'Were you going out long?'

'Six months or so. She was a gorgeous girl, Jenny. She didn't deserve that. She'd never been with anyone else. She knew I knew that. I should have stuck by her. I should have. But I didn't. You should have seen her face. The way she looked at me. Like she couldn't believe it was really me saying those words. She said as much. She was so angry. Told me she was a fool to have ever loved me, that she never wanted to see me again. I admired her for that. Almost gave in. Wish I had. A friend of ours looked after her, was very good to her. When Alan was born, he married her. Never spoke to me again.'

'Do you ever see Alan?'

'No... If he knows about me at all, he probably hates me.'

'You don't know that.'

'His mother hates me.'

'Do you know where they live?'

'Yes.'

'Would you like to get in touch?'

'I couldn't.'

'But you would like to?'

'Only if I thought it would do some good.'

'Do you?'

'I don't know. If he got to know me, grew to like me, maybe. If I could help him, in some way, to become a man. That's what I'd like. To be part of his life, have a role, even a small one. He's in Junior Cert, this year. D'you know what I'd love? To be able to help him with his exams, English maybe. They do media studies, don't they?'

'I don't know.'

'Know what else I'd love? To cheer him on at rugby. To say, "come on, son".' His voice softens. 'I sometimes go to see him play, hide in the crowd. He is captain of the team, you know.' The pride in his voice brings tears to my eyes. 'But it's been fifteen years. I can't just land myself on him and expect him to care about what I want. I'd only mess things up for him.'

'But maybe he does know about you. Maybe he'd like to know you. Maybe he's wondering why you left. Maybe he blames himself. Maybe he's like Charlie, always wondering about his father, longing to see him.'

'Is Charlie like that?'

'All the time.'

'Even though he's only four?'

'Yes, Jack.'

'But Alan has another father, who has been there from the beginning. It's different.'

'Maybe. I don't know. Fifteen years. It sounds a lot but is it, I mean, in a whole lifetime? Not compared to all the years you could have together.'

He doesn't look convinced.

'Look at it another way, then. What if he gets leukaemia? What if he has it right now and doesn't know it? What if he only has two more years left? Don't look at me like that. It happens. I should know. You might've only two years left to get to know Alan. Can you waste any time? You get one life, Jack. One. You made a mistake, don't let your whole life become one. If you regret what you did, do something about it.'

'Jesus.' He is running the palms of his hands along his trouser legs.

'Maybe if you'd asked someone else, they'd tell you forget it, it's not worth the hassle. But you've asked me. And if there's one thing I know it's that there's no point wasting time.'

'But it's not just about me. It's about the boy, and what he wants.'

'So find out what he wants. Quietly, behind the scenes, if you can.'

'I don't want to open a Pandora's Box.'

'Jack. Live life. While you have it. That's all I'm going to say. No actually, it's not. I think you'd make a great father.'

'You do in your arse.' He laughs.

'I absolutely do. You always get it right with Charlie. You always know what he wants, you understand him.'

'That's because he's a lad.'

'Just as well you've a boy then.' I smile. 'Now get up and pour me another Bailey's.'

When Jack has gone, I sit on the couch, thinking. About the male point of view, the father, something I've happily ignored for years. I think of Dave and I'm glad we did the paternity test. And sorry we waited this long. I've always seen Charlie as mine. But that's not the case. Charlie has a dad, who deserves a chance to know him, get involved, be there. If he wants. If it's Dave, Charlie will benefit so much. If Simon, well, we carry on as normal. We don't lose anything.

At midnight, I sit down to write my article about Charlie, about our battle with leukaemia. I keep it simple, pared down. No frills. And yet, I know it will move people. Getting it down helps, giving structure to what has happened. I can look at it from the outside now, detach myself. It helps me focus on what I need to do. I save the article and go to bed feeling like I've achieved something. I'll edit it tomorrow.

Two days after Stephen's Day, I ring Simon to see if he's heard back from hospital administration. He hasn't, so I still don't know if the hospital will test samples donated by people as part of my campaign. My impatience must come across because he talks about proper channels, about dealing with administration as probably the most frustrating part of his job and about negotiation. Oh, and about it taking time and the likelihood of finding an ultimate match being extremely unlikely.

I wonder if I can bypass the hospital. At two in the morning, I think of it. The solution. There is a register already in existence, a system in place. Surely, it must be possible to enrol more people to join it. It's so simple I wonder why I didn't think of it sooner. *We could do that, surely? Increase the size of the register. Everyone would win.* I leap out of bed and rush to my laptop. I search the website of Ireland's bone marrow support group for details on how to join the register. I find what I'm looking for, jot down the contact number, then open up my article and insert it. I e-mail the piece to Jack and cross my fingers. If this works, people will read our story and join the register. Not everyone, of course, but even a few more donors will make a difference, if not to Charlie, then to someone else who is waiting, hoping. I go back to bed and have the best night's sleep I've had in ages.

thirty-two

The morning of 25th January is as bleak as they come. I'm putting up surprise balloons, Happy Birthday banners and streamers for Charlie, who is over at Dara's, when the call comes through. Simon. He wants to come over. Why, he won't say. He sounds upbeat. Which is odd. It's his wife's anniversary.

He's grinning when I open the door. I've never seen him grin before. It's kind of weird.

'We've found a match!' he announces before he even steps inside. When he does, it's to grab me in such a tight grip that I stop breathing. Sausage goes berserk, barking as if I'm being attacked.

'Down, Sausage, down.'

When he sees it's Simon, he relaxes, snuffles back to the fire, winding down his tail-wags with each swing.

Simon lets me go.

I'm laughing. And crying. 'I'm sorry. I'm just so happy. I can't believe it…Are you sure?'

He's smiling and nodding. 'We've done a tissue test as well as a blood test.'

'There has to be a catch.'

'No catch.'

'What kind of match is it?'

'Not perfect but good enough.'

'From the register?' *How else?*

'No, Jenny. Can we sit down?'

'Of course, sorry. Come in.' I close the door behind him and follow him into the sitting room, all the time thinking, *who? If not from the register, then who could it be? Everyone was negative. Have I forgotten someone who was tested and didn't get results? I go through the list. Mary? No. My parents? No. Jack? No. Dave? No. Me? No. Simon? No. Well, who, then? No one else was tested. Unless we got a false negative.*

He sits on the couch.

I perch on the edge of a tub chair.

'It's Debbie,' he says.

'Debbie? But *how*? She wasn't tested.'

'Actually,' he pauses. 'She was. She volunteered. Coming up to Christmas, she was missing her mum. It's never a great time for us. She started asking about leukaemia, about Charlie, about his chances. I explained about the Philadelphia Chromosome and that Charlie needed a bone marrow transplant and that we weren't having much luck finding a donor. I wasn't in great form myself because I'd just found out I wasn't a match.' He sighs. 'Anyway, Debra wanted to be tested. She was adamant. She has always felt guilty that she couldn't help her mother in some way and was very down about not being able to visit Charlie in hospital. This was something she could do. It was important to her. I was afraid she'd get her hopes up so I was straight about her chances of being a match. That's when she decided to do it anonymously. She didn't want you to get your hopes up either, especially after all the disappointments you've had.'

I touch my heart. Can barely speak. 'She's so amazing. You must be so proud.'

He smiles.

'Does she understand what she has to go through, though?'

'Yes and she'll have counselling.'

'Actually, what *does* she have to go through?'

'She'll have an anaesthetic, then some of her bone marrow will be removed. It's important to get enough cells, so it's good that Debra is bigger than Charlie. She'll be out of hospital in twenty-four hours and will be sore for a day or two. The biggest challenge is usually psychological. But her expectations are realistic, and as I say, she'll have counselling.'

'So, she should be OK?'

'I think it will be good for her, Jenny. As for Charlie, it's a very simple procedure, the marrow is just injected into his Freddie, and it finds its own way home to where the bone marrow was.'

'Will it be completely gone?'

He nods. 'We have to kill it before the transplant, using radiation and chemotherapy. That will take a week. Charlie will be very weak and vulnerable during this time, Jenny.'

'But it's our only hope?'

He nods.

'Well, then, we have to do it. And we have to tell Charlie.'

'Where is he?'

'At his friend's house.'

'Well, when the time is right, we can tell him. Together if you like, the way we told him about his diagnosis.'

'First I need to know more about what's going to happen.'

'I'll arrange a meeting with Stephanie, the transplant coordinator. She'll take you through everything, answer anything you need to know.'

'I can't believe it's actually going ahead. I have to ring Deb and thank her.'

He smiles. 'It will give her a boost. Especially today. She'll need good news today.'

'Poor Deb. I'm so grateful. So incredibly grateful... '

'She'll be delighted to hear that.'

'When do you think the transplant could go ahead?'

'We'll have to queue. Then, when we have a slot, we'll take Charlie in for a week of chemo and radiation. He'll have to have the radiation at St Matthew's Hospital. So there will be a bit of to-ing and fro-ing. He'll need to be in isolation to protect him, Jenny, because his defences will be completely down.'

'You said he'll be in hospital for six weeks?'

He nods. 'And no school for nine months. He'll be on medication to stop his body rejecting the transplanted cells. Have you thought about what you'll do with Sausage?'

'God, no, I hadn't.'

'He'll need to be away for nine months.'

'Right. OK. I'll sort something out. '

'We could…'

'You've done enough, thank you, Simon. Honestly. I'll work something out. So, this is it. What we've been waiting for.'

He smiles 'Yes.'

I could kiss him. I could definitely kiss him. I push that thought from my mind. Another one replaces it. *Does Debbie being a match mean that Simon is Charlie's father? Or is it just a coincidence?* I sit staring at him. But I can't ask. It's almost six weeks since we did the test. I can wait. Actually, I'm not sure I want to know.

I ring everyone. Dave, first. Then Mary, my mother and Jack. With each phone call, it becomes more and more a reality. The euphoria is contagious. When they arrive for Charlie's party, the mood is celebratory. Everyone suddenly upbeat. Even Charlie notices.

'Everyone's so happy that it's my birthday!'

I look around and realise the absence of children around him. Just Dara. But that will change. Everything will return to normal. It will take time but once this transplant is over, we can work towards building a normal life.

I open the door. A smiling Debbie bursts in and throws herself at me, then jumps up and down. I'm laughing.

'I can't believe it,' she says, eventually letting go. 'It's so amazing, isn't it?'

'Thank you so much, Debbie. You've no idea how much this means to us.'

'Where is he?'

'In the sitting room with his birthday presents. But Deb...' I say, stopping her from rushing ahead.

'Yes?'

'He doesn't know about needing a transplant yet. We didn't want to tell him until we found a donor.'

'Well, here I am,' she beams.

'Yes, but we should probably wait for your Dad to tell him. He's very good at talking to kids about these things, explaining honestly but in a way that they don't worry. I was glad he was there when we had to tell Charlie about having leukaemia.'

'Oh, OK, Sure,' she says, sounding disappointed.

'It's just that Charlie will need to go through some intense treatment beforehand and we need to explain this. And we need to explain about having to wait a little while. But, you know, I bet when he hears it's your marrow he's getting, he'll be thrilled.'

She smiles again. 'Maybe I could be there when you tell him?'

'I think that's a great idea,' I say with conviction, but then wonder how we might do that if Deb doesn't want to come to the hospital.

'This is the best day. I was so depressed. It's my mum's anniversary. But then, Dad told me the news. And suddenly it felt like a new day. I can do something for somebody after all. It's the best thing that could have happened today, you know?'

I smile. 'Your dad must be so proud of you. And your mum.'

She blushes.

'Come on, let's go in to see the birthday boy,' I say, putting my arm around her.

thirty-three

Our GP's surgery is like countless others, clean, neutral, just bigger than small, with desk, doctor and plinth. Dr Finnegan's desk is probably tidier than most but does support the obligatory prescription pads, handkerchiefs, stickers, clock and calendar, all sponsored by pharmaceutical companies.

Dave and I sit on one side, Dr Finnegan, the other. She is by no means lounging but compared to us she is, our spines as erect as, well, one of Charlie's standing pencils. We take up the front third of our chairs. I have my clammy hands pinned between my knees. Dave has his tucked under his armpits.

She reaches across the desk to hand me an envelope that I see has already been opened.

'The results come addressed to me,' she explains. 'Registered mail. I have to open it. Some cases can be sensitive or difficult, that's why they like GPs or solicitors to give the news.'

I examine the front of the envelope. URGENT PATHOLOGY REPORT, addressed to Dr Finnegan.

'Would you like to take it home and read it in private?' she asks.

'Yes,' Dave says.

'That's fine.' She stands and extends her hand. 'If you've any questions, or want to talk about it, just give me a ring.'

Passing a bin on the street outside, I'm tempted to fling it in. Leave everything the way it is. Safe. Not knowing. We reach the car and sit in. Look at each other.

'Ready?' he asks.

'No.' I laugh, nervously.

'Want me to open it?'

'No...I'll do it.'

I take a breath, look down at it, then up at Dave. This will change everything.

I take out the yellow sheets of paper. Heart pounding, I unfold them. I stare at the words, black and definite. I flick to the second and third pages to see if there's anything else. It's just legal jargon. I already know all I need to. Wordlessly, I hand it to Dave. His eyes follow the words. He takes an audible breath. He looks up. I will his eyes to meet mine. Instead he looks straight ahead.

'Dave?'

He doesn't answer.

'Dave?'

'Yeah?'

'What're you thinking?'

'You know what? I'm going to walk back,' he says, handing the document back to me, avoiding eye contact.

'But it's freezing. And it's at least two miles.'

'Yeah I just want to be on my own for a bit, OK?'

'OK. But you are coming back to the apartment, aren't you?'

'Yeah. Yeah. I'll see you later.'

I watch him go. Hands stuffed deep into the pockets of his navy reefer jacket, black-capped head down, shoulders forward against the cold. I look back down at the document I've ended up holding and feel like tearing it into confetti. Now, too late, I understand what Jack meant about a Pandora's Box. We have disturbed everything. There is no going back. I know who Charlie's father is. And I'm disappointed. I try to be positive, tell myself the news is good. I was right not to marry Dave, expect him to accept a son that wasn't his. But that's rubbish because I know that if we'd stayed together, Dave would have been a father to Charlie, a real father, been a presence in his life, loved him as a son. Now, Charlie has nothing more than he has always had – an anonymous and absent dad. So Charlie loses. And Dave loses. He wanted it. I know he did. I turn on the engine to clear the condensation.

I'm not going to sit here, getting upset. But I don't know where to go. I'm not ready to face Mary, who's minding Charlie. She'll want to know the result. So I just drive, without a destination. Until I find myself parked outside my old home.

My mother opens the heavy door of the period house.

'Oh, Jenny, it's you. How wonderful. This is a surprise. How are you? Where's the little man?' She sticks her head out as though trying to find his hiding place.

'He's at Mary's.'

'Oh. Well, come in, love,' she says and I know she's wondering what has brought me here without Charlie, the only reason we've been seeing each other again. 'Your father has just popped to the shops to get a few chops for dinner. He won't be long.'

'You've him well trained.'

She looks at me quickly as if trying to tell if I'm being sarcastic. She says nothing, though.

I follow her through the hall. It hasn't changed. Same pale blue used-to-be-plush carpet, same wallpaper (the type you get in country homes – beige with pale pink rustic scenes), same matching curtains. Same smell. Not one you can pin to anything specific, just the smell of home.

She waves a hand as she walks. 'Ignore the décor. It's my next project.'

'It's nice as it is,' I say, suddenly not wanting it changed.

Another sarcasm check from her.

Am I really that bad?

She offers me coffee.

'Let's have it in the conservatory,' she suggests. 'You go on ahead. I'll be there in a sec. No sugar, lots of milk, or have you changed?'

'Nope, same as ever.' I continue on into the conservatory. I don't feel like sitting, so I wander around checking the names on the plants, filling her little red watering can with the long spout and starting to water. It's automatic. I used to do this when I was left to potter around on my own in the house as a child. It was the one thing I liked. She noticed, appreciated it, I remember.

Of course, I stopped as soon as the poor-little-rich girl routine kicked in.

Every action designed to annoy. Nothing to please.

I trip over something, stumble and grab the arm of a wicker chair. I look down. It's a heap of books, stacked up beside the chair. I bend down to sort the books back into a pile. That's when I notice what they are. Books on leukaemia, living with cancer, communicating with people who have cancer, medical encyclopaedias. I pick one up, flick through it. She has underlined and made notes beside chunks of text. I remember her doing this to newspapers on the rare occasion I was allowed into her office. I hear her coming now and look up.

'I see you've found my light reading.' She's smiling as she carries in the coffee on a tray.

'You've been busy,' I say, putting it back.

'You know me, have to keep on top of things.'

'Any good?'

'They've answered a lot of my questions.'

It hadn't struck me that she'd *have* questions, but of course she must have. And she must have gone through the same uncertainty I did, but with no one to talk to, no one to ask.

'You should have asked,' I say.

'I didn't want to get in the way. And anyway, the books are fine. Funnily enough, I like the psychology ones, though I'd never any time for that kind of thing in my former life. You know, I never thought I'd survive without politics but I have to say I'm learning more than I've learnt in a long time.'

'Charlie helps.'

She smiles. 'I've never known so much technology. Your father and I play chess on the laptop now. He wouldn't admit it but he likes the hints the computer gives him.' She chuckles as if fond of him. Which, I have to admit, she always was.

'Dave isn't Charlie's father,' I blurt. Don't know why. 'I know you never wanted us to split up. I know you thought I was a fool but there was a reason. Now you know it.'

Her face is totally, surprisingly, relaxed. 'What I think of Dave is not important. I was wrong to interfere. I know that now. Your life is your life. All I saw was the surface of it. I didn't know you then, though I thought I did. I didn't understand your point of view, your reasons. I just thought you were throwing everything good away like you did when you were a teenager. But I was wrong, Jenny. We're different, you and I. And I'm very proud of you, the way you've brought Charlie up on your own. You're stronger than I'd have been. And he is a wonderful child, a special child. Thank you for allowing us to see so much of him.'

'He loves you,' I say simply. Because it's true.

'And we love him.' She reaches for a hankie.

'It's alright,' I say but keep my distance.

'I know, I know, I'm sorry, just a silly old woman.'

'You're not old. Or silly,' I quickly add, in case she thinks I'm making a point.

'I could be worse, I suppose.' She smiles.

'Look, I'm sorry for keeping Charlie from you. I just didn't think it would be good for him. I see her hurt expression and add, 'Obviously, I was wrong. You've really helped him; you were there when he needed you.'

'Thank you, Jenny.'

'Do you want to know who Charlie's father is?'

'Only if you want to tell me.'

I tell her about Brussels, about Simon. She listens in silence.

'What should I do?' I ask, finally.

'It's up to you. If there's one thing I've learned it's that I don't know what's best for you. You do.'

'But if you were me, what would you do?'

'I don't know, Jenny. What do you want?'

'What do you mean?'

'What do you want from Dave? What do you want from Simon?'

'I don't know. Nothing.'

She throws me a be-honest-now look.

I take a deep breath, let it out slowly. 'I just want Dave to be happy. I'm sorry for dragging him over, upsetting his life – for nothing.'

'And Simon?'

'I don't know. Well, actually I know what I would *like*. But I also know it's impossible.'

'What?'

'I'd like him to be a presence in Charlie's life. No, more than that. I'd like him to be a father to him. Charlie would so love to know his father. And he likes Simon already. It's important for boys to have a father figure. But that will never happen. Even if I tell Simon he's Charlie's father, that's where it will end. He can't be a father to Charlie, not publicly. He has a daughter – who really doesn't need to know her father was unfaithful to her mother. Her dead mother. Even though it wasn't like that. How could she possibly understand – and why should she have to? She's fifteen.'

'You can't control other people's actions. Maybe all you can do is give them the truth and see how they handle it. At least Dave knows. That's good.'

'Charlie will miss him so much.'

'We'll be here for Charlie.'

'I know.'

'And if Simon wants nothing to do with Charlie, there's nothing you can do about that either. But you can tell him. And you've nothing to lose in doing so – he already knows there's a chance. You'd just be clearing the uncertainty.'

'I know.' I sigh. 'Poor Dave, though.'

'Maybe not. Maybe Dave is better off in the States, starting out in marriage with no strings.'

'Yeah.' I look at her. 'You've a pretty clear head.'

'I'd want to have. The bullshit I've had to put up with for thirty years. How did I ever get into politics?'

'You loved it.'

'You know, I never stopped to think about that. I just got caught up in it.'

'You talk like it's addictive.'

'That's exactly what it is. I'm glad I'm out of it. You've done me a favour. And Jenny? I'm sorry. For everything.'

'I know.'

'Friends?'

'Friends.'

'Hug?'

I smile. And hug her. She's alright. Maybe it was me, or a clash. I don't know, but I'm so glad it's over.

thirty-four

I drive by the apartment on my way to Mary's. The light is on in the sitting room. Dave's back. I need to know what he's thinking. Feeling. Planning. We won't be able to talk once Charlie's home. So I park and go up. Wanting to get there, but not.

'Hey,' he says, from the couch.

I throw my coat on a chair. 'Hey.'

'Where were you?'

'My mother's.'

He looks surprised but lets it go.

'You OK?' I ask.

He nods.

I sit beside him. 'Well?'

'Well, what?'

'I want to know how you feel about it, Dave.'

'I thought you knew how I felt. I thought you knew what I wanted.'

'But did you want it? Really, Dave? Think about it. Sickness, uncertainty, maybe...worse? Who would want that? Your life will be so much simpler, happier. Back to the States, getting on with it. No guilt. No strings.'

'Maybe I wanted strings.'

'Living with cancer...'

'You think I can just walk away from him now?'

I look at him.

'We should never have done that stupid test.'

'I did it for you.'

'And I did it for you.'

'Oh God.' *Stupid, bloody Fiona.*

'I didn't want to know,' he says. 'I just wanted to help. Be there for you. I told you, five years ago, I didn't want to know. I was committed to *you*.'

'But it must have mattered, subconsciously...'

He slaps his hand down on the couch. 'I would have been a good father. It would have been easy – he's such a great kid. I knew he would be. He's yours.'

Welling up, I look down at my hands.

'Maybe we could get it back?'

I look up. 'What d'you mean?'

'Marry me, Jenny.'

'What?' I ask quietly.

'Marry me. Let's be a family.'

'What about Fiona?'

'Fiona.' He sighs. 'I've seen a different side to Fiona. It's so easy when everything's light and it's all socialising and parties and fun. But I've seen her with you. And I've seen her with Charlie. She has no warmth. No understanding of what you're going through. She sees everything from her own point of view.'

'She's young.'

'Maybe.'

'Dave.' I put my hand on his.

'That's a no.'

'No, it's not a no, but it's not a yes. I've so much to think about now. So much to do. With the transplant.'

'I see.'

'Dave, I'm being honest. It's not a no. It's just, I can't think about anything else, right now, anything but the transplant. And I don't expect you to wait around either. You've done enough of that.'

'But you will think about it?'

'Of course, I will. But I want you to think about it too. Take time to. Away from us. You're reacting to the news. It's a shock, a disappointment. But maybe, in time, you'll realise it's for the best. Maybe you don't need this in your life.'

'Maybe I do.'

'Go back to New York, Dave. Think about what you'd be taking on...'

'I know what I'd be taking on.'

'I can't promise you anything. Not now, Dave. Not yet.'

'I understand. I have to go back to talk to Fiona. I have to end it...and in a week or two, I'll come back – if she doesn't murder me. Will you call me when the transplant is going ahead? I'll be over on the first plane.'

'You don't have to do that.'

'I want to.'

I know what it would mean to Charlie. 'Are you sure?'

'Jenny, I want to be with you, care for you, for Charlie. It's what I want. So don't feel guilty about it. It's what I want to do. OK? '

'I don't deserve you,' I say, hugging him.

'You go get Charlie. I'll make dinner.'

Mary and I are in her kitchen, out of earshot. She's looking at me like she's dying to know.

'It's Simon,' I tell her.

'Simon.'

'You sound surprised.'

'I thought, because it was a one-off thing and you were in a relationship with Dave... Who did *you* think it was?'

'I didn't want to think. But I kind of hoped it was Dave. He's been so amazing, so good to Charlie.'

'They both have.'

'Simon is his doctor. He kind of has to be.'

'No. He doesn't.'

'But Dave wanted it. He'd have been proud to be Charlie's dad. Can you imagine what that would have meant to Charlie? Especially now. These could be his last months, Mary.' Because no one's saying it but the transplant might fail.

'Don't talk like that,' Mary says firmly. 'We've got a donor. At last. After all our worrying.'

'I know.'

'And maybe Simon will surprise you.'

I smile. 'Even if he wanted to, he can't.' I explain about Debbie.

She goes quiet for a second. Then: 'Crap. I hadn't thought of that.'

'Maybe it doesn't matter.'

'What d'you mean?'

'He asked me to marry him.'

'*Simon?*'

'No. Dave. How did you even think Simon?'

'I've seen the way he looks at you.'

'You say that about everybody.'

'No, I don't.'

'Yes, you actually do.'

'We're getting away from the point. When did this happen?'

'Just now.'

'Oh my God. And?'

'I said I'd have to think about it.'

'What's there to think about?'

'The fact that this could just be a reaction to the news, the disappointment.'

'You think?' she asks doubtfully.

'I don't know. I don't even know what I feel. I don't know if I love him.'

'He's gorgeous, helpful, loves Charlie, has been so good to you...'

'And I don't want all those things to confuse me. I have to ask myself, honestly, do I love Dave, the person, not Dave the friend, the carer? And if I do, would I need to ask? And anyway how can I even think about this now?'

'So what did you say to him?'

'I told him I couldn't think about it till after the transplant. I told him to go back to the States...'

'Go back to the States?' she asks like I'm mad.

'He has to anyway. He says he's going to end it with Fiona.'

She gives me a look that says, 'this is significant.' Then she frowns. 'What if he changes his mind when he's over there? What if she works on him?'

'At least then I'll know it was a reaction and he should be with her.'

'I need another coffee.' She gets up and puts on a fresh pot.

'Make it strong.'

She does.

'So,' she says when she sits back down. 'Are you going to tell Simon he's Charlie's dad?'

'I don't know.'

'You should.'

I'm suddenly angry. 'Why? If I'm supposed to rush off and marry Dave, why tell Simon?'

'He knows you've done the test,' she says simply. 'He'll want to know.'

'Maybe he won't. Did you ever think of that, maybe he won't want to know at all. And does it really matter when it's not going to make a difference anyway?'

'How do you know it won't?'

'Look, the man has made it clear he wants nothing to do with me. And that's fine. Fine. I'm not giving him any opportunity to think I want his involvement in any way.'

'When?'

'When what?'

'When did he say he doesn't want anything to do with you?'

I start to blush. 'After Jessica's funeral,' I say quietly.

Suddenly, she's hyper alert. 'I knew something had happened between you.'

I sigh. And tell her. She'd only drag it out of me anyway.

'Why didn't you tell me?'

'I wanted to forget it.'

'So he *does* like you.'

I shake my head. 'It meant nothing.'

'D'you really think he'd have had sex with you if he didn't like you?'

'He did before. When he didn't even know me.'

'That was different, his wife…'

'It wasn't different. He was upset both times.'

'Yes but he said, "If things were different…"'

Why did I tell her that? 'But things aren't different. And anyway, it's so easy to say stuff like that, it's a typical wimpy cop-out used by people all the time.'

'Well, I think you should tell him. And I don't think you should send Dave off to the States. Honestly, Jen, sometimes I believe you don't want a man at all.'

'I don't. I want a father for Charlie. And it looks like that's never going to happen now.'

'Not if you can help it.'

'You see, this is why I don't tell you things.'

'I'm just being honest. You don't do yourself any favours, Jen. You never trust people to come up to the mark. Sometimes they do – if you just give them the chance. Now, come here and give me a hug.'

'You are so bossy.'

She smiles. 'I know.'

'I will kill you some day, you do realise this?'

'Impossible.'

'Why impossible?'

'You love me too much.'

'Actually, I do. You've been the best friend, Mary,' I say, starting to get teary. 'You've been so good to us.'

'You know what you need? A holiday. As soon as Charlie recovers from the transplant, we're going somewhere. I don't know where yet but I've a few months to plan. Dolphins; I'm thinking, dolphins.'

'Jack's given me some vouchers.'

'Nothing stopping us then.'

Except fate.

Another day of chemo. Dave stays with us for most of it but has to go catch his flight.

'But why do you have to go?' whines Charlie.

'I have to talk to Fiona.'

'Can't you ring her?'

'Well, I have to tell her something sad and I should really be there when I tell her.'

'What?'

'You're very nosy,' says Dave, pressing his nose with a finger.

'No, I'm not. What sad thing are you going to tell her?'

Dave looks at me to see if it's OK to talk about relationship break ups.

I shrug.

He turns back to Charlie. 'I have to tell her that I don't want to be her boyfriend anymore.'

'Yes!' He punches the air.

'Charlie,' I say.

Dave laughs. 'Don't you like Fiona?'

'No, Dave.'

'Why not?'

'She doesn't smile. When are you coming back?'

'Very soon.'

'When soon?'

'Maybe next week.'

'OK. Dave?'

'Yes, Charlie?'

'Will you be looking for a new girlfriend, now?'

'I don't know, I might take a rest for a while.' He smiles at me.

'Well, when you're finished the rest, I know someone really nice. And guess what?'

'What?' Dave smiles.

'You know her already. And you like her too. And she's pretty and she's a good cook and she's great if you're sick.' He frowns. 'She doesn't smile so much anymore, but she still smiles much more than Fiona,' he adds hopefully.

'She sounds lovely, alright.' Dave smiles. 'Are you sure you don't want her for yourself?'

'Daw. I'm too small for girlfriends, Dave.'

'When I come back, you can tell me a bit more about her.'

'OK. And she might get her hair cut properly by that stage.' He sneaks a look at me.

I raise an eyebrow at him.

I walk Dave to the door. I'm already starting to feel an emptiness and he hasn't even gone. We hug and I don't want to let go. We stay like that for a long time. Until I see Simon swinging through the doors. Before I can look away, our eyes meet. He turns suddenly to say something to Dr Howard. She laughs.

'Good luck with Fiona,' I say to Dave.

'I hate letting her down. She's so focused on the wedding.'

'Then don't say anything. Go home, wait a few days and see how you feel. Then decide.'

'I'm going to do it, Jen.'

'You owe us nothing, Dave.'

'It's not about owing. I'll text you when I get there.'

'Or Skype.'

'You'll be in bed.' He holds both my hands in his. 'I'll be back.'

'I know.'

'As soon as you've news on the transplant date, call me.'

'I will, Dave, thanks.'

I watch him go until he disappears around the corner at the end of the corridor.

I return to the room and my life. He's left me with so much to think about. But I can't let myself. Not until he comes home and I see how he feels then. I do love Dave. But how much and in what way? It's not something I can think of till all this is over.

'Dave's gone,' says Charlie to Simon.

'Is he?' asks Simon, rolling up Charlie's top.

'Yeah, he's gone back to America.' Charlie helps hold up the top.

Simon just nods.

'But he won't be long. He's just going to tell Fiona that he doesn't want to be her boyfriend anymore.'

'I see,' says Simon, putting the stethoscope into his ears.

'Then he's coming back.'

'Charlie, Simon can't hear you. He's got the thing in his ears.'

He stays quiet for a moment but keeps looking at Simon, waiting to continue the news bulletin.

I wish I knew what Simon was thinking. That the results are back? That Dave's the father, not him? Why else would he be breaking off his relationship and coming home? Is Simon relieved? His professional face is on. I can't tell.

'That's a great heart you've got there, Charlie,' he says finally.

'You say that every time.'

'Well, it's true every time.'

'Can I tell you a secret?' Charlie asks him.

'I don't mind, if your Mum doesn't.'

'Charlie, secrets aren't nice.'

'Just one, Mum.'

'Alright, go on then.'

The thing about Charlie's whispering method is that it's not perfected. I hear everything. Unfortunately.

'Dave needs a new girlfriend. I think Mum would be good, what do you think?'

Simon's reply, 'I suppose that would really be up to your Mum, wouldn't it?' is directed not at Charlie, but at me. He looks at me as though daring me to decide between him and Dave. Which is ridiculous. He's not interested in me; he's made that clear. He turned himself off like a tap after the last 'mistake'. So what is he doing? What is he saying? Does he even know what he wants? Or is he just one of those men who only wants something if he thinks someone else wants it? Not for the first time, with Simon Grace, I've no idea what's going on.

'I'll have a chat with her,' whispers Charlie.

'OK, Charlie,' he says patting him gently on the shoulder and heading for the sink.

We have to stay overnight because Charlie needs a blood transfusion and the day ward is closing. We're transferred to the oncology unit, where there's a single room free. Someone is being admitted tomorrow, but we'll be well gone by the time they arrive. I'm sitting in semi-darkness with Charlie asleep beside me. It is strangely peaceful. And for once, I have time to think. To work out what Simon wants, what Dave wants, and what I'd want if they knew what they wanted. Obviously, it's a waste of time.

'Jenny?'

I jump.

'Sorry, did I frighten you?' he whispers.

'No, I just wasn't expecting anyone. I was miles away. Is everything OK?'

'Yes, fine. I just wanted to ask you something.'

'Sure.'

'Do you mind if I sit down?' *Oh crap.* 'I was just wondering,' he says, sitting without waiting for a reply, 'did you get the results of the paternity test? It's just that I've been thinking a lot about it since you told me about the possibility that, well, you know, Charlie could be my son. I'd like to know, Jenny.'

'Simon, I have the results but I think it was a mistake doing the test. It's upset things. Maybe it's best to leave everything the way it was.'

'He's my son, isn't he?'

I hesitate.

'He is, otherwise you'd have denied it already. He has to be. He was born the day Alison died.'

'That was a coincidence.'

'I don't believe that.'

If I didn't know before, I know now. He still hasn't got over his wife. 'Simon, I'm not sure that...'

'He is my son,' he says with a certainty I can't argue with.

I nod, suddenly, weary.

'Thank you. That's all I wanted. Just to know.'

We're both silent.

'Any idea where we go from here?' I ask and regret it instantly.

'We get him better,' he says with certainty.

thirty-five

Morning. Simon comes to discharge us. He sits beside Charlie and chats as if he has all the time in the world. I notice it instantly. The difference. The softness in his voice. The tenderness in his eyes. The way he slides Charlie onto his lap. The way he tilts his head to listen. Simon has always been gentle, caring. This is different. This is father and son. It shocks me. I'm not ready for it. Charlie is my son. He's always been mine. *I* make the decisions. *I* decide.

'OK, time to go,' I say, standing.

Simon looks up. He seems to understand. Lifts Charlie onto the floor.

'Well, Charles, I'll see you soon.'

'OK, Simon, see you soon.'

I feel suddenly guilty.

For the next two days, we stay home, Charlie recovering from the chemo, me painting the kitchen, cleaning out the cupboards, keeping busy, trying not to think. About Simon and what he wants or doesn't want. About Dave, who hasn't called. About Charlie and getting him through.

On the third day, Mary calls over with Dara, just back from Cork, where they were visiting her mother. The best friends busy themselves trying to save Scooby Doo from the Faceless Rider.

'Get him, get him, yeah, yeah, you got him.'

We watch from the kitchen over coffee.

'How're you doing?' Mary asks.

'He knows.'

'Who knows what?' she asks, her Cork accent returning after the visit.

'Simon knows about Charlie.'

'You told him? Good girl.'

I smile. 'You'd think I was five.'

She laughs.

'He asked, Mary. It was weird. He just seemed to know and just wanted me to confirm it.'

'How was he so sure?'

'Charlie was born the day his wife died.'

'Jesus.' She puts down her cup. 'That's spooky.'

'It's just a coincidence.'

'Actually, Jenny, it's spooky.'

'He thinks that he's been given something in place of his wife. He misses her so much, he's prepared to believe that.'

'Maybe he's right. Who knows?'

'Mary.'

'Well, we don't. Strange things happen, that's all I'll say.'

And I think of Great and the smell of roses and her inheritance arriving on her birthday.

'So what did he say when you told him?'

'Just that he knew it.'

'Did he make any commitment?'

'No. Just talked about getting Charlie better.'

'Well, that *is* the priority.'

I sigh. 'He was all over him like a rash the next day.'

'Aw, Jenny, that's sweet.'

'I didn't like it. He can't just waltz in and behave like a father. Especially when he's never going to admit it.'

'Jenny. You've done it all by yourself for so long, of course it's going to feel strange. But think of Charlie. Think of how good it will be for him.'

'What, a bit of attention? Simon will never admit to anything. Not openly. Even if he is around more, it won't be as a father to Charlie.'

'Simon's a good man, Jenny.'

'Who has his daughter to think about. And who is still in love with his wife. Anyway, it doesn't matter. I don't want anything from him. The last man who offered me something is back in the States four days and hasn't even called.'

'No.'

'Yes.'

'I told you,' she says, pointing at me.

'Doesn't help.'

'Look, don't worry. Maybe he's waiting till he has everything sorted; made the break from Fiona.'

'How long does he need?'

'You told him to take his time. Now let him.'

'I know but…'

'He's not going to rush back to Little Miss Snooty.'

'It's not about that. I just want him to call. Let me know he's OK, that's all.'

'You said yourself you can't concentrate on anything until the transplant is over. So don't.'

'You're right.' I sip my coffee. 'How was Cork?'

'You'll never guess what happened!'

'What?' I ask glad of a diversion.

'Remember we took the boys ice skating at Smithfield, two weeks ago?'

I nod, remembering the happy family scene I imagined when she told me she was going.

'And you know Phil fell?'

'No. I didn't.'

'Well, he did. Anyway, turns out he broke his elbow.'

'Oh no. When did you find out?'

'Today, when I got back.'

'Only today?'

'He had an X-ray as soon as I left for Cork. I know. I kept telling him "ah, you'll be grand; it still works doesn't it?" If it were any of the boys, I'd have had them X-rayed, straightaway. You know, he'd never even have got it looked at only for a guy in the office. After two weeks of listening to Phil moaning, he told him to shut up and get an X-ray. He'll never let me live it down.'

'So is he in a cast?'

'No, it's too late to do anything now. They'd have put it in a sling two weeks ago. But there's nothing they can do now.'

'Crap.'

'I'm mortified.'

'Well, I'm relieved. You're human after all.'

'Damn. Another fan bites the dust.'

I pass her a fresh coffee.

'Anyway, need any shopping? I'm going,' she says.

'It's going to be a bit harder than that.'

'Than what?'

'To get back up on my pedestal. A little bit of shopping, I don't know…'

'God, the pressure…'

'Oh, all right then. But you're getting away lightly.'

'Ah, thanks Jenny, you don't know how much this means to me.'

And we're laughing.

When Mary's gone, I think about ringing Dave. That's as far as I get. I don't want him to feel under pressure. I turn my attention to Charlie. We settle down, cuddle up with Sausage and read *The Gruffalo*. I can do it right now. And I know he's enjoying the togetherness. It's so easy to be with him but not *with* him.

I'm saying, 'The End,' when the doorbell rings.

'Debbie! What a nice surprise,' I say, delighted to see her, as is Sausage who has dashed out to her, barking excitedly and making pathetic but cute little jumps where all four legs lift together off the ground.

There's another surprise. Debbie's not alone. Her father's standing, a little awkwardly, to her right. And I'm stupidly blushing.

'Hi, Jenny. I hope you don't mind. I was dropping Debbie off and thought I'd just pop up to see how Charlie's doing.'

Debbie shrugs and pulls an I-couldn't-stop-him face.

'Hi, guys, come in,' shouts my son from the couch.

'Hello, son.' Simon walks straight over to him.

Does he realise what he's just said?

He sits in the exact place I've just been.

'What're you reading?' he asks, looking younger, more relaxed. Happy even? If only Charlie knew he was sitting beside his Dad.

'*The Gruffalo*. Dave bought it for me.'

There's that vulnerable expression I'm such a sucker for.

'It's very good. D'you want to read it?'

'Maybe we could do some Lego,' suggests Simon, spotting a Lego mountain on the coffee table.

'Yeah, OK. But watch me first; I know what I'm doing.'

'Righty-oh.'

Debbie looks at me as if to say, 'What's going on?'

'I think your Dad's just trying to get Charlie to feel comfortable with him so he's not as worried when it's time for the transplant.'

'You haven't told him yet?'

'No.'

'Maybe we could tell him now? Since we're all here.'

I nod. 'Let's just let them play for a while and then I'll get your dad's attention.'

'OK.'

'How are you, Deb? Nervous?'

'No. I just so want it to work.'

'It will.' As I say it, I regret it. I shouldn't get her hopes up. Charlie has only been given a sixty per cent chance of this working. If it doesn't, she'll blame herself. Donors always do.

'Did you know that after the transplant, Charlie and me will have the same DNA? Brothers and sisters don't even get that close. We'll be blood brother and sister.'

If only she knew. 'Have you spoken to the counsellor?'

'Yeah.'

'So you know it doesn't always work, Deb? Because I dont want you to be disappointed if it doesn't.'

'It will work.' She looks over at Charlie, her jaw firm.

'You're a very special girl. You're very special to Charlie and to me. I hope you know that.'

She smiles, then joins the construction site while I make refreshments for the builders.

Finally, they take a break, apart from Charlie, who's 'nearly finished'.

I talk to Simon. He is all for telling Charlie now, especially with Debbie here.

'Charlie?' he says.

Charlie glances over. 'I'm doing a great job, amn't I?'

'Great, Charlie, very creative. Charlie, we'd just like to have a chat with you about your leukaemia.'

'But I'm in the middle of this tower.'

'OK, do you want to finish that and then we can talk?'

''K'

Once the tower's complete, we all sit on the couch, Debbie with Charlie on her lap. Simon and I on either side.

'Charlie, you know what leukaemia does to the bone marrow?'

'Yeah, the bad cells kill the good cells.'

'That's right. And you know the medicine is to kill the bad cells?'

'Yup.'

'Well, we need to do something else, to help the medicine.'

'What?'

'Well, we want to give you brand new bone marrow.'

'Can you *do* that?'

'Yes, we can.'

'Well, why didn't you do it before so I wouldn't need all that medicine?'

'Good question.' He sounds proud, like a dad. 'Well, two reasons. Firstly, we had to get rid of the bad cells. Secondly, we had to find the right bone marrow.'

'Where did ye find it? In a shop?'

'You'll never guess.' Simon smiles at Debbie.

'Debbie found it?' asks Charlie.

'I have it in my body, Charlie. It's my bone marrow and I'm going to share it with you. Isn't that cool?'

'How?'

'I'm going to have, like, a bone marrow biopsy thingy so they can get it from me. And then they'll just give it to you into your Freddie.'

'Don't you need yours?'

'I'm only giving you a bit. I'll have loads left.'

'It's not nice, Deb. They make you go to sleep and you dream about space ships.'

'It's OK, Charlie. I like space ships. And I love going to sleep. It won't hurt. I'll be fine. And you know what? Afterwards we're going to have the same bone marrow. If you rob a bank, they could blame me.'

'Really? That's so cool. When can we do it?'

Debbie looks at Simon.

'In a few weeks, Charlie, but first you have to come into the hospital for a few days and have lots of medicine and things like X-rays.'

'Oh no, I don't want to.'

'I'll come in and see you every day,' says Deb.

We all look at her.

'I'm going to have to go in anyway. Might as well get used to it.'

'Will you be able to stay with me?'

'For a good while, but not all day and not at night. OK?'

'OK.'

'And I'll be there too, Charlie,' I say.

'Me too,' says Simon.

'OOOOK,' says Charlie. As if he has a choice.

And then, much quicker than I expected, we're given a date for Charlie's transplant. Ten days from now. I'm relieved and terrified at the same time. This is our only hope. Our last chance. In three days, Charlie will be admitted and his body bombarded, his bone marrow destroyed along with a host of innocent bystander cells. It's like waiting for a time bomb to explode inside my baby. Where is Dave? Why hasn't he called? He said to ring when I had the date. I've texted the date. Maybe he can't decide. Maybe he is back with Fiona and doesn't want to tell me. But maybe something's happened. Finally, I call him.

'Dave?'

'Jenny?'

'Everything OK?'

'I'm sorry, Jen. I should have called. It's just that, it's more complicated than I thought.'

I say nothing.

'Fiona didn't take it well. I'm worried about her, Jen. I'm worried she might do something, you know, stupid. It's just something she said. She's…' he lowers his voice, '…vulnerable.'

Try manipulative.

'She depends on me more than I'd realised. You're not saying much.'

'I'm listening. Go on.'

He clears his throat. 'I think maybe I need to stick around here for a bit. Fiona's very down. I can't leave her. It'd be too risky. I'd never forgive myself if anything happened.'

'Fine.' My voice is flat.

'How's Charlie?'

'Fine.'

'I'm sorry I haven't rung, Jen. It's just that I got a bit of a fright when Fiona started, you know...'

'Threatening to pop herself?'

'I don't think that's very sensitive.'

'So you're staying there, then?'

'For the moment. You don't mind?'

'Why would I mind?'

'You're strong, Jen. A coper. You don't need me.'

'You're right, I don't.'

'Don't be like that.'

'Like what?'

'Snappy.'

'I'm not being snappy. I'm being honest. I've brought Charlie up on my own. Without anyone. You're right. I *am* a coper.'

'I'm sorry.'

'What for? You don't owe us anything.'

'Jenny, it's not about owing, you know that.'

That's when I realise, that's exactly why he wanted to marry me. Owing. And guilt. I am so glad I didn't say yes.

'Are you OK?'

'Yep. Bye.' I hang up.

He calls back. 'I'll ring you.'

'I'd prefer if you didn't.' I hang up again.

He rings again.

'I'll come over soon.'

'Dave. Leave it. Please. You've made your choice. That's fine. So let's just leave it. OK?'

'I haven't made any choice. It just that...'

'I know. She needs you.'

'For now, Jen.'

'OK, listen, I've got to go. I'll talk to you, OK?' I put the phone down, close to tears. He did offer to marry me. Has he forgotten that? You can't just go around proposing to people left right and centre and then not even ring them. I know I didn't say yes. But I didn't say no either. Can't he see what she's doing? But it's OK. Because he doesn't love me. He just wants someone to need him. And I don't. He can shag bloody well off.

thirty-six

It's time to go in. Home for the next six weeks will be in an isolation room with specially filtered air. No visitors apart from Deb. And even she has to wear special clothing so that she doesn't bring germs into the room. I keep in touch with Mary, Jack and my parents by phone. I don't know what to do about Elaine, not wanting to remind her that my child is still alive. I write, tell her I'm thinking of her and that she should call me to talk, any time. I say where I am and, briefly, what's happening.

In here, I have Anne, Siobhan and Simon. There are others of course, helpful and caring in their own way, but these three people are my rocks, my lifelines, people I'd trust with my life, people I do trust with Charlie's. Unfortunately most of the time, they're on the other side of the door, mostly it's just Charlie and me. And so, the countdown begins. Fasten your seat belts, prepare for blast off. We will be in orbit for six weeks. Charlie is five. But he knows this is serious.

'Mum?'

'Yes, sweetie.'

'Would you be sad if I died?'

I look at him, shocked. 'Of course I would. I'd be so *so* sad.'

'Why?'

'Because I love you very much.'

'Do you?'

'Of course I do, you big eejit.'

He smiles.

'Would you cry?'

'I think I'd be too sad to cry.'

'Would you whine?'

'I'd probably scream.'

'Really loudly?'

'You'd hear me in Timbuktu.'

'Where, what's Timbuktu?'

'A place in Africa.'

'A dump?'

'I don't know what it's like. I think it might be like a desert.'

'Oh. And you'd hear me in, in, in, that place, if I was in Ireland and you were there?'

'Yeah.'

'Wow.'

'But Charlie.'

'Yeah?'

'You're not going to die.'

'I know Mum.'

'Good, now go to sleep, monkey.'

'Ooh, ooh.'

He has the chemo. He has the radiation. Bam. Bam. Bam. He becomes so weak he can't get out of bed. He is floppy. Lifeless. At night, he sleeps like a corpse. And most of the day. I am so scared. Simon is around constantly. Perhaps this is normal for such a sick child. Perhaps he is more attentive than he would usually be. How do I know?

He's gentler when examining Charlie now. He holds his hand

and strokes the back of it when he talks to him. He explains what's going to happen with great care, making sure Charlie understands. He talks about the future, not a future with him of, course, just a future of normality, school, hair, football. A future. The future. Something to focus on. Aim for. Strive for.

There are messages from Dave, Mary says. I don't want to know about Dave. Fiona needs him. Well, let Fiona have him and his so-called strength. I tell Mary to delete the messages.

The day comes finally. I am strong. Or so I tell myself. I'm beside Charlie all the time, holding his hand, pretending to myself that Simon is here as his father. That he has both parents with him now. Supporting him. Which he has. It's just that we're not together, not a family. But I don't see why I shouldn't have my own little fantasy, my own way of coping.

I have to wear a mask. They've told me about this but I hadn't imagined how it would hide my face so, at a time when Charlie needs familiarity so badly. My breath hot behind it, I feel I'm suffocating. I could panic. But won't. Charlie and I watch in silence as the transplant coordinator holds up a packet of Debbie's marrow, dark red, almost brown, smaller and darker than a blood transfusion, but otherwise similar. She draws it up in a giant syringe. I think of Deb and pray she's alright. The transplant coordinator, dressed in scrubs, smiles as she approaches Charlie with the syringe. I see him swallow. I smile encouragement but he can't see it. She attaches the syringe to Charlie's Freddie.

'Now, Charlie,' she says. 'This might feel a little cold, sweetheart.'

His eyes widen.

I squeeze his hand. I hold his eyes with mine. Force myself not to blink.

'You're the best boy,' I tell him over and over.

And he is. For the last few months he has put up with so much, the last week, pure torture. And now it's all over. At last. Now, all we can do is we wait. And hope. And pray that it works.

thirty-seven

After two weeks of waiting and worrying, Charlie's blood cells start to creep back up, which means that his bone marrow has kicked back into action. *Thank, You, God.* Another biopsy shows that 99% of the leukaemic cells have been killed. Better than expected. He is plagued with mouth ulcers, nausea and vomiting and has to be fed through his Freddie, but, slowly, he is beginning to regain some strength. Debbie, allowed home the day after the transplant, is on a high, and allowed to call to see him every day. We joke about the protective clothing she has to wear. She helps keep our spirits up.

Another week passes and Charlie's white cell count is high enough for them to stop isolation. The doors are opened. We can walk in and out. It's like we're human again.

We concentrate on building Charlie up. He starts to chatter again, making me realise how quiet he had become.

Week five and I'm marvelling at the resilience of children.

Tomorrow, we go home.

I'm not the same. Isolation did something. It made me think. Realise. Open my eyes. I see now how close Charlie has become to his father. And I finally admit how I feel about that father. I brighten when he walks into the room. And flatten when he leaves. Can't help it. I think of him when he's not here. Don't want to help it. I wonder what he's doing, whether or not I ever make it into his thoughts, what those thoughts are, what his dreams are, if he allows himself to dream. My heart softens to see them together, father and son. I notice things I haven't before, tiny mannerisms that he and Charlie share. The way they scratch behind their left ear when nervous, the way they breathe through their mouths when concentrating, the way they smile a little higher on the left than the right. Ever so slightly. No one would notice. Only me.

Simon, though, doesn't see me, focused only on Charlie. And that has to be enough. I'd be lying if I said I didn't dream of a cosy family unit: Simon, Jenny, Debbie, Charlie, Sausage. I've pictured it. Played around with it. Dismissed it. The first time Simon and I met, he turned my world upside down and disappeared. The second time, he didn't disappear, because he couldn't, but he would have if he'd had the choice. That is the way it is between us. Wham! Poof! When Charlie's discharged, it will be poof again.

It could be worse. I could have married Dave. I know now what was missing. What I feel for Simon. Passion, not just physical, though that's there, but an enthusiasm for everything about him – what he says, does, doesn't say, what he looks like, everything. His hands, eyes, scar, mouth with its crooked smile. His confidence. His awkwardness. His way. I wonder did I know, deep down, five years ago, what was missing from my relationship with Dave but never admitted it to myself. I wonder did something lead me to Simon back then, just in time. Maybe Simon didn't ruin my life after all. Maybe he saved it.

We leave tomorrow, prognosis good. Better than good. It doesn't mean I won't be holding my breath for the next five years. Nothing is certain. But nothing ever was, I know that now.

And maybe I appreciate things a bit more for it.

Once we go, so will our excuse to see Simon. And his excuse

to see his son. It will be over and I'll go back to writing my columns at night and minding Charlie full-time during the day. Jack's been great, as usual, setting me back up with my health column. It was the least he could do, he said, holding me responsible for giving him the push to do something about his son. Jack approached Alan's mother. After her initial shock, taking some time to think, and talking with her son, she said she wouldn't stand in Jack's way. So they met. Alan and Jack. It wasn't the great reunion that dreams are made of, but it wasn't a disaster either. And they're meeting again. For Jack, it's more than he'd ever hoped. One positive outcome from Charlie's illness.

There have been a few. My parents are part of our lives now, something I never wanted, but should have. I don't know what happened back then, loneliness, resentment, rebellion. I don't dwell on it. Point is, it took leukaemia to force me to face my mother. I'm not too proud of that. But I'm looking forward now. We've got to know each other. And I see things I never did before. A sharpness, a wicked sense of humour. But also a warmth. She is great with Charlie. And she is going to teach him. The Department of Education never agreed to home tuition. Charlie is too young, they said. My mother jumped to the rescue like an enthusiastic puppy. I'd forgotten she used to teach before becoming a politician. Even if I'd wanted to, I couldn't have stopped her. And the weird thing is, I see so much of Great in her now, the same enthusiasm for life, honesty, sense of fun, things I didn't notice when her energy was focused elsewhere. She is also going to mind Sausage for the next nine months. She keeps saying how her life has started over. She's got a second chance at it. And claims to be feeling 'light years younger'.

I hold the leukaemia responsible for something else, the friendship I have with Mary. Yes, we'd have been friends but nowhere near as close as we are. She went so far for us. That kind of friendship is special, something to treasure. And I do.

The leukaemia has helped Debbie too. By donating her marrow, she has helped beat cancer, the disease that took her mother. It's given her strength, hope. And a new blood brother. It was the leukaemia that started her talking with her father again, listening to him, communicating with him, respecting him. They have a relationship now, a good one. I know how proud he is of her.

Charlie's illness has been a nightmare but it's made me face issues I'd avoided for years. Who Charlie's father was; the fact that my mother and I had no relationship. I've changed. I face things head on, now but one step at a time, one breath at a time. If Simon wants to see Charlie, I'll be so happy. If he doesn't, I'll be gutted, but I'll cope.

Elaine rang me as soon as she got my letter. She was going through a particularly bad time and needed someone to talk to. Everyone else was shying away, afraid. All she wanted to do was talk about Jessica. Just talk and talk and talk. Keep her alive by talking. I listened. I wanted to. And in a strange way, it helped me too. Over the last six weeks we've helped each other through. She's setting up a charity for families who lose children to cancer. I'm going to help.

The article I wrote about Charlie was published, though we found a donor. The register grew and I hope that somebody, somewhere has benefited. When I've built up my strength again, I'll join it myself.

Debbie pops her head into the room. 'Hey,' she says cheerfully.

'Debbie,' says Charlie. 'I'm going home tomorrow!'

'I know, isn't it great?' She sits him up on her lap. They talk about all the things they're going to do. She calls him blood brother. He calls her blood sister.

I start to pack up our things. I enjoy every minute.

After a while, Simon calls in.

'All set?' he asks, smiling.

I smile back. 'I've never been more set in my life. Thank you so much for everything.'

'It's my job.' He looks at Debbie. 'Debra, do you think you could let Jenny out for a little walk?'

I look at him, surprised.

'Sure. I was going to offer anyway.'

'Are you sure, Deb? I don't mind. We'll be going home tomorrow anyway.'

'No, honestly, I was going to offer.'

'Go on, Mum,' says Charlie, who wants Debbie all to himself.

'OK, great, thanks.' But I'm nervous. Is there something he needs to tell me? Some catch?

I get up, grab my bag. All the way out, I'm expecting him to say something, ruin the peace I've come to know. But he says nothing. And as we walk towards the exit, I start to think that maybe I was wrong. Maybe there's nothing he wants to say after all. Maybe he just thought I needed fresh air. We reach the main doors of the hospital. I expect him to turn and go back in.

'Goodbye, then,' I say, awkwardly.

'Sorry,' he says. 'Do you want to walk alone?'

'Oh. Sorry, I didn't realise. You're coming?'

He looks awkward now. 'If that's alright?'

'Yeah, sure. I didn't realise, sorry.'

'Right then.'

We fall into step. Both silent. Then we both talk together.

'You must be happy to be going home?' Simon.

'You must be happy to get rid of us.' Me, joking. Badly.

Then together again.

Him: 'No, of course not.'

Me: 'Yes, dying to get out.'

Then both, 'oh.'

Then silent again.

I decide to keep quiet.

Eventually he says. 'So Charlie won't be my patient.'

I panic. 'Why, will someone else be looking after him in the clinic?'

'No, no, sorry. I'll be seeing Charlie in clinics. I just mean he won't be an inpatient.'

'Oh, right, yes.' *Phew.*

'So,' he says, again. 'How's Dave?'

'Dave?'

'Yes, Dave.'

'Fine, getting married.'

'You're getting *married*?' His head swivels towards me.

I squint at him. 'What? No. He's marrying his American girlfriend. Fiona.'

'Oh. I thought he was ending that.'

I feel like laughing. 'That was the plan.'

'I thought you were back together?'

'No.'

He stands back to let a woman with a buggy go by. I wait for him.

'Jenny?' He says my name like no one else. 'Had you given any thought to how I might see Charlie now?'

'Simon. It's up to you. Of course, I'd love you to see him as much as possible. And I know *he'd* love to see you. But I'm not sure how you'd do that. Wouldn't Debbie wonder? She'd probably think you were going out with me or something.' I laugh now, awkward again.

'Would you?'

'What?'

'Go out with me?'

I'm so stunned I laugh. Then I see his face. 'Sorry. I didn't mean to laugh. I just got a bit of a shock.'

'I'm not very good at this. I'm too straight. Say what I mean.'

I want to kiss him. Which makes me realise just how clear I have to be. 'Simon. Please don't ask me out just so you can see Charlie.'

'I'm not.'

'We can work something out. You could see him sometime during the day. I don't know. When Debbie isn't around.'

'Jenny, stop! I asked you out. Nothing to do with Charlie. I'm sorry. I'm out of practice. I should've just asked you to dinner or something. Not made it such a big deal.'

'You want to take me to dinner?'

'We could start with dinner.'

'So you really are asking me out?'

'If it doesn't suit...'

'But you said...'

'What?'

'You said the timing wasn't right.'

'It wasn't.'

'But what about your wife?'

His face falls. *All I seem to do is hurt him.*

'I'm sorry, Simon. But is there room in your life for someone else? We've done this. Been together and it's always been a disaster...'

'Jenny.' He stops walking, turns to me, takes my hands in his. His wedding ring has gone. 'This isn't easy for me. I'm not going to pretend it is. But I'd like to give it a try. Couldn't we do that? Give it a try? If you're interested...you might not be interested.' He stands awkwardly, looking like he doesn't know what to do with my hands now that he has them in his.

I help him out, take them back. I can't risk getting thrown aside again because he's feeling guilty about Alison or has changed his mind or who knows why.

'It's just that I think I might love you. No, I do, actually. I think you're marvellous.'

I want to laugh again. And cry.

'I admire you so much. The way you've brought Charlie up on your own. The way you have handled all this. The way you've coped.'

Here we go again, a coper. 'Simon, admire is different to love.'

'I know, I know. What do you want me to say? I'm passionate about you?'

'That would do it.' I smile.

'But I thought you knew that. Why else would I have got carried away like I did, not once but twice? I am absolutely, one hundred percent, passionate about you. I can't help it.... I've tried.' He brushes my hair aside with a tenderness that doesn't surprise me, he kisses me with a gentleness that doesn't surprise me but then hunger and passion take over again, reminding me of the first time, the second time and I wonder how I could have doubted how he felt. He looks at me now and I know I'm about to give in. That face. I love that face. 'I told myself you were too young. I told myself it wouldn't be fair on Alison, on Debbie. I told myself Charlie was my patient. I told myself you weren't interested. That was the easiest to believe. Especially when I saw you with him in the corridor, the way he held you. Debbie had told me he was staying with you. And then Charlie said he was going to end his relationship and come home. But then I couldn't let you go. I knew you were leaving tomorrow and I couldn't let you out of my sight again. I couldn't face it. I had to say something. Tell you how I felt. Every time you're not there, I miss you.'

I smile. 'Me too.'

'Really? You're not joking again?'

I shake my head, then kiss him.

The side of a mountain when a cloud's shadow clears away, that's his face now.

'Oh, Jenny.' He smiles. 'Can I pinch you?'

'No.' I laugh. 'But I'll pinch you if you like.'

He brushes my hair back again, then holds my hands again. He says quietly, 'I didn't think I had a hope. I just wanted to tell you how I felt. I thought that if I was lucky, I might get a chance to convince you that you were making a mistake, and that it was us who should be together. But really, in fairness, I thought you were gone.'

'I'm going nowhere.' I smile. 'In fairness.' I lean forward and kiss him.

He takes me in his arms, in full view of the hospital. I worry that we might be seen. I pull back. 'Is this OK, in front of the hospital?'

'Probably not, definitely not.' He laughs and kisses me. 'You're gorgeous.'

'No, you're gorgeous.'

'No, you are.'

And we laugh.

'So where are you taking me to dinner?' I smile and take his hand in mine.

epilogue

'Come on, Mum,' Katie shouts, racing up the path ahead of me, the pink soles of her shoes flashing as each foot kicks back in the air. She makes it to the door. Jumps to reach the bell. Misses. Tries again. And again.

'Katie, I have the key.'

'Oh, yeah.'

I open the door. In she runs. Almost into Charlie who is standing holding the handlebars of his bike, about to head out. Sausage is jumping up on him, whacking his tail from side to side.

'Helmet, Charlie,' I say, stepping out of his way.

He mutters something I can't hear, leans the bike against the wall, grabs the helmet from a hook under the stairs and is off. 'See you later.'

'Where you going?'

'Dara's.'

'Back by dinner, OK?'

'OK.'

'And remember, we're going out. I need you back by half-five.'

'OK.'

'And Charlie?'

'Yes.' Impatient, now.

'Don't go too fast. Sausage is getting old, you'll give him a heart attack.'

'OK.'

I drop the box of groceries on the kitchen table.

'Hi, Deb. Didn't expect you home.'

'Lecture cancelled,' she says, without looking up. 'That guy never turns up. They should fire him.'

'Can I've my ice cweam now?' asks the girl with the curls.

'You can have some in the restaurant.'

'Aw.'

'Where's your dad?' I ask Deb.

'Upstairs.'

'Down in a sec,' I say, going to look for him.

'I'm hungwy.'

'Deb, get her a mandarin would you, love?'

She reaches for the fruit bowl without taking her eyes off her textbook, feels around for a mandarin, peels it, also without looking. 'Here Squirt,' she hands it to Katie.

'Tanks, Deb, whatchadoing?'

'Reading about hearts.'

'Can I see?'

'OK, but don't get juice on the book,' she says, lifting Katie up on her lap. 'Now, you know, your heart? Well, this is a picture...' Their chatter becomes inaudible as I head up the stairs. It's friendly, though, because they adore each other.

He's not in the bedroom.

'Simon?'

'Hello,' comes a voice.

'A bit more specific?'

'Attic.'

'What are you up to?'

'Getting Charlie's surprise.'

'D'you need a hand?' I call up.

'Yeah. Can you grab it?' A brown cardboard box appears through the hole in the ceiling followed by my husband's arms and head. 'Hello,' he grins.

'Hello, yourself.'

I lower it carefully to the floor. He hoists himself down onto the stepladder.

'Will it take long to put together?'

'Don't know yet; let's have a look.'

We rip off the cardboard.

'Actually, all you do is screw on these legs.'

I watch him assemble the snooker table. I pick up a ball, it's heavy and cold, and I roll it round in my hand. 'He'll love this.'

'Do you want a go?' he smiles, 'a trial run?'

'OK, but give me a few free goes, I'm useless at snooker.'

He stops and looks at me. Says quietly. 'Can you believe it's five years?'

I slip into his arms and look into his eyes. 'No, Dr Grace, I can't. Five years.' There will be yearly tests for the rest of Charlie's life, I realise that, but this is the big hurdle, and we've jumped it. We hold each other. I rest my head on his chest.

The restaurant is Italian. Relaxed, casual and friendly, with genuine flamboyant Italian waiters and the best pizzas. It suits all ages. Which is just as well, because that's what we are. Simon, forty-five; me, thirty-two; Deb, twenty; Charlie, ten and Katie, three. And that's not counting Mary's lot or Jack. Or, indeed, my parents, who haven't arrived yet. When they do, we'll have a representative here from every decade up to seventy, which is fitting as this is a celebration of life. We've reached a day that five years ago, I was afraid to dream we ever would. But here it is.

I smile across at Mary. She winks back, while fixing a bib on the little girl she and Phil always wanted but were too practical to plan. Amy had to spring herself on them. She is an angel. No, really, an actual angel sent to thank Mary for all she did for us. A present from Great. At least, that's what I think at times like this, when I've every reason to feel soppy.

Jack's here with his new girlfriend, someone we know, as it happens. Anne. They met at the hospital. But it took fate to intervene, putting them together in the same evening class – psychology. Jack, not an evening class man, was trying to pick up a few tricks on fathering, seeing as he now sees Alan, twice a week, for golf, another something Jack would never have tried on his own. Jack keeps in touch with Dave. I'm not supposed to know, but he and Fiona are going to counselling.

Debbie hasn't brought her latest boyfriend, though we did invite Gareth.

'We're only going out, like, six months, Jenny, it's not like we're married or anything.' Debbie's studies come first, as serious as her father about curing the world. In her year is Mark, Charlie's super-hero, also doing medicine, also determined to make people better. And what better doctor than one who knows what it's like to be on the other side.

I glance at Charlie. He's becoming more like Simon every day. I admire his thick, now dark, hair and have to stop myself from reaching out to touch it. He's very precious about it, always gelling it some way or another, always conscious of it, something that was taken away and given back. To look at him, you'd never tell he had leukaemia. The only way you might guess, is his attitude. So philosophical for one so young, so accepting, not worried about the small stuff. He understands things that other kids his age wouldn't notice – like why people leave flowers at the place where they lost their loved ones. Charlie knows that this is the last place they were alive, and the flowers are to say, 'we haven't forgotten you'. He told me that once as we were just driving along. It made me stop short, remember, how close we got. There is a special bond between Charlie and Debbie that I don't think anything will ever be able to change. She saved his life. He needed her but she needed him, too, in a way. A part of her will always live in him, literally. It's not something you forget. I'm so proud of them both. And so grateful to have them here.

Katie wriggles up onto my lap. Our little girl. Who wasn't in my happy-family dream five years ago. But here she is now. A born survivor, always finding her way to the top of any queue, never going hungry, never being left behind. I sometimes wonder if it's a genetic thing – that the last mix of genes had some fault in it that produced leukaemia and this time they weren't going to make a mistake? She's so plucky it makes me laugh, and her strength is, frankly, a relief. She, too, has her father's dark hair. It's already almost black. Her eyes are bright blue sparkly discs, innocent but strangely knowing. Deb and Charlie take her in their stride, very casual with her, never fussing over her because she's not the kind of kid who needs or wants a fuss. Yet I know if she was ever in trouble, they'd kill for her.

We're a family now, but it wasn't always easy. From the beginning, Simon and I were in a rush. We didn't just want to meet for dinner and go our separate ways. We wanted to be together. Go home together. Share our lives, ourselves, with each other. We didn't want to wait. We'd both faced death and knew that there is only so much time we're all given and we have to make the most of it while we have it. We didn't want to waste a second. But we had to tell the children. We had to be honest with them before we made any commitment, even before we started seeing each other properly. So we decided. No hiding from what had happened. If we wanted this to work, we had to do it right, from the beginning. We had to deal with things. Face them.

But how do you tell a fifteen year old that her father, let's face it, had sex, with another woman when her mother had just been diagnosed with cancer? With difficulty, that's how. The deliberation! The preparation! The nerves! But it had to be done. What gave us the final push was that I got a 'fright' of my own. A breast lump that turned out to be innocent. (That took some convincing.) But it frightened us enough to push us over the line.

We couldn't be together without being honest with Debbie. How to tell her, though, that was the problem. I felt that if we did it as a couple, it would be harder for her, as if we were teaming up against her or something. I was also afraid it would embarrass her, put her in a position where she couldn't scream and shout, and be honest. So Simon had to do it. He was terrified. There were things that helped Debbie accept it. We were being open with her. What happened in Brussels was an accident and there was no contact after that. When I did bump into Simon again, I tried to avoid seeing him and would have cancelled the babysitting if she and Charlie hadn't got on so well. But the main thing that helped Deb to accept what happened was that she already saw us as a potential family. Charlie was her blood brother and she had already instigated a plan to try to get Simon and I together, the Make My Dad More Marketable plan, involving movie trips and recommended reading. Which is also why she was so uncomfortable seeing Dave 'sleep over'. We had all been through so much with Charlie and the enormity of that lessened the importance of other things. And, finally, she came to me and we talked about it, honestly and openly.

I've tried to be sensitive with Deb. I've never tried to be a mum to her. Instead, I've told her I'll always be here for her, to listen, to do things together. I suggested that we could catch up on all the shopping we'd missed out on by having absent mothers. She liked that idea. So that's what we did. Went shopping, to the movies, had 'girly time'. Now that she's with Gareth, I don't see so much lot of her. But she's happy. And that makes me happy.

As for Charlie, when he heard he had a father, well, 'wow'. And that his father was the same father as Debbie, double wow. And that it was Simon. And that he knew him all along. And liked him. And that he was going to be around, available, there. His face looked like it had that time we were watching the firework display. He did want to know why we hadn't told him before and that was awkward. How much can you say to a five-year-old? But we worked something out.

We managed to hold on for six months before getting married, to give the children time to adjust. When we did, it was a low-key affair, conscious as we were of Deb. But it was a very special day, surrounded by the people we love. Charlie was best man (so cute!). Debbie, bridesmaid (so pretty!). My father got very nervous about giving me away and was delighted that the wedding speeches had a time limit of two minutes. My mother was tremendously happy. I couldn't help thinking that she finally got her wish of having a doctor in the family. It's hard to just get rid of a lifetime of cynicism towards a person, but actually, except for the odd moment, I seem to have managed it. And she is great. What she missed out on as a mother, she is more than making up for now, both with her grandchildren and me. She adores Katie, but will always have special affection for Charlie who brought us back together as a family. Her life is so filled now, it's hard to imagine her the way she was. In fact, when politicians call to her house to canvass, she runs them.

And then there's my husband, the man I used to wonder about – what he liked, what made him happy, angry, how he got the scar on his cheek. I will tell you. He likes Bruce Springsteen, looking out at rain from somewhere cosy, poppadums, and the way I have a freckle on each of my erogenous zones (his discovery, not mine). He also likes yoga, which he took up, saying that anything that allows him see me with my bum in the air has got to be worth doing. What makes him happy: family, making me laugh, sex and his patients recovering. What makes him angry: the only thing that makes him angry is when he loses a patient. And that anger makes up for all the times he doesn't get angry at the small things. He got the scar on his cheek when he tried shaving at the age of four with his father's razor – his first hospital experience. He comes from a family of four. (Charlie got six instant cousins.) I was wrong about his age. He was a few years younger than he looked. But, actually, he looks younger now than he did then. The worried, tense pull has left his face. His smile-per-day rate has gone way up. He has a pretty cheeky sense of humour. A new side to Simon Grace has emerged. A fun side. He has learned to laugh again. I'd say he was happy, if I wasn't aware of the next corner and what might be around it. Then again, when you've made it around one corner and survived, maybe it gives you something special – a will to treasure the simpler moments, like making a fool of yourself with a whisk on the kitchen dance-floor or pretending to be Papillion beside a swimming pool in France. 'Le Roi de la Piscine'.

He looks across at me, now, and smiles, his face saying, 'look what we have'. And I want to leap over the table and kiss him. Yes. We are lucky.

THE END

Made in the USA
Middletown, DE
27 July 2019